MURDER NOW AND THEN

An utterly gripping crime mystery full of twists

FAITH MARTIN

DI Hillary Greene Book 19

JOFFE BOOKS

Joffe Books, London
www.joffebooks.com

First published in Great Britain in 2021

ISBN: 978-1-78931-876-0

CHAPTER ONE

Former DI Hillary Greene jumped off the prow of the *Mollern*, her narrowboat home of more years than she cared to remember, and onto the towpath of the Oxford canal. She stood for a moment, breathing in deeply of the slightly damp but warm early spring air, and cast an assessing eye on the sky.

From the branches of an about-to-bloom pussy willow nearby, a hedge sparrow sang with his usual gusto, and was answered by a rival male from the farmer's field beyond. Deciding that it probably wasn't going to rain within the next ten minutes or so, she set off briskly on the short distance up the towpath towards the village of Thrupp and the car park of the Boat pub, where she regularly parked her car.

Thankfully, her ancient Volkswagen Golf, Puff the Tragic Wagon, was feeling in a benevolent mood that morning, and despite the moist air started on the first turn of the key.

Her commute to the Thames Valley Police HQ in Kidlington was less than five minutes (maybe ten if she got caught in the rush hour) as Thrupp was on the outskirts of the large village — or was it the town? — of Kidlington. Hillary knew that the locals had long been unable to agree on the status of Kidlington, and she was far too wily to pick

1

a side. Stick your head above the parapet on that one, and you were likely to get it knocked off.

She left Puff in her favourite spot in the HQ car park, more or less underneath the spreading branches of a horse-chestnut tree, her bag slung over one shoulder.

Once inside the lobby, she traded the usual and mandatory friendly insults with the desk sergeant and headed downstairs into the bowels of the building.

The CRT (Crime Review Team), where she worked as a civilian consultant solving cold cases, wasn't a high priority with the top brass, hence the less-than-glamorous digs. However, since retiring as a DI, she'd become almost used to being treated like a mole, and rarely noticed the lack of natural daylight any more.

She passed the large computer-packed office (where the majority of the CRT officers hung out, using computer databases and the newest technological breakthroughs to constantly check old cases for modern-day matches) to the much smaller communal one where she and her tiny investigative team were based.

The powers-that-be had recognized that some cases needed the old-fashioned touch of an experienced detective, and thus had recruited Hillary to lead a small team dedicated to working unsolved murder cases or other serious crimes. Alas, cutbacks had dwindled her team to just herself and two others: a former police sergeant, Claire Woolley, who'd worked for years in a rape and domestic violent unit, and a civilian ex-soldier, Gareth Proctor, who'd recently been invalided out of the army.

She saw that neither one had come in yet — but that wasn't surprising. She was nearly always early. Unlike her days as a DI, she and her team were supposed to stick strictly to a nine-to-five regime, as overtime was utterly unheard of.

She carried on to her own office, which had — literally — once been a stationery cupboard. She had room to open the door, squeeze past the small desk, pull out a single chair which hit the back wall almost instantly, giving her just enough room to slither between it and the desk. If she was ever to put on weight, she'd probably have to be reassigned another room. A former toilet stall maybe?

She logged on to her computer, checked her emails, and then impatiently bided her time until Superintendent Roland 'Rollo' Sale, head of the CRT, called her in to his office. She'd filed her report on the case they'd successfully been working on and had closed only yesterday, and now she was looking forward to seeing what they'd be working on next.

She had to exercise patience (not her strongest point) for another half an hour or so before finally getting the phone call. Once it came she walked quickly to his lair — one of the few with a window near the ceiling that allowed you a nice view of people's feet as they walked past on the pavement above.

She was, as usual, wearing one of her civilian 'uniforms', which today consisted of a skirt and jacket in dark green, with a plain cream-coloured blouse. Now in her mid-fifties, her bell-shaped cut of dark brown hair with chestnut highlights owed a little more to hair dye than Mother Nature, but it wasn't something that particularly worried her.

When she tapped on the door and walked in, her eyes went instantly to the large folder on the desk in front of her boss, unaware that her sherry-coloured eyes were gleaming.

Rollo Sale, though, smiled happily as his best detective fastened her eyes avariciously on the file and once the pleasantries were over, wasted no time in filling her in on the case he'd selected. She listened, as usual, without saying much, but making copious notes.

The superintendent was glad to see her back on top form again. The last year and a half had been extremely rocky for her, following the death of her partner, the former head of CRT, Steven Crayle. She had lost weight and still looked rather thin, but he was relieved to see that her old stamina had returned, and that she'd regained her dry sense of humour.

Half an hour later, Hillary went to brief her team on their latest assignment, feeling pleased with the case Rollo Sale had selected.

Claire Woolley was a hefty woman in her early fifties, with short black hair and brown eyes, and stood five feet ten inches in her stockinged feet. She was a warm, motherly sort of woman by nature, but after years of seeing the worst of humanity, she had a backbone of steel.

Although Rollo Sale was technically in charge, he let Hillary do things her way and just get on with it, which was how everyone liked it. This was not surprising, since her solve rate as a full-time DI had been second to none, and that had continued with her move to cold cases.

'New case, guv?' Claire asked hopefully.

'Yes, murder this time,' Hillary confirmed. Their last case looked set to put away a serial rapist for the rest of his life.

Hillary noticed Gareth Proctor sit up a little straighter at the word 'murder'. He was the latest recruit to her team, but she thought, overall, that he was settling in well. Never having trained as a police officer, he'd come through a steep learning curve with flying colours so far. Although his tendency to bark respectful answers at her — as if she were a colonel in the army — could wear thin occasionally, she had no issues with either his work ethic or his discipline.

He was, as ever, dressed as neatly and immaculately as you'd expect from a former soldier in a dark blue suit with what she supposed was a regimental tie, and his blond hair had been recently trimmed to its usual very short length. His only concession to sartorial diligence was his habit of taking off his jacket and hanging it on the back of his chair, which wasn't surprising. The heating down in the basement levels tended to be fierce, the ancient radiators seeming only to function on two levels — blast furnace in the winter and, thankfully, stone cold in the summer.

Intelligent blue eyes watched her thoughtfully. As was his habit, he sat with his left hand in his lap, hiding from view the scars that ran from his hand up the entire length of that limb. When he walked, he used a stick to help support his left leg, which was withered and weakened, a legacy of being too near a bomb when it exploded.

At thirty-six, he'd been divorced for a few years now, his marriage being unable to withstand the pressures put on it by his near year-long hospital stay and his loss of job, friends and former life.

Hillary's team had never been funded as well as anyone would like, and she'd had to work with a variety of people over the years, most of whom came and went quite quickly. Chief among these were students who thought they might like to make the police their career (and then quickly decided that they didn't!). But there were also people like Claire, who'd retired from the job, and then found time hanging heavy on their hands and decided to return, albeit in a less stressful role.

Hillary was used to training the uninitiated and working with whatever skill sets they brought, while trying to bear in mind that she was lucky to have 'staff' at all. Naturally, some worked out better than others, but so far, the former soldier looked as if he was going to be a good fit and, with luck, might stick around for some time to come.

She understood his reasoning for taking this particular job only too well, for while they might not be the army, he appreciated the chain-of-command mentality of police work, and understood and approved of the gravity of what they did.

Nodding at both of them, she walked to the white board, now wiped clean of the specifics of their previous case, and began to fill them in on their latest assignment.

'All right. This is Michael Beck.' She put up a not par-ticularly good photograph of a young man with nondescript brown hair and eyes. Neither good-looking nor ugly, he peered impassively back at them from a photograph that had probably originally been given to them by his family. 'He was twenty-two years old when he went out on his bicycle one morning and never returned. His body was discovered that evening in the water meadow not far from where he lived in the village of Woodeaton.'

She named a village that was on the outskirts of Oxford, and was unfortunately used as a rat-run by commuters who worked in the hospitals that proliferated in the nearby suburb of Headington. 'This was in early September 2011. He'd not long finished doing a BA in Ancient History at Bristol and had had to move back into the parental home while trying to find a job and a place to live.'

Claire, mother of three grown kids, grunted. Oxford was notoriously difficult when it came to finding affordable housing. Her eldest was still living in rented accommodation that she wouldn't have thought big enough to house a kennel.

Hillary's lips twitched at this wry comment. 'Quite. A local dog walker found him in the late afternoon near Islip, which is more or less the next village down from Woodeaton — a distance of maybe two and a half to three miles or so. According to the files, there's a weir in the river nearby where the Ray flows into the Cherwell. The water meadows there are a popular spot with villagers in the summertime.'

'Do courting couples still like to roll in the hay these days?' Claire mused.

'The dog walker was a man in his seventies,' Hillary said with a grin. 'And, according to the original report, had only his mutt for company. He saw the body and gave the alarm. According to the pathology reports, Michael had been hit over the head with something oddly shaped, vaguely rounded, and was probably made of some kind of metal rather than wood. Unfortunately, the pathologist wasn't able to match it to any of the usual suspects.' She meant things like a cricket or baseball bat, poker, sandbag or some other hand-made kind of bludgeon like a rock in a sock, but she didn't think this needed spelling out to her team. 'It was a single blow only, but it cracked his skull sufficiently to kill him, with death resulting probably within a few minutes. He certainly didn't drown, as the medical reports later made clear.'

'He was probably dropped in the river sometime later?' It was Gareth who asked the question and sounded slightly tentative. He was very much aware that he was still green when it came to police work, but he'd gained enough trust and confidence in both women to feel comfortable asking questions.

'I think so,' Hillary said cautiously. 'If he'd been standing by the river and fell in immediately after the blow, he'd probably have *some* water in his lungs as his death wasn't instant. When you've copied the files, you can go over the medical report for yourself and take in the details. You'll see that the doctor thinks the angle of the blow indicates that the victim was hit almost on top of his crown — which means with a distinctly downward stroke.'

'Meaning, unless the killer was a giant, <u>Beck</u> was either sitting or kneeling,' Claire said. 'Did he get hit from the front or the back?'

'Back, they think,' Hillary said.

'Well at least the poor sod didn't see it coming,' Claire muttered.

'The original senior investigating officer, DI Weston, has now retired and is living in Spain,' Hillary carried on, 'which is nice for some! But it means he's not readily available for us to pick his brains. From what Superintendent Sale told me, he's confident the original team did a good job, but they simply couldn't bring it home to anybody. They did, however, identify two strong suspects.'

She paused to place two more photographs on the board.

'This,' she tapped the photograph of a middle-aged man with reddish-brown hair, which had clearly been taken at an outdoor event of some kind, 'is Dr Timothy Durning.' A lean and tall man, with thin but good-looking features, he looked like the academic she already knew him to be. He was wearing a neat bow tie and old-fashioned waistcoat: a look that suited him, but one that not everyone could bring off. 'One of the victim's tutors at uni, Michael laid a charge of sexual harassment against him, that wasn't upheld, but which nevertheless resulted in Dr Durning leaving the university under the proverbial cloud. DI Weston's notes say that although the university's inquiries couldn't prove Michael's claim — there being no independent witnesses — they were uneasy enough about what they discovered to suggest that the good doctor resign. Which he eventually did, but not without some rancour on his part.'

Claire heaved a heavy sigh. 'Don't tell me — he's now probably working in some posh public school earning a mint without a stain on his character.'

'Well, we'll soon have to find out,' Hillary said and added, with a wicked little grin, 'and since you seem to have taken such a shine to him, perhaps you'll have the task of tracking him down, Claire.'

Claire groaned good-naturedly.

'Gareth, you can find out all you can about this woman, with her current whereabouts a top priority.' Hillary tapped the second photograph. 'Dr Mia de Salle. She and our murder victim had been "going steady" for over a year before splitting up. According to Michael's family and friends, it was not an amicable break-up. Michael ended it, and Dr de Salle did not take it well. There were vague mutterings about her becoming a bit of a stalker.'

Gareth nodded. 'Yes, ma'am,' he said smartly.

The woman in the photograph looked distinctive rather than beautiful, with long black hair and wide hazel eyes. She had the kind of thin, aesthetic face you sometimes saw in old master paintings.

'Mia de Salle was twenty-five years old at the time of the murder,' Hillary swept on. 'They met at Bristol, where she was doing a PhD in . . . something or other.' She knew she'd need to take at least the rest of the day in order to fully absorb the data, but it annoyed her not to have the details already at her fingertips.

'According to the original reports, Dr de Salle had no alibi, but there was no forensic evidence linking her to the crime and no witnesses placing her in the vicinity either. And although DI Weston thought she was "squirrelly" — and that's a direct quote from his notes — she denied any and all knowledge of Michael's recent whereabouts and activities.'

'Well she would, wouldn't she?' Claire said dryly, paraphrasing the famous courtroom quote from the Profumo scandal. Hillary's lips twitched again, but she doubted Gareth understood the reference. All of that was old news, wasn't it? And unlikely to interest him.

'All right,' Hillary said briskly, 'you know the routine. Claire, you need to get any paper files from records, and make copies for everyone. Gareth, help out with that — it'll be a mammoth task and will probably take a few days. Do it in batches and then go on to something else, or you'll set fire to the old photocopier!'

The CRT tended to be a repository for old and outdated equipment passed down from above — not quite like manna from heaven. Not that they weren't grateful.

'Download digitally whatever you can,' she added with a sigh. 'I'll start the Murder Book going, and make my own notes. By the end of the day, I should have a list of assignments for you. As usual, most of it will be tracking down up-to-date info on our witnesses and suspects. But let's see if, after a decade, we can't unearth something new that'll help us get justice for Michael.'

'Guv,' Claire said amiably.

'Ma'am,' Gareth said crisply.

Hillary retreated to her office to devour all the notes she'd been given from the original investigation and the rest of the day passed quickly. She tried to put herself back in 2011, but when it came to remembering what had been important in her life ten years ago, she couldn't come up with anything specific. But she assumed that her work had been her priority.

She only hoped that others had a better memory of that time than she did, and that the people who knew him hadn't forgotten Michael or what had happened to him.

But if they had, they were about to be reminded — and in no uncertain terms.

* * *

Six months ago

Simon Newley unlocked the back door of what he always referred to as his antique shop, stepped into a dingy passageway, and punched in the alarm code on the machine on the wall. It was something he did automatically, although when he stopped to think about it — which wasn't often — he wondered why he bothered. The system was ancient, none of the CCTV cameras actually worked, and even if they did, he'd never been robbed in all the years he'd owned the shop.

There were many reasons for this. For a start, the shop, situated not far from the worst estates the city of Oxford had to offer, was full of total tat. His more law-abiding customers regularly brought him knackered stuff and received mere pennies in return. Old radios that didn't work, sofas with springs that had given up the ghost before the turn of the millennium, Aunty Mary's vase with the crack a mile wide down the side and shiny yellow metal trinkets that had about as much gold content as a daffodil.

Nobody ever came in to buy. But that was all right, it was only for show anyway. Although he kept a fictitious set of books to show the taxman or any coppers that might come calling, indicating that he managed to earn a very modest living from his 'antiques'.

But many knew that the real service that Simon provided had nothing to do with second-hand goods. Which was another reason why he was never robbed. The locals all needed him too much.

The token 'security' measures seen to, he slouched wearily into the front room of what had once been a regular house. Years ago, he'd knocked a sizeable hole in the wall and installed a large single window (back in the days when you could do such things without historical societies and planning officers throwing a hissy fit), which was now so dirty it barely let in the daylight.

A doll (minus a leg) sat in the front windowsill looking out over the narrow street beyond, its dress long since bleached into an indeterminate colour.

He wound his way through the narrow and cramped central aisle, where old wooden kitchen chairs were stacked in piles that almost reached to the ceiling, and through the far door into his office, where he deposited the ledger that he'd been carrying under his arm.

Formerly the kitchen of the house, it still retained the old kitchen sink, and a kettle stood on the draining board nearby. But rows of old-fashioned filing cabinets now lined the walls, along with smaller, card-index cabinets, testimony to Simon's distrust of computers. He didn't want his online movements tracked, thank you very much, and he knew far too many hackers to risk getting himself caught up in blackmail. No, pen and paper suited him just fine, as did the big, old-fashioned ledger.

Although he was only fifty-five years old, Simon was aware that in appearance he could pass for a good ten years older than that. But that's what inhabiting the sleazy side of life did for you, he supposed. Bald, with watery blue eyes, he tended to dress as his grandfather had, in warm woollen trousers, a thick check shirt, and a chunky cardigan. Nice and warm on a cold autumn day, they lent him the totally misleading appearance of a harmless old man.

Underneath his desk, though, he kept a sawn-off shotgun, and out in the attached garage was a very large dog that didn't take kindly to strangers, but had been trained not to kick up a racket unless urged to by its master. He couldn't have the dog barking every time someone knocked on his door. But being within easy call through a huge dog-flap, he knew that he could always rely on Brutus to come running whenever he whistled.

Not that he ever had much call to use the dog. People in the neighbourhood knew all about Brutus and his nasty personality. They also knew all about Simon Newley, and *his* nasty personality.

That chill October morning was like any other for Simon. He'd left his wife and the three of his five kids that still lived at home behind in their former council house in Kidlington, and driven into the city, cursing, as always, at the amount of traffic.

He set up his cash box and then turned the notice on the front door to indicate that he was open for business.

His first customer was a teenage likely lad from Blackbird Leys who had twenty iPads he needed to offload sharpish. There was the usual haggle about price, with the kid finally and ungraciously accepting Simon's terms to come and collect his money later, and cash changed hands.

The moment the disgruntled teenager slouched out, Simon was on the phone to a man he knew in Milton Keynes who would be very happy to accept the merchandise on offer and would send someone round for it after dark.

He noted the transactions in his ledger (which he always took home with him at the end of the day and slid under his mattress), marking down both the buyer and seller only by the nicknames he gave them. He was careful to use a code of his own devising for telephone numbers and other pertinent information — that way, if his system ever fell into the wrong hands, nobody would be dropped in the shit — least of all himself.

In all the years he'd been in business, Simon had never served prison time, and he didn't intend to. His reputation for being clever, dependable and — within limits, fair — had stood him in good stead for nearly thirty years, making him something of an institution in his neighbourhood.

Not that he always had things easy. Right now, business had been going downhill for a bit, a fact that Simon had been very careful to keep well hidden. It didn't do for the jackals in this world to scent blood. But he also knew that the downturn was only temporary — he'd been through lean times before, and they always picked up, so he wasn't really worried.

But he had just had to reorder his finances somewhat and take out a 'loan'. Unfortunately, the loan had recently become more of a pressing problem than he'd anticipated, leading him to have to make some painful choices.

But he was confident that it was all sorted out now, and his loan shark had been happy with the compromise he'd suggested. If nothing else, Simon knew he was a natural born survivor. Maybe not a noble predator such as a lion or a tiger, but something far more useful — something indestructible — like a cockroach. Didn't they say if the bomb ever went off, cockroaches would inherit the earth?

And like all born survivors, he knew that if you had to throw someone else under the bus in order to walk away unscathed yourself, well, that was just life, wasn't it? Everyone — well, at least everyone who lived in his kind of world — knew that you had to look out for number one first and foremost.

It was getting on for eleven when Simon put on the kettle and settled down with the morning paper, his eyes running thoughtfully over the horses running at Haydock, mentally checking their form, the record of the jockeys riding them, and which nags preferred soft ground and which didn't.

The second caller of the day was a woman with a wedding ring for sale and a black eye that Simon was sure he could actually see was still throbbing.

He bought the ring cheap (the gold was the lowest carat there was), and wished her the best of luck. He knew her husband, and if she didn't get away free and clear before he staggered home from the pub when his money ran out, the black eye would be the least of her problems.

Outside, the October day grew a little darker as storm clouds blew in, and soon the gusting winds were blowing raindrops against the dirty windows.

Someone thumped on the back door and Simon sighed. Not everyone, for obvious reasons, liked to be seen going into his establishment, and he felt no presentiment of foreboding as he left the office and shuffled through the passageway towards the rear.

The glass in the rear door was pebbled (to stop nosy coppers peering in and spotting something they oughtn't) so all he saw was the vague outline of a male figure.

He opened the door on its chain with his usual caution, but seeing only the face of a long-time and lucrative customer that he'd nicknamed Teddy Bear, he slipped the chain off the latch, and pulled it open.

'Ah, it's you again. The usual is it?' He stepped back, watching his visitor thoughtfully. He wasn't unduly concerned, since he was sure that Teddy Bear could have no idea — yet — of what Simon had been forced to do in order to keep his loan shark happy. He'd only come to the arrangement with Lionel Kirklees yesterday, so he doubted Lionel would have put the bite on him this soon.

But in that, as it soon turned out, Simon was mistaken.

The first indication that something wasn't quite right was when Teddy Bear made an odd movement with his right arm — raising it to chest level. The second indication was when Simon heard this strange noise and felt his whole body convulse with pain and a strange, hot, alien sensation racing across and through him like liquid fire.

He found himself on the dirty floor of the passageway, his limbs jerking in an odd, macabre dance. He felt utterly disorientated and totally confused. His brain didn't seem to have control over anything. He couldn't even open his mouth to yell for Brutus. He felt pain, but also a sensation that he knew he'd never felt before. Most bizarrely of all, he was sure he could smell something burning.

Was he having a stroke?

Then Teddy Bear was standing over him, and when Simon looked down the length of his still jerking body and saw two small metal pins, with their telltale wires sticking out of his chest, he finally understood what had happened to him.

He'd been shot with a taser, and his body was still paralysed by the electric current that had knocked him off his feet and out of touch with reality.

He tried to open his mouth, to plead, to try and make amends, to promise Teddy Bear anything he wanted, anything at all, if only he would let Simon be. But he could produce no sounds other than a kind of silly 'uh, uh, uh', and his eyes widened in fear and panic as he saw his visitor lean back through the open door and reach behind him for something.

The moment he saw what it was, Simon Newley finally had to accept that he was wrong about being a natural born survivor after all.

Dead wrong.

CHAPTER TWO

By the next morning, Hillary's team were all well on their way to being up and running on their latest case. Most of the really important documents had either been photocopied and distributed as hard-copy files or else downloaded onto their digital devices. Better yet, Gareth and Claire had tracked down the latest addresses or contact details for a good percentage of the witnesses and suspects involved in the original investigation.

Arriving dead on the dot of nine o'clock for once, Hillary found both Claire and Gareth already in and raring to go. For a moment she stood in the doorway, regarding them both, and then smiled.

'Claire, feel like coming with me to talk to Michael's parents?'

She'd telephoned the Becks yesterday afternoon to warn them that their son's case was being looked at again, and had arranged a visit with them for ten o'clock that morning.

'Great,' Claire instantly accepted. In her view, anything that got her out of the office for a few hours was not to be sniffed at.

'On the way there, we can stop off and take a look at where the body was found,' Hillary suggested.

Although the medical evidence hadn't been able to determine one way or the other if the place Michael Beck's body had been found was the same as where he went into the water, it seemed to her to be unlikely. Given the current in the river, the original team had theorised that the murdered man must have entered the river somewhere upstream. Unfortunately, despite their best efforts, they'd been unable to find the spot. The surrounding fields for some miles around had either contained cows, sheep or horses, most of which regularly went to the river banks to drink, and thus might have obliterated any evidence.

'It probably won't tell us anything useful all these years later, but it'll at least give us a feel for things and get the lie of the land fixed in our heads.'

'Good idea, guv,' Claire agreed happily. 'A walk in the countryside won't hurt, either!'

Hillary knew how she felt. She gave Gareth an apologetic look. 'Gareth, I need you to get in touch with the original SIO and pick his brains. I doubt he'll have anything to add to what's in the files, but we can't overlook it. Who knows, a call out of the blue might jog his memory about something.'

Claire rolled her eyes at the likelihood of this but wisely said nothing. In her experience, once retired coppers got the smell of sand and sea in their nostrils, then their old life might just as well have never existed.

Gareth accepted his less-appealing assignment with no visible expression but a calm nod.

Since Hillary didn't like to ask too much of her ageing car these days, they set out in Claire's more recent and reliable little runabout, heading out towards the villages of Islip and Woodeaton in a brief burst of bright spring sunshine. Early daffodils gave the Kidlington roundabout a daubing of cheerful yellow, and through the clouds, now and then, a blue sky promised better things to come.

There was still a chill breeze blowing, however, when fifteen minutes later Claire pulled the car off onto the side of the road opposite a water meadow and switched off the ignition. Over beyond a stand of trees lay the attractive village of Islip, and as they set off walking towards the riverbank, Hillary could hear a colony of nesting rooks kicking up their usual racket.

The fields were bare of wild flowers so early in the season, and the trees were yet to don their mantle of green but the river still managed to look beautiful as it wound its way towards Oxford. It didn't take the women long to find the weir where Michael Beck's body had been caught up by the detritus that had congregated in the lower section of the water. Painted a rather utilitarian grey, the protective railings stretched over the waterway, with a central concrete partition in the centre, sending the river flowing either side of it.

'I love the sound of rushing water,' Hillary mused out loud as the two women stood together, regarding the unlovely structure thoughtfully. 'He was killed in September,' Hillary swept on more briskly, 'so the water would have been much more overgrown with vegetation than it is now. Both river weeds, like water crowfoot, which grow in the actual flowing water itself, and things like river mace or rushes, rosebay willowherb and meadowsweet would all have infringed down from the banks and colonised the outer edges.'

Claire, also a country girl, nodded. 'Yes — it's easy to see why his body would have snagged here. You're thinking he didn't travel that far?'

Hillary sighed. 'It's impossible to say. Because his home is only a short distance away . . .' she turned, getting her bearings, and then pointed vaguely, 'over there, it's tempting to assume that he was killed near to home and then dumped in the river at the closest point to Woodeaton, if only because his killer would have been anxious to get away from the proximity of a dead body as soon as possible. But there's no real way of knowing. We mustn't get lured into one-dimensional thinking,' she said, warning herself as much as Claire. 'For all we know he could have been killed miles away, and then driven back here in the back of some vehicle and dumped close to his home just to lay a false trail or confuse the issue.'

Claire nodded. For a moment, the two women stood companionably in the field, watching the hypnotic motion of the river flowing over the weir. Somewhere a yellowhammer called, and a chiff-chaff, probably newly arrived from its impressive migration from much warmer climes, was encouraged to join in. With the grazing cattle in the next field, the place looked bucolic, calm and innocent.

'Not the sort of place you expect to find a dead body, is it?' Hillary said quietly.

'Not really, no,' Claire agreed, then shivered in the chill wind. 'Seen enough, guv?' she asked hopefully.

Hillary smiled. 'Sure. Let's go and warm up.' With a bit of the luck, the Becks would offer them a hot cup of coffee.

* * *

William and Martina Becks, according to Claire's research, had both retired relatively early from their respective professions, and had not moved away from the family home.

Hillary didn't read anything into this. Sometimes, the relatives and loved ones of murder victims couldn't wait to move away from the place where they'd suffered such a traumatic loss. Others felt the need to stay close by, perhaps because the familiar surroundings helped keep their memories more vivid.

William Beck, who'd sold his business providing greenhouses and conservatories to the well-heeled barely two years after losing his son, turned out to be a tall, thin man with fine pure white hair and pale brown eyes. Dressed in elegantly tailored black slacks and a warm cream woollen pullover, he answered the door with a strained smile and invited them in the moment they showed their identification.

The Becks' house was a large detached cottage situated in a small lane by the church, just off the main street. Much extended and built of the local stone, it was wonderfully warm inside and decorated in muted pastels. He showed them through the small entrance space and straight into a newer kitchen-cum-diner, where a sofa at the far end sat facing a log burner, flickering with flames.

The walls were covered, not with paintings, but with photographs of local scenes and wildlife. A grey heron, caught on a misty morning on a recognizable bank of the River Cherwell at Oxford, was framed in pride of place above the sofa. A close-up of a wagtail, perched on a stone in the middle of shallow stream, sat on the wall above the kitchen sink. They looked not quite professional, but all of them had merit, and she wondered which one of the Becks was the amateur photographer.

Hovering by the sofa, they found Martina Beck waiting for them, wearing the same strained smile as her husband. She looked younger than her spouse by some years, but that could have been put down to good clothes and flawlessly applied make-up. She too had white, rather than silver hair, but in her case she'd kept it long, and held up in a becoming chignon. She had large dark brown eyes and a face a little too rounded for conventional beauty. Like her husband, she wore well-fitted slacks, this time of a deep velvet brown, with a rose-pink pullover, very similar in design to that of her husband.

Wordlessly, William Beck set about making tea.

'Thank you for seeing us, Mr Beck, Mrs Beck,' Hillary began formally.

'Please, sit down,' Martina said, retrieving two kitchen chairs from beside the kitchen island, rightly assuming that the two women would prefer not to sit crammed together on the sofa with their hosts.

'We were surprised but very pleased to get your phone call yesterday,' she continued, returning to the sofa and sitting down at the same time as Hillary and Claire. 'Naturally, we've always wanted to get justice for Michael, and we're only hoping that you can find who did it this time.'

Hillary didn't take the implied slight personally. 'As do we, Mrs Beck,' she simply said gently.

Without prompting, Claire got out her notebook and pen, and proceeded to somehow disappear into her surroundings. It was a talent Hillary appreciated.

'And I'm glad that you feel that way about a second investigation,' Hillary added. 'Obviously, we're aware that taking a second look at cases such as your son's is bound to stir up a lot of pain and bad memories, and that not everyone is happy to rake over such times.'

'Oh, we don't mind that, if it means you might catch whoever did it,' William assured them, coming forward with a tray of steaming mugs. Hillary accepted one, took a sip and then set it down on the small coffee table between her and the sofa, Claire doing the same.

Neither of the Becks, she noticed, had elected to drink themselves. They were probably feeling way too tense and anxious to do so.

'As I said yesterday, I'm a former detective inspector, working as a civilian consultant for Thames Valley Police,' Hillary began to explain. 'No unsolved murder case is ever officially closed, and every now and then the Crime Review Team will take a second look at these cases. We find, with the passage of time, and with a fresh set of eyes, it's some-times possible to tease out some new lines of questioning, or unearth facts that might not have been uncovered by the original team. This doesn't mean that Inspector Weston's original investigation was flawed or shoddy in any way,' she emphasized clearly, 'it's just that, in the first rush of a new case, of necessity, some things tend to get prioritised. And under the pressure to get as much done as quickly as possi-ble, sometimes minor things don't get scrutinized as much as we'd like. As you are probably aware, the first forty-eight hours of a murder investigation are crucial. That puts an enormous pressure on officers working the case. Where we have the advantage over them is in having the luxury of being able to take much more time and care, and explore everything that perhaps didn't look very promising at the time.'

She paused to take a sip of tea. 'And this is going to be the focus of our investigation this time. There is no point, obviously, in simply going over the same things that DI Weston did back in 2011.'

The Becks were watching and listening to her intently, and Hillary paused to take another sip of her tea, giving them time to process what she'd said.

'Also, after a long period of time has passed, witnesses that might have been reluctant to speak at the time, for whatever reason, might now be persuaded into speaking more candidly,' she added, and let that sink in too.

Martina nodded, her face tight. 'They might not be so inclined to lie or cover up for people, you mean?'

'Well, that too, yes,' Hillary said, careful to keep her voice calm and unemotional. 'Also, sometimes their priorities change. What might have seemed so important or significant to them at the time could seem less important now. For example — witness "A" might have been having an extra-marital affair, and if he or she saw your son on the day he died, he or she might not have said so, for fear of being discovered in their infidelity. Their evidence might or might not be relevant, but until we uncover it, we have no way of knowing. But now, years later, they may have divorced or separated, or be more willing to be helpful.'

William Becks nodded, but said nothing. His wife merely sighed.

'You'd also be surprised how much people hold back simply because they don't want to get mixed up in a murder investigation. And again, here, the passage of time is a help to us. Things are less raw or frightening, and they find the courage to actually be cooperative. Then there are those people who simply didn't realize that some little snippet of information they had might have been of interest to the police, and so they didn't come forward because they didn't want to waste police time. Again, years later, if we come knocking on their door and actually ask them to talk about the day Michael died, they'll quite happily tell us.'

'Yes, I can see how that could happen,' Martina agreed.

Hillary, watching her closely, said casually, 'Then there are those who didn't want to say anything in case it caused trouble for people that they were sure could have had nothing to do with what happened to Michael. And in this, they may be right — or of course, they may not. But it's still an interesting psychological fact that these people often feel safer to talk about such things when a lot of time has passed than they did when a full-on murder investigation was under way. That's why these second looks into cases are so important.'

'Yes, we can see what you're getting at,' William Beck said, a touch impatiently.

'Do you have any reason to think that your neighbours or Michael's friends, or anyone else for that matter, had been less than honest about what they told DI Weston at the time?' she asked curiously, watching Martina more closely than her husband.

Michael Beck's mother flinched slightly, and cast a brief, questioning glance at her husband. 'We can't be sure. You have to understand, our emotions were all over the place at the time. But I never liked that girl Michael was seeing.'

'Mia de Salle?' Hillary clarified.

'Yes. She never seemed right for him somehow. I felt they were totally mismatched. I was glad when Michael broke up with her, to be honest. What's more, I don't think she was ever a particularly truthful person.'

At this, her husband stirred a little uneasily at her side. 'But that was just an impression we formed, you understand,' he added scrupulously. 'We never caught her telling outright lies.'

Martina laid a hand across her husband's knee and patted it. 'My husband is right, of course. But even he will admit that she was rather odd.'

'Can you be a bit more specific?' Hillary appealed.

'I don't know if I can. She just seemed to be not quite . . . I mean, oh, what's that expression? Off with the fairies?'

At this William sighed, but didn't contradict her.

Hillary thought about this statement for a moment, and decided it still needed clarifying. 'By that, do you think she was . . . what, mentally ill?'

'Oh no, I wouldn't go that far,' Martina said at once. 'She seemed to function perfectly well. And she was very clever, of course, getting a PhD in environmental studies and all that. It's just that . . . Oh, it's hard to describe. You'd have to have met her yourself to understand what I mean. It was as if she wasn't really living on the same planet as the rest of us somehow.'

'Did Michael say anything about Dr de Salle's, er, eccentricities?'

'No, not to us,' Martina admitted reluctantly.

'Did they ever argue violently?'

'No, not that we saw,' again the answer came grudgingly. 'At least, not while they were a couple. After they split up, she became . . . well, the only word I can use is obsessive.'

Hillary turned her attention to William. 'Do you agree with that, Mr Beck?'

William shrugged. 'I suppose so. She had a very strong personality, which made her very passionate about things. Especially about saving wildlife. I think that's probably what attracted Michael to her in the first place.'

He indicated the photograph of the heron. 'Michael's first and enduring love was always ancient history, but he loved animals and nature almost as much. Whenever he took up a new hobby he always threw himself into it with everything he had. Researched it, read all about it. He was a born scholar, that boy.'

'Michael took all these,' Martina broke in, indicating the photography on the walls. 'He was only twelve when he started. They're quite good, aren't they?'

'They certainly are,' Hillary agreed, but wasn't to be distracted. 'Do you know why he broke off their relationship?' she asked bluntly.

'Not really. I think she just got too much for him,' it was the boy's father who answered. 'From what we hear about her now and then, she's made a success of her life, but she could be a bit . . . intense, I think is the best word for her; a bit over the top. I think Michael simply found it a bit overwhelming after a while. Our son was very much a normal sort of chap, and she was . . . well, not.'

He shrugged helplessly.

'I understand she didn't take the break-up well,' Hillary tried next, and Martina all but snorted.

'She certainly didn't! For ages afterwards she kept ringing here, asking to speak to him. He'd blocked her calls on his mobile, and on social media and all that sort of thing,' Martina said. 'It got embarrassing in the end, having to pretend he wasn't in when she called.'

'Might it not have been easier for him to talk to her — convince her that it was over?' Hillary asked mildly.

'Oh, he *tried*,' William said sharply. 'But the woman just wouldn't take no for an answer.' He sighed wearily. 'Or perhaps that's being a bit harsh. I have no doubt that she was deeply hurt by it all. To be fair, she did care, very intensely, for Michael. But she just didn't seem to have the coping mechanisms in place that most of us have. When Michael left her, it seemed to shock her to the core. It was as if she just couldn't *believe* it was over.'

Hillary nodded, then said calmly, 'Do you think she killed him?'

For a moment, there was an electrified silence, and the two older people looked first at her, then at each other. Some kind of silent communication passed between them, because Martina gave a small sigh and a shrug.

'We simply don't know, do we, William? Somebody killed our son, and they must have had a reason for doing so. And it seems to us that she was really the only one who *might* have done it, the only one with a motive, you know? Michael hadn't an enemy in the world — he wasn't the sort of boy who got people mad at him. He was into his history and his latest favourite hobby, but apart from that he kept pretty much to himself. He wasn't a womaniser, or someone who went to the pub and drank too much and became a pest. If he wasn't studying or applying for jobs, he was here at home with us for most of the time. Apart from anything else, he didn't have much money to go gallivanting around. So where would he have crossed paths with someone *capable* of killing him?' she asked, the question clearly rhetorical. 'Mia, on the other hand, was . . . well, like I said. She was odd.'

Hillary decided she'd learned enough about Mia de Salle for now, and it was time to shift the focus. 'But Michael *did* have one enemy, didn't he?' she ventured.

'You mean that lecturer who groped him?' William Becks said, and his wife made a brief sound of disgust.

'Oh, *that* pervert,' she said grimly.

CHAPTER THREE

Hillary waited patiently, and eventually William Beck sighed heavily. 'Dr Durning,' he said with a grimace. 'But DI Weston was never able to place him and Michael together on the day that Michael died.'

Hillary, who'd read the file, knew that. But what she wanted from these people were their own thoughts on their son's life around the time of his death.

'Michael accused Dr Durning of making improper advances towards him in Dr Durning's office. Is that right?' she asked.

'Yes,' Martina said with another grimace. 'Michael was really upset about it. Apart from anything else, he said it really surprised him.'

Hillary blinked a little at this. She could tell Claire found the comment unexpected too, since her pencil momentarily stilled over her notebook.

'I'm sorry,' Hillary said, 'I'm not quite sure I understand.'

The dead boy's father smiled briefly. 'No, sorry, let me explain. After the incident happened, Michael returned home for the weekend. This was during the final year of his BA studies — the spring term. He was due to sit his final examinations that summer. He'd always *liked* Dr Durning, that was the thing, and he felt, apart from being shocked and repelled and angry and all the obvious things, as if he'd been really stupid in not realizing what must have been going on. At least, what had been going on in Dr Durning's *mind.*'

Hillary nodded. 'I think I understand. He felt somehow culpable because he felt that he'd been naïve in not realizing that his tutor had a predilection for him?'

William Beck shifted a little on the sofa, and sighed gently. 'Michael admired him as a teacher, you see, and Dr Durning had always been his favourite tutor. Our son was really into ancient history, right from the time he was a little boy. He grew up on the legends of King Arthur and the whole Camelot thing, and from that, his interest grew into the realms of proper history and became a real passion of his. And he always said that Dr Durning felt the same way. That he hadn't allowed himself to become jaded or bored, like a lot of his tutors had. Michael was particularly interested in the Saxons and Romans, but also in pre-history. He spent as much time as he could at the Rollright Stones, for instance, and Dr Durning always encouraged his research.'

Hillary nodded. She knew that the small, ancient circle of standing stones wasn't that far away, being just within the Oxfordshire border out near the pretty Cotswold villages known as the Tews. Nowhere near as famous or impressive as Stonehenge, of course, or the circle at Avebury, they were nevertheless still fascinating in their own right. 'Was that because they're close by?'

'Partly, yes, and also because they're less well-studied. He also loved visiting the white horses,' William said.

Again, Hillary immediately understood the references. There were ancient depictions of horses that had been carved into the chalk hills by ancient man in several nearby locations in Oxfordshire, such as Uffington, and even more in the nearby county of Wiltshire.

'And Michael wanted to make ancient history his career. He wanted to go on to do a PhD and teach it to university standards. Maybe even write text books,' William continued.

'Which is why he allowed himself to become so close to Dr Durning, in all innocence, because Durning always encouraged his ambition.'

'I imagine that's a tough field to break into,' Hillary murmured. 'So few good appointments, and far too many candidates. Not many people with degrees manage to get university postings, surely?'

'No, you're right. So many of them have to settle for jobs in related but lesser fields than pure academia. And Michael knew that. But according to him, Dr Durning was always very supportive of his chances of achieving his goals, and sponsored him all the way. And Michael, up until that moment in his office, had always thought that his encouragement was genuine. And . . . well, pure, for want of a better word.'

'But it seems Dr Durning had other, less altruistic motives?' Hillary supplied.

'Yes,' William said flatly. 'When he asked Michael to come to his office that last time, he used the excuse that he'd found some rare books in a private collection that he thought would interest Michael. But when they were alone . . . Well, according to Michael he seemed to think . . . well . . .' But here the older man seemed to be lost for words.

'He asked Michael for sexual favours in return for access to the books?' Hillary encouraged.

'No, not in so many words,' William said carefully, as if anxious to be seen to be fair. 'From the way Michael explained it to us, it was more as if Dr Durning thought and fully expected that Michael would be interested in starting a relationship with him. It surprised Michael no end, because, well, for a start, he'd been seeing Mia for a while by that time, and he was sure Dr Durning must have been aware that he wasn't gay.'

'So what happened?' Hillary asked. Of course, Michael Beck's version of what had happened next, along with the subsequent investigation by the university, were all included in DI Weston's files, but Hillary wanted to see if the Becks' memories of that time contained anything new.

'Well, Michael said at first that he was just stunned. He couldn't think what to do or say. He said he just stood there, speechless and embarrassed.'

'Perhaps,' Martina injected, 'that might have given the wretched man the wrong impression. Maybe he mistook Michael's silence for acquiescence. Anyway, he tried to seduce Michael. Physically, I mean,' she finished disdainfully.

'He tried to kiss him?' Hillary asked, more bluntly.

'Yes,' William said. 'And he pushed him against the wall, touching him inappropriately.' It was said in a quick, flat tone, as if the older man had had to say the words before, but didn't really want to hear them.

Hillary could understand why. 'I understand this is all very distasteful and upsetting,' she said gently. 'I take it Michael fought him off?'

'Yes,' William said briskly.

'And then reported Dr Durning to the head of the university?'

'Yes. But not straight away,' William said, after a moment's hesitation. 'Michael said he felt hideously embarrassed at first, and just wanted to forget about it. After all, this was the man he'd always admired, and who'd been his greatest champion. Then he began to wonder if, somehow, it was his own fault that it had happened. You know, had he somehow given his tutor reason to believe that there was something between them.'

'Yes, that often happens with victims of sexual harassment,' Hillary agreed quietly, with a quick glance at Claire. She, having dealt with abused women for most of her career, knew all about this sort of thing. She saw her companion grimace, but knew that Claire wouldn't give a lecture on it right now. She wouldn't want to interrupt the flow of the interview.

'They start to second-guess themselves,' Hillary explained matter-of-factly. 'They start to look back on things and wonder if some innocent remark they'd made could have sounded like a come-on. Or whether a purely innocent gesture could have been interpreted as an invitation.' Although, as both she and Claire well knew, it was far more often women who had this type of experience, she knew that men were not immune from this sort of false reasoning.

'Exactly. It took him a while, I think, to come to terms with it all. To see that he'd actually done nothing wrong — nothing at all. And that his tutor had no right to put him in such an invidious position. That he'd used his position of power in order to try and, well, persuade him into doing something that he wasn't comfortable with. And when he finally reasoned all that out,' William shrugged, 'he finally became angry.'

'You say he *finally* became angry,' Hillary slipped in smoothly. 'Was Michael usually slow to anger, would you say?'

'Oh yes,' the boy's mother said at once. 'It sometimes worried me. He was such a placid child. And even when he grew older, he had such an even, amiable nature. It took a lot to make him angry, didn't it, darling?' She looked over at her husband.

'Yes.'

Hillary nodded. So it was unlikely that their murder victim had been killed because his hot head had got the wrong person riled up. Unless . . .

'But when he *did* lose his temper, did he lose it violently?' Hillary asked. Some people who were slow to anger could really blow their top when they finally did. And if that was the case here, then it was possible that Michael, unused to being angry, had really lost it on the final day of his life, and whoever he'd taken his frustrations out on had returned the favour in kind and then some.

'No, not really,' Martina said thoughtfully, again looking at her husband.

'When Michael was upset about something, he tended to become quieter if anything, and very stubborn,' he said.

'Yes, that's true. Normally he would just go along to please people, you know? But if he was seriously riled, he'd dig his heels in and be very mulish.' Martina smiled. 'I

31

remember him once as a boy refusing to do something or other I'd asked of him, and nothing could move him.'

Keeping her voice carefully neutral, Hillary continued her questioning. 'Do you think that's what happened with his tutor? Was he just being stubborn in going through with the complaint?' It was not that she didn't applaud the dead man for the courage of his actions, but she needed to get a feel for the victim. Was he a vindictive sort? Was he quick to be offended? Did he always retaliate? It didn't seem so, based on what she'd learned about him thus far, but if he was, it was far more likely that Michael had more enemies than his parents seemed to think. And that was something she needed to be aware of.

'No, it wasn't that so much,' Martina explained wearily. 'Michael never wanted Dr Durning to get the sack, for instance, did he?' She turned to her husband, who was already shaking his head. 'In fact, we had to stop him writing a letter to the university about it.'

'He just didn't want another student to go through the same thing, you see,' William Beck said with a small, sad smile. 'I think, in his own mind, he'd convinced himself that Dr Durning had been guilty of nothing more than a bad lapse of judgement. That he had misunderstood their relationship and Michael just wanted him to be more careful in the future. So that he didn't do it again and upset another student, or be drummed out of teaching altogether. In spite of it all, I think he still credited the man with being a good teacher.'

'So he felt guilty when Dr Durning had to leave the university?'

'Yes, in a way. I told him it was silly to feel that way,' Martina said, anger creeping back into her voice now. 'The man got exactly what he deserved.'

'But Michael wanted to retract his accusation?' Hillary persisted, still not sure that she fully understood the dynamics of what had happened between her murder victim and his tutor.

'No!'

'No!'

Both the Becks spoke forcefully and at the same time. After another quick, silent glance passed between them, it was Martina who carried on.

'As we pointed out to him, after he spoke up and the university began an investigation, several other young men who'd been students of Dr Durning came forward and testified that similar things had happened to them,' she said indignantly. 'As I told Michael, it wasn't as if the university had taken Michael's word for it alone. Well, they wouldn't, would they?' she said bitterly. 'If they'd been able to, they'd have swept it under the carpet and avoided a scandal at any cost.'

'Now, I'm not sure that's altogether true, Marty,' her husband put in, but his wife, for once, ignored him.

'But with others backing Michael up, they couldn't,' she added, with evident satisfaction.

Hillary nodded. 'Did Dr Durning make any threats against Michael after he left the university? And would Michael have confided in you if he had?'

'No, I'm sure he didn't,' Martina said, clearly confident of her answer. 'Michael had proper support from the university when it became clear that Dr Durning was a serial offender, I'll give them that, at least. He was appointed a proper counsellor that he could always talk to, as well as a member of the Student Union to keep an eye on him. I'm sure if anything more had happened, one or the other of them would have known about it. I felt so helpless being here while Michael was finishing his final term, but it did help to know that he had someone he could go to at Bristol.'

'Would Michael have told them things, do you think?' Hillary mused. 'Would he have been happy to talk about such private matters with strangers?' Again, she was not judging, only trying to understand Michael's personality.

'Yes, I think so,' the dead boy's mother said, beginning to sound tired now. 'He was never a secretive sort of boy.

Never the kind to keep things locked up. He was an only child, so we were always a bit worried that he might not be very sociable, but we needn't have been concerned on that front,' Martina smiled. 'He made friends easily, and his best friend, Kevin, was almost like a brother to him. They'd known each other since they were eleven. He was always enthusiastic, and shared his toys, even as a toddler.'

Hillary nodded and decided that it was time to leave it there. Both of her witnesses were beginning to look as if they'd been put through the wringer, which was not surprising. She could always come back for a second interview once the case inevitably started throwing up more things that she'd need to ask.

'All right, Mr Beck, Mrs Beck, I think that's all we need for now,' she said, beginning to gather her things around her and rising from her chair. 'I might like to come back some other time to talk some more, if that's all right with you?'

'That's more than all right with us,' William said, also rising. His wife, still looking weary, stayed on the sofa.

William walked them out in silence, but on the doorstep, he looked Hillary in the eye and said, 'Please find whoever killed him.'

Hillary swallowed back a hard lump that had risen in her throat, and promised simply, 'I'll do everything I can, Mr Beck.'

* * *

Six months ago

DI Robin Farrell peered through the back door of the dingy shop but made no move to step inside. The police photographer and the scene-of-crime people were still working around the pathetic figure of the dead shop owner, and he was not averse to waiting until they'd finished.

He glanced curiously around the neighbourhood, feeling a little depressed by the rows of tiny back gardens, most of them overrun with weeds, nettles and rusting objects, the run-down garages all but falling apart and used more for storage than shelters for cars, and the ubiquitous rain-soaked overflowing gutters.

'At least finding a witness who saw our man come and go should be easy enough, guv,' the young and green constable standing beside him said, looking hopefully at the many rows of windows in the surrounding drab council houses and the back ends of a few other shops. '*Someone* must have seen Mr Newley's visitor.'

Robin gave a brief grunt of laughter, which held nothing of amusement in it. 'I doubt it, Constable,' he predicted tiredly. 'Most of the homeowners will prove to have been out at work or spending their universal credit at the pub, and even those who were home won't have been looking this way, mark my words. And as for the commercial premises,' he glanced at the grubby rear windows of the betting shop next door, which had its blinds firmly drawn, 'I think you'll find that they were all too busy with their own customers to take notice of Mr Newley's business.'

It never ceased to amaze the DI how good people were at managing not to see things going on right under their noses — especially in districts like this.

The constable glanced again at the houses, hoping that the senior investigating officer was just being pessimistic. After all, it would be he, along with some other constables, who would be spending the rest of their day talking to the neighbours, and the prospect of meeting with a belligerent wall of silence, or wide-eyed fake innocence, was depressing.

'It's not a nice area, is it, sir?' he finally muttered in forlorn agreement — and massive understatement.

Robin Farrell didn't bother to answer, but moved back out of the way as one of the white-suited lab technicians stepped past him with a box of bagged evidence. His absence from the narrow rear passageway revealed the doctor who was kneeling beside the fallen body and examining it closely. Once the medical man had finished and was packing up his case, Robin sent the constable about his unenviable task, and prepared to have a brief word with the expert.

The doctor wasn't someone Robin knew, but he greeted the SIO with a smile and a brief handshake. 'Dr Coltrane. And don't ask for miracles,' were his opening, rather discouraging words. 'But I'm prepared to say that he's probably been dead not more than two hours. And it looks, from just my preliminary inspection, as if cause of death is likely to be the blow to the head, made by an oddly shaped weapon, probably made of some kind of metal. But don't hold me to it until after a full autopsy.'

Robin glanced at the form of the dead man lying in the hallway, and sighed.

'Right,' he said heavily.

When he'd been given the assignment and learned that the victim was a man killed in his shop, he'd immediately assumed the chances were high that he would be dealing with a more or less straightforward robbery gone wrong. Now, he was beginning to wonder. Most thieves who killed did so because their victims confronted them in the shop in the act of actually stealing, or in the office, caught trying to steal the petty cash.

But the old man here had been killed at the back door, and according to those who were first on the scene, the cash box had been found intact further inside.

'One thing of interest,' the doctor said, making the inspector's ears prick up, 'I found two unusual marks on his chest. I was first alerted to them by a slight brownish stain on the front of his shirt.'

'Knife wounds?' Robin asked.

The medical man looked at the SIO with interest, seeing a man somewhere in his mid-to-late forties, not quite six feet tall, with thinning fair hair and wide grey eyes.

'No. I think it far more likely that they were made by two points of electricity coming into contact with his skin, having penetrated the thin material of his clothing.'

It took the inspector only a moment of quick thought to come up with the answer. 'You think he was hit by a taser first?'

'I think that's the most likely explanation,' the doctor confirmed cautiously. 'I'll be able to say for sure once I've got him on the table.'

Robin frowned. This was looking less and less like an opportunist robbery the more he learned about it. 'I see. Anything else you think I should know about?'

'Not at this stage, Inspector,' the doctor said with a wry smile. 'I think I've stuck my neck out far enough as it is.' He cast the dead man a brief look and sighed. 'Good luck. I'll be off now.'

The inspector nodded and thanked him, then set off around the side of the building to the front of the shop, where the first officer on the scene — an old hand from the local station — was guarding the front door. Not that it needed much guarding, as the street was conspicuously empty. It wouldn't have taken long for word to get around that the police were out in force, and not even nosy kids had been allowed out to see what it was all about.

'Constable Wrighton, isn't it?' he said briefly to the man standing stolidly in front of the door.

'Yes, sir.'

'Know the victim, do you?'

'Yes, sir, he's pretty well known to us. Simon Newley. He's had these premises for going on thirty years now.'

Robin nodded, not surprised by the news that his victim had come to the attention of the locals. It had taken him but one glance at the premises to guess that the owner of such a place was hardly likely to be a paragon of virtue. Shops such as this one were shops in name only.

He glanced through the almost impenetrable grime and peered into the interior. 'What a load of tat,' he commented. 'He never earned his daily crust from selling that lot,' he nodded his head to include the items within.

The constable's lips twisted. 'That he didn't, sir.' He regarded the SIO with the calm patience that a lot of long-serving, lower-rank officers usually reserved for the high-flyers. He knew, vaguely, of DI Robin Farrell's reputation. Decent enough bloke, recently divorced (who wasn't?), with grown kids. Too good-looking for his own good, so the rumour mill had it, and his missus had found him playing away. Worked out of Thames Valley HQ in Kidlington. Played golf, hoping to catch some bigwig's eye, no doubt. Had ambitions, so it was said.

Well, the constable had no problem with that. Although he doubted he himself would ever even make sergeant he was happy to have a steady job and a steady wage.

'Receiver of stolen goods, our Mr Newley,' he said helpfully. 'Fence. Unofficial pawnbroker. Did a bit of smuggling of ciggies and booze too, I shouldn't wonder,' he added.

'Bit of an all-rounder then,' Robin said with another mirthless smile. 'Sounds like the old-fashioned sort.'

The constable grinned. 'That about sums him up, sir. Made a living, kept to himself.'

'Form?'

'No, sir,' the constable surprised him by admitting. 'Our Simon was too canny and too timid to really stick his neck out. We nearly had him a couple of times over the years, but nothing stuck. You know how it is. Nobody around here would grass him up — they needed his services too often. And he was a known quantity too. You could trust him — well, within limits, like — and he'd been here so long he was almost an institution. A local mascot, so to speak.'

Robin nodded and sighed. 'I get the picture.'

The constable regarded the SIO for a moment, then sniffed. 'Funny thing, this,' he jerked his head back towards the shop. 'Can't really understand it. Old Simon never struck me as the sort to go and get his head bashed in.'

'Oh? I'd have thought a man in his line would have made plenty of enemies?' Robin countered mildly. 'Some junkie who didn't think he gave him enough for his mother's best wristwatch or wedding ring maybe?'

'Nah, I can't see it myself,' the constable said helpfully. 'Like I said, he was careful. He knew who to do business with, and who to avoid. He knew every petty villain and third-rate crook for miles. As I said, he just wasn't the sort to stick his neck out.'

'Could be straightforward robbery?' Robin floated the idea without much hope.

'Never kept that much cash here, he didn't, and everyone knew it. And as for finding something worth lifting in there . . .' He eyed the interior of the shop and laughed out loud.

'A stranger to the area?' Robin Farrell hazarded next.

The constable shrugged without enthusiasm. 'Possible, I suppose,' he said doubtfully, looking around the narrow backwater ostentatiously. And Robin took his point — the place was hardly on a main thoroughfare. You'd have to know it was here to find it.

'Personal woes?' he asked next.

'Nah — married for over thirty years to the same long-suffering woman,' the constable said. 'Lives in a nice little place in your neck of the woods in Kidlington. Sensible woman, had a brood of kids by him and was fond of him in her own way, so rumour has it. I can't see her bashing him over the head with a rolling pin. But you never know. And he wasn't what you'd exactly call a ladies' man, our Simon.' He grinned openly at the thought. 'No jealous husbands had it in for *him*, I reckon. No, it won't have been personal,' he predicted confidently.

Robin nodded. That all rang true enough.

Besides, the inspector believed that he already had a pretty good idea who was behind all this, and why, and he suspected the helpful local did too. But whether or not Robin and his subsequent investigation would be able to prove it remained to be seen.

But he'd give it a damned good go.

CHAPTER FOUR

Hillary and Claire returned to the office from Woodeaton around eleven o'clock. Claire immediately put the kettle on and brought out the communal biscuit tin. Happily dunking a custard cream into her mug of steaming tea, she sighed in bliss as she munched and began to type up her notes, somehow managing not to spill a drop of liquid or scatter a crumb on her keyboard. It was her boss's habit to keep a running 'Murder Book', which everyone contributed to as and when they'd completed a task, thus keeping it regularly updated with anything they came across. This ensured that everyone could refer to it and know what was what, and there was less chance of repetition of tasks or any snippet of information falling through the cracks.

Hillary made a point to always read it through last thing at night before leaving, and she was glancing through it now as she sipped from her own mug of coffee.

As Claire typed, Hillary gave Gareth a verbal account of what they'd learned at the Becks' house, then asked him if he'd managed to track down the original investigator in Spain as she'd asked.

'I did, ma'am,' Gareth said smartly. 'He was actually at home, and we had a long telephone conversation. I've almost finished typing up the report.'

'Give us the highlights then,' Hillary instructed, sitting down on the edge of his desk. It was always kept so clear and tidy that she was in no danger of dislodging anything with her backside, which, in the past, had tended to be broader than she'd have liked. (She wouldn't dare try this manoeuvre on Claire's end of the desk though!)

'Ma'am. DI Weston remembered the case after a little prompting,' he began, rifling through his notebook for reference, though Hillary suspected he didn't really need it. 'At first, he concentrated on a possible drugs angle,' he said, frowning slightly, 'although I couldn't see, from reading the case files so far, that drugs were ever really an issue?'

Hillary nodded. 'No, but it was a logical starting point for him,' she explained. It was part of her job to teach Gareth as much as she could, and give him training as they worked. 'Any officer, on being confronted with the death of someone young, especially if they've recently been — or still are — a student, is to look at the drugs angle. Simply because more often than not, they turn out to be at the root of it.'

Claire sighed over her third custard cream. 'Either dying of it because they took too much, or it was a bad dose, or they just had a bad reaction to it, or because they sold it on somebody's else patch, and pissed off the local pusher,' she chipped in.

'Exactly,' Hillary agreed.

'But there were no signs of drug abuse in Michael Beck's autopsy,' Gareth pointed out. He was not arguing, Hillary knew, just trying to learn. 'And his parents were adamant that he was not a user, and had no need to be a dealer. And he did come from a fairly affluent family. He wouldn't have needed to sell stuff, would he?'

Hillary nodded. 'What you need to take into account when dealing with family members and their evidence is this. Some parents actually *do* have a very good understanding of their children, and really *are* the best people to give you pointers as to a victim's circumstances, personality, and movements. So don't ignore them or dismiss them. However, others really don't have a clue.'

'The problem is, of course, you can't always tell which is which,' Claire put in, contemplating the biscuit tin and wondering whether to switch her allegiance to Jammie Dodgers, but forcing herself, with regret, to put the lid back on instead.

Hillary smiled grimly. Wasn't that the truth? 'DI Weston wouldn't have been able to take the Becks' word for it that their son wasn't involved in the drug culture. Yes, the autopsy suggested he likely wasn't a user, but dealing them was still very much a possibility.'

Gareth absorbed this, then nodded thoughtfully. 'Now you've met them, ma'am, what do you think of them?'

Hillary cast a quick look at Claire, who shrugged, and carried on typing.

'They seemed a nice couple, genuine and honest as far as I could tell,' Hillary began cautiously. 'I think, from what they said, they probably *were* close to their son. I certainly didn't get the vibe that there were any tensions between them, and the fact that Michael was back home and living harmoniously among the family seems to bear that out. But he *was* an only child, and it's always possible that his parents might have been the clinging type and that he was desperate to get away. He was actively seeking work, but that's only to be expected. He couldn't afford a car, which suggests that even though his parents didn't exactly lack money, they didn't over-indulge him either. They paid his university fees though.'

Claire, listening to this recital, was impressed with how much Hillary always got out of her interviews with witnesses. She hoped young Gareth was taking it all in.

'Could be they didn't buy him a car because they liked to keep him close to home,' she chipped in, but Hillary sensed that she spoke more as devil's advocate than because she had sensed possessiveness in the Becks.

Hillary shrugged. 'But all this is speculation. Carry on with DI Weston's take on things,' she nodded at Gareth to continue.

'Yes, ma'am.' He turned a page of his notebook and nodded. 'When his team couldn't find any evidence of his involvement with drugs, he turned to the victim's personal life. He told me, right from the start, that Dr de Salle . . . er . . . quote "pinged my radar" unquote. Says he thought the young lady might be . . . quote "a bunny boiler" unquote.'

Claire snorted over her nearly empty mug of tea, but otherwise didn't comment.

'I take it DI Weston hadn't attended many seminars on sensitive policing,' Hillary put in dryly, making Claire snort even louder.

Gareth looked uncertain how to respond. No doubt in the army one didn't tend to disrespect officers within the hearing of other officers. Hillary spared him having to make a comment on the ex-DI, and said briskly, 'But he confirmed he wasn't able to find any evidence linking her to the victim that day?'

'That's right, ma'am. As you know, according to the Becks' original statement, their son was in the habit of leaving the house more or less every day on his bicycle, either to cycle to Oxford to look for work, or to indulge in his hobbies.' Hillary recognized this as an almost verbatim quote from the original case files, and she wasn't surprised that her latest team member was already well on his way to memorizing much of the paperwork.

The more she got to know him, the more impressed she became with him, and she could only hope that he'd stay in the job long-term.

'They were rather hampered by the fact that, right from the start, they didn't know what the victim intended to do that day,' Gareth swept on. 'His best friend, Kevin Philpott, didn't know either and Mia de Salle also pleaded ignorance.'

'For all DI Weston knew, he could have gone to the city, left his bike somewhere and met up with someone who had a car,' Hillary mused. 'In which case the bike was probably stolen from Oxford. Or he might have been off in the local area taking his wildlife photos. In which case, whoever killed him must have come across him out and about and, after murdering him, disposed of the bike somehow.'

'Yes, ma'am. DI Weston said they searched everywhere in the local countryside for the bicycle but it never showed up.'

'Not surprising,' Claire said gloomily. 'All the killer had to do was leave it propped against a lamp post somewhere in town and it would be gone and repainted before you could spit.'

Hillary nodded. Oxford had a massive bicycle-theft problem.

'Well, we know the only sighting of Michael on that day was right after he left his parents' house and was seen cycling through the village, heading towards Oxford,' Hillary said. 'Which isn't exactly helpful. Did the DI say if he ever came up with a favourite theory? Something too nebulous to put in writing maybe?'

Sometimes, she knew from being a DI herself, you often got a 'feel' for something that you just knew your superiors would never wear, and thus never officially recorded it anywhere. Nevertheless, that didn't stop you forming your own theories.

'No, ma'am, not really. He didn't have total recall of the case, or details, only his vague memories. He didn't take any of his notebooks with him to Spain, so he couldn't help out much. But he did say that he remembered feeling as if the victim was not the sort to get himself killed, and he couldn't find anyone with a bad word to say about him — apart from the jilted girlfriend and his former tutor, of course.'

'A waste of a phone call then,' Claire opined gloomily, still eyeing the biscuit tin wistfully.

Hillary shrugged. 'Well, that's the way it—' She was interrupted by the straightforward ringtone of Gareth's mobile. Not for the ex-soldier a jaunty theme tune.

He answered it with a quick, guilty look at Hillary. He rarely received personal calls when he was at work, and he was surprised that he had now. But the moment he recognized the voice on the other end of the line, he felt a small jolt of worry pass through him.

'Hello, Jase, what's up?' he said quietly.

'Can you get away from work for a bit? I need to see you, mate.'

Gareth cast another quick, worried look at Hillary, who raised an eyebrow.

'Is it urgent, mate?' Gareth asked.

'Oh, don't bother,' his friend snapped. 'I wouldn't want to get you in shit with the big boss lady.'

'No, don't hang up,' he said urgently. He'd heard his friend in this kind of mood before and he knew it didn't bode well. 'Hold on . . .' Gareth closed his eyes briefly. His friend sounded as if he'd been drinking. Never a good idea if you also suffered from severe depression.

'Problems?' Hillary said quietly, and saw his eyes snap open again. In truth, it wasn't much of a leap on her part — she could read his indecision and unhappiness clearly on his face.

'Yes, ma'am. Would it be possible for me to take a few hours off? I can make it up by working late,' he promised hopefully.

Immediately, Hillary nodded. 'Sure, go ahead.'

'Thank you, ma'am. Jase, where are you? Are you at home?'

'Where else would I be?' his friend asked bitterly and abruptly hung up.

Gareth rose, pulled his jacket from the back of his chair and reached for his car keys. His car, adapted so that he could drive it with his limited mobility, had been one of the many things that he had at first resented, but had now come to cherish. 'Thanks again, ma'am,' he muttered awkwardly, and left as quickly as his limp would let him.

Both Claire and Hillary watched him go in silence. Once the sound of his footsteps had faded along the subterranean corridor, Claire sighed. 'Do you think that was his friend — the chap he was in the army with? Suffering from PTSD, isn't he?'

Hillary shook her head. 'I don't know. I just hope it's nothing bad,' she said. But her eyes were watchful as well as concerned.

This wasn't the first time she'd had cause to speculate about Gareth Proctor and his links with his former pals — or enemies — in the army.

* * *

Gareth drove within the speed limit and with his usual customary care, even though his heart was thudding uneasily in his chest. It wasn't often that Jason Morley phoned him and the fact that he had now worried him.

Although Jason hadn't been able to settle down to a job for any length of time after leaving the army, he'd always *seemed* genuinely pleased that Gareth had found a new career for himself. And one that Gareth thought might finally give him some sort of focus in life.

Of course, Jason had always ragged him about being a 'police lackey' with no real power to call his own, but underneath his friend's cheesy grin, Gareth had often sensed some deeper, hidden feeling. Contempt maybe, a touch of envy, or maybe just sardonic amusement — or a combination of all three?

When he arrived at his friend's tiny flat, he knocked on the door, still unsure what sort of state Jason might be in.

He had to knock a second time — wait and then knock yet again — before the door was finally opened. By that time he'd begun to run through worst-case scenarios, so he breathed a sigh of relief when he met his friend's baleful and slightly bloodshot eyes.

As Gareth had expected from the slight slur he'd detected in his friend's voice over the telephone, Jason had been drinking heavily. He clung to the door, making it creak in protest. He blinked blearily for a moment, finally recognized his visitor and then gave a wide, sardonic smile that revealed yellowing, uneven teeth. A waft of sour body odour emanating from his direction told Gareth that he hadn't showered in some time, and his chin was rapidly beginning to grow a beard.

Remembering how smart he'd always looked in his uniform, and the painstaking care he'd taken to keep his boots and kit clean, it made Gareth want to either swear or cry.

'Well, well, if it isn't PC Plod,' Jason growled. As a friendly greeting, it left a lot to be desired. 'Whad'ya want?'

'You called me. Remember?'

Jason frowned, as if about to debate the truth of this, then merely shrugged and turned around, lurching back into the living room beyond.

He made it to the room's sagging sofa and fell into it.

Gareth sighed gently and closed the door behind him. Without a word, he spent the next half an hour vacuuming and dusting the small space, washing and drying the dirty dishes clustered around the sink in the tiny kitchen, and emptying and taking out the bin bags.

All the while his friend watched him in total silence.

When Gareth had finally finished and sat down in the battered armchair opposite the sofa, he almost felt as tired and depressed as his friend.

'Feel better now?' Jason asked quietly, without a trace of the savage grin of before.

'No,' Gareth admitted wearily. He knew, as did his friend, that his compulsion to see everything kept neat and tidy was his way of trying to keep control of his destiny, and to keep the random chaos of life at bay. Which was about as successful as the proverbial rearrangement of deckchairs on the *Titanic*.

Jason Morley regarded his best friend for a long moment, and then laughed. 'A right pair we are, aren't we, mate?' he said softly.

'Yeah,' Gareth agreed, rubbing his face with his undamaged hand. 'So. What's up?'

His friend looked at him bleakly. 'I shouldn't have called you.'

'You can call me anytime. I told you that, and I meant it. Not thinking of jumping off any bridges, are you?' Gareth tried to keep his voice light. 'Because with my gammy leg and useless arm I'm not the swimmer I once was.'

'You'd have more sense than to jump in after me,' Jason gave another wide grin.

Gareth gave a small grunt that might have indicated agreement — or might not. 'Seriously. How are you doing?'

'You don't want to know.'

'Right. That's why you sent out the SOS. To tell me something I don't want to know?' he allowed himself to sound just a little exasperated. 'So long as you're not about to rob a bank, I'm listening.'

Jason nodded. 'I forgot you were working for the boys in blue.'

'No you didn't,' Gareth said levelly.

For a long moment, the two ex-soldiers simply looked at one another. Then Jason slowly nodded. 'No. You're right. I didn't. I wanted to tell you . . . I mean, I've been wanting to tell you something for months.'

Gareth felt himself tense, as if for a blow. He became aware that he was feeling slightly sick. Was this going to be the day that his friend finally said something that, once spoken out loud, could never be retracted? Was this going to be the day when his loyalty to his stricken comrade was finally going to be put to the ultimate test?

And if it was, just what the hell would he *do*?

Feeling a little panicky, Gareth flexed his injured hand, feeling the usual stiffness just tinged with pain that had now become the norm. It had become a habit of his, whenever he was under stress, to do something to test the limits of his injuries. No doubt a psychiatrist would have had a field day with that, should he ever be foolish enough to admit it to one.

'Oh shit, Gary,' Jason said heavily, making Gareth's heart sink further still. Jason only used that version of his name when he was really agitated. 'I just . . . Things are getting on top of me, that's all. I needed to speak to someone about . . .'

'The army?'

'No.'

'What happened to you over there?'

'Shit no!'

'What happened to me?' Gareth attempted a smile, and held up his mangled hand and waggled it.

Jason grunted with laughter. 'Hell no. *You* wanna talk to *me* about that?'

'Hell no.'

Again, they both grinned aimlessly at each other. Then Jason's face hardened, and again Gareth's heart rate rocketed, anticipating the worst.

But even as he braced himself, Gareth saw the determination leak out of his friend's haggard face, and his eyes shifted restlessly away. He gave a long, shaken sigh and let it out noisily.

'Look, let's just forget it, yeah?' Jason said flatly. 'I shouldn't have called you. It's just . . . you're my best mate and . . . but you've got some sort of life back and I don't want to . . . Just forget I called, will you?'

He forced himself out of the chair and into the kitchen, where he drew a bottle of beer from the small fridge. He levered the tin cap off it expertly by leveraging it under a protruding, open drawer, and took a long swallow, walking back to the living room.

He didn't look at his friend, which was just as well, because he might have seen the relief, tinged with guilt, written clearly on Gareth's face.

But the truth was, ever since Gareth had learned about the murder of a former soldier in Reading, he felt as if he'd been walking a tightrope. Never daring to ask Jason what he knew about it because he was always scared of what the answer might be. But never being able to quite forget about it either.

And here he was, still performing the same old circus trick. Wouldn't it be better to face it, square on at last? To stop being afraid of the bogey-man under the bed and drag him out into the light of day? At least then they'd know what they were dealing with. But what if he'd got it wrong — about everything? After all, there was no proof, none at all, that Jason had done something unthinkable. There were only his suspicions and fears. And he might be way off beam. Wasn't it that possibility that had kept him silent all these months? To let his best mate realize that he suspected him of doing something utterly awful — when in fact he hadn't — would kill their friendship stone dead.

Feeling even more nauseous, he swallowed hard. 'You know I'll do whatever needs doing if you're really in a fix, mate,' Gareth said, watching his friend's back. He could clearly see Jason's shoulder blades sticking out underneath the dirty T-shirt. 'No matter what, I'll stick by you, Jase,' he added.

There. He couldn't say more than that, could he? The offer was there. It had been made. All his friend had to do was take it and . . . But even as he thought it, he felt the tension set like rock in the pit of his stomach, and he wished he'd left the words unsaid.

Because if Jason did unburden his soul — and it was as bad as he suspected — what then? What, exactly, would he, Gareth Proctor, do?

Slowly, Jason's shoulders hunched in despair. 'Yeah, I know you would,' the former soldier said bleakly. 'That's what worries me . . .' he added in a despairing mumble.

Gareth felt his throat go bone dry. A cool sweat broke out on his forehead. And suddenly he knew for sure that there could no longer be any doubt. This *was* about that bastard Corporal Francis Clyde-Brough.

But even as he opened his mouth to ask, Gareth knew that he didn't dare actually say the words.

'Just go, all right,' Jason said finally, still with his back turned to his friend. He suddenly sounded very sober.

With some difficulty, Gareth managed to get out of the decrepit chair. And still he didn't dare mention the bastard's name. Nearly a year dead, and still former Corporal Clyde-Brough was doing his usual damage . . .

'Jase,' Gareth said helplessly.

'Just piss off, mate, yeah?' Jason said gently, still not turning around to look his friend in the eye.

And slowly, reluctantly, his heart hammering in his chest and every instinct telling him to stay, Gareth left.

When the door had finally shut behind him, Jason Morley stared at a crack that ran almost the entire length of one wall, and stood for a long time, thinking and drinking beer.

He didn't know how much time had passed, but he found himself nodding, as if in agreement about some decision that he wasn't aware had been made.

Eventually he went back to the sofa and slumped into it.

He needed to do some proper thinking.

One thing was clear. Gareth knew. He might not be able to bring himself to say it out loud, but he *knew* what he, Jason Morley, had done. All those months ago, on that dark, dreary night in Reading.

Gareth, his good old mate Gareth, his comrade-in-arms Gareth, upstanding, law-abiding Gareth Proctor, knew. Good old Gareth, who was now a policeman in all but name, knew that he'd committed murder.

Jason closed his eyes for a moment, and then nodded some more.

Yes. It was finally time to *do* something about all this. He could put it off no longer. He was getting too tired, and really, what was the point in prolonging things? It had to be sorted out, one way or another.

Once and for all.

CHAPTER FIVE

Six months ago

The killer of Simon Newley sat behind the wheel of their parked car and waited, nervously but patiently, feeling glad that the afternoon light was now fading and that soon it would be dark. Although it had been many hours now since Newley had died, and the killer wanted nothing more than to go home and have a strong, fortifying drink, it simply was not possible.

The horrors of the day were not yet over — and what had to be done now had to be done quickly, before the next victim heard about Newley's death and was alerted.

The killer patted their most prized gadget, which was now fully recharged and ready again for action. It hadn't been easy to acquire, of course. But there were always ways and means for someone who was determined — and willing to pay.

Around the unremarkable-looking car, the street lamps started to come on. Since it was autumn, the lights reflected glorious hues of reds, oranges and golds, giving the leafy city side street an almost storybook atmosphere, but the driver barely noticed.

The next victim was due home any time soon, and if he wasn't on his own . . . well, then, things might not be so easy. The moment would have to be postponed, and who knew, by then, what protection Lionel Kirklees might have put in place? He would certainly make himself a far harder target once he knew the danger he was in, and would be bound to keep bodyguards close.

The uncertainty of not knowing if the moneylender to most of Oxford's less-than-upstanding citizenry would be vulnerable or not was giving the car's occupant the heebie-jeebies.

The killer patted the little gizmo again and regarded it anxiously. If Kirklees was alone, then nerves would have to be fortified once more, and a sick stomach firmly ignored. Killing someone seemed easy when you read about it in crime novels, or watched it on the cinema screen. But there was nothing easy about it in real life. It was frightening, dangerous, scary and ugly, and it didn't feel right, or good, or normal.

But when you had no choice . . .

The killer swallowed hard and hoped their next victim would come soon, and be alone. The waiting was almost too much. Again, the restless and agitated hand reached out and stroked the taser's small form.

It had better not malfunction. It had already been used once today, and although it was recharged, the killer was no technical expert and supposed that any equipment could fail, at any time, and for any number of reasons. And if it did . . . well, things could go catastrophically wrong.

The figure in the car felt the skin on their body become cold and clammy at the mere thought.

Newley had been an older and overweight man, and even if the taser had failed with *him*, the so-called antique shop owner could probably still have been dealt with without too much trouble.

But Kirklees was a different matter altogether. Younger, fitter and much, much nastier, Kirklees was in another class of criminal altogether from the pathetic Newley. If, for some reason, he wasn't sufficiently incapacitated first . . . well, the killer was under no illusions about their chances of winning in a straight physical fight.

Trying to settle already fraught nerves, the occupant of the car recalled all the research they'd done on the handy little gadget waiting so patiently to be used for the second time that day, in an effort to reassure.

Tasers fired two small barbed darts, intended to puncture the skin and remain attached. They should also penetrate clothing up to two inches thick, so really there was nothing to worry about. *Was there?*

A woman passed by, carrying shopping bags and giving the car, parked in a respectable residential street in leafy north Oxford, not so much as a second glance.

The killer watched her go and then glanced in the rearview mirror for what felt like the hundredth time. And for the hundredth time, saw no signs of Kirklees's car. The clock on the dashboard said it was gone six o'clock now though, so the crook's return home from a hard day of loan-sharking, extortion, and who knew what else, was imminent.

Not for the first time, the killer roundly and silently cursed Newley. If it hadn't been for him, this nerve-wracking day would never have been necessary.

The watcher in the car settled down to wait for as long as it took, and returned to contemplating the taser. The barbed darts were connected to the unit by thin insulated copper wires, and delivered a modulated electric current designed to disrupt voluntary control of muscles. The resulting neuromuscular incapacitation, according to the literature on the subject, apparently, fooled many witnesses into thinking the victim was unconscious.

Had Newley looked unconscious?

Suddenly, headlights coming up close behind had the occupant of the car instinctively ducking down, and a few moments later, Lionel Kirklees's sleek slate-grey Jaguar turned into the driveway just in front of the parked car.

Of course, there were all sorts of cars parked in this side street of desirable residences, and the killer felt confident that Kirklees would have had no reason to be interested in one car out of the many.

Knowing they had to move quickly now, the killer of Simon Newley grabbed the taser and the long implement which had been lying between the front and back seats, opened the car door, got out, closed it quietly and sprinted to the entrance of the driveway. There the figure, dressed in dark clothes bought especially for the occasion, knew that they must reach it and slip inside before the automatic gate (which Kirklees had probably opened from his car fob) began to close again.

Therefore the figure in black rested the long implement down just inside the gate, and had only a moment to peer at the car parked in front of the impressive house and make the call. Was Kirklees alone, or would he have a minion with him? Because the vicious crook had a veritable army of young, violent men working for him. Men he used to keep his string of clients motivated to pay back loans at his outrageous lending rates, and deal painfully with anyone foolish enough to object or challenge Kirklees's methods.

But even as the killer peered through the dark October night into the private, enclosed garden, Lionel himself emerged from behind the wheel, and the automatic light inside the car revealed that he carried no passenger with him.

The killer's heart leapt in a combination of elation and dread. It was now or never. There would never be a better opportunity to catch Kirklees alone, and in the dark and relatively private surrounds of a garden littered with cover.

The killer felt sick and far less confident than they had earlier that day, at Newley's tatty shop.

But it had to be done.

The killer was wearing black trainers, and, careful to avoid the gravel on the drive, ran only along the grass lawn bordering the shrubs, moving as fast as possible towards Kirklees, who was now standing in the motion-triggered light that had come on in his porch.

Lionel Kirklees, at thirty-two years of age, was fit and lean, a regular attendee of his local gym. Born in London, he'd come to Oxford because he'd not been able to rise as high as he'd have liked in the capital. But in the years since his arrival in the university city, he was more or less content with his rise up the criminal ladder in a much smaller but still very lucrative pond. Not all his clients were from the lower echelons, desperate to keep the wolf from the door. Oxford was an expensive city, and keeping up appearances was vital to many across the social strata. In fact, his client's list could, at times, read like a veritable list in 'Who's Who'. Bankrupts, living precariously in mansions. Businessmen who needed that extra hundred thousand to make a scoop, just when the banks were being so unreasonably cautious.

Cultivating the custom of such lucrative milch cows hadn't been easy, and he had, perforce, come to the attention of some rather nasty rivals. But right now, he was confident . . .

A sudden rustling noise had him turning in surprise. Something had disrupted the bushes growing along the drive. But he had no real sense of danger, even then, confidently expecting to see either a neighbourhood cat, or maybe a fox or stray dog slinking along. This was hardly gangland London, after all.

But there was nothing wrong with his reflexes, and the instant he comprehended the figure causing the disruption was human, his right hand was reaching out and behind him for the throwing knife that he kept in his back pocket.

Even so, he was just a little too late to use it.

The taser was discharged and did its work with admirable efficiency. The two barbs hit him square in the chest, and before he could quite establish what was happening, Lionel could feel gravel biting uncomfortably into his face, and he realised he was down on the ground.

And he couldn't seem to move. Unable to lift his head, he could see only what was at his immediate eye level — which were a pair of black trainers, visible in the light spilling over from the porch, moving away from him towards the gate. Instantly, he felt a sense of relief that whoever was stupid enough to attack him had thought better of it, or had lost their nerve at the last minute, and was retreating. He closed his eyes and tried to concentrate on breathing, hoping he'd get control of his limbs back sooner rather than later. He felt horribly exposed and vulnerable in the dark, damp night.

The relief he felt didn't last long.

The crunching sound of footsteps running across gravel had his eyes snapping open again. He could see only the black trainers, growing almost monstrous in size as they came ever nearer before coming to a stop a few inches from his face.

He tried to speak, but, as Simon Newley would have been able to tell him had he still lived, speech wasn't possible in the circumstances.

Lionel sensed, rather than saw or felt, something rapidly approaching him, but his wits were too scattered to figure out what that meant for him. So it was that when the unusual-shaped metallic object hit the back of his prone head, he still hadn't figured out that he was being murdered.

The killer, feeling sick now, and unknowingly sobbing with a mixture of tension, fear and an excess of adrenaline, backed off and glanced wildly around.

The houses on either side, built in more affluent times, seemed reassuringly far away, and each had their own generous garden in between. Nobody had seen or heard anything, it seemed. Certainly no faces appeared at windows, peering out, looking and wondering.

And from the street behind the banks of shrubs, the city traffic swept past uncaring and oblivious.

It was actually over. At last.

With Newley and Kirklees dead, the killer was safe once more.

On knees that felt distinctly rubbery, the figure in black walked to the gate and thrust the murder weapon over the top. Then with shaking hands and weakened limbs, they clambered inelegantly over the gate and almost staggered onto the pavement beyond, bending down to retrieve the object lying on the ground.

Luckily, it was only a few yards to go to the car.

The killer opened the door, slumped behind the wheel, and sat breathing hard.

But not for long — just in case.

With shaking hands, the key turned in the ignition and, with great care, the nondescript car pulled out into the road and drove sedately away.

* * *

When Gareth got back to HQ after his disturbing talk with Jason, Hillary gave him the task of finding out in more detail what had become of Dr Timothy Durning in the last decade. At some point they'd need to interview him, and the more ammunition she had, the better.

Of course, it was possible that Michael Beck's former lecturer had led a pristine life over the past decade. But she wasn't holding her breath.

'It'll be interesting to see if our Dr Durning has garnered any more complaints from pupils in the intervening years,' she mused out loud to her team of two.

'I bet he hasn't,' Claire said. 'The near-miss with our victim will have made him far more careful,' she added cynically, when Hillary raised a surprised eyebrow at her.

'Hmmm, possibly,' Hillary said, but she wasn't so sure. People with compulsive personalities, she'd found, were the least able to change their habits — even if it *were* necessary for self-survival. 'Tomorrow, Gareth, we'll go and talk to Michael's best friend and see what he has to say about the murder victim. Especially about how he was behaving and what he thought was going on with him in the last few weeks of his life. While parents might not know everything that goes on in a young adult's life, it's far more likely that their best friend will.'

She liked to be fair with the allocation of tasks, and since Claire had been out in the field today it was Gareth's turn to escape the office. Besides, he needed more opportunities to learn how the job was done than Claire, who was an old hand at such interviews.

'Yes, ma'am,' Gareth said, his voice and face both carefully neutral, but both women could tell that he was pleased with the assignment. Paperwork, no matter how vital, always palled after a day or two without a break from it.

And thinking of admin . . . Hillary gave a general mumble of farewell and returned to her own stationery cupboard in order to catch up with her fair share of the boring tasks that never seemed to come to an end.

When she left promptly at five o'clock, she wasn't surprised to see that Gareth was still at his desk, fully intending to work the extra time that he'd taken off earlier that day.

She was tempted to tell him that he needn't bother, but knew that the former soldier would feel happier if he was allowed to keep his word, so she simply nodded at him on her way past the open office door.

She climbed up the wide cement stairs, crossed the foyer and emerged out into the chilly car park, walking towards her ancient Volkswagen Golf with a thoughtful frown.

Gareth had looked a little pale when he'd returned to the office.

She slid behind Puff the Tragic Wagon's steering wheel, telling herself firmly that the private life — and woes — of her co-workers were no longer her concern. That she was no longer an active DI — and if anyone would be needed to sort things out, it should be Superintendent Rollo Sale.

Puff started on the first turn of the key, as if in agreement with her.

But as she drove back the short distance to her narrowboat's mooring at Thrupp, she couldn't shake off the feeling that she wasn't going to be let off so lightly.

Leaving Puff in his favourite place, parked close up against a large, sheltering, overhanging hawthorn hedge, she stepped onto the Oxford canal towpath and headed towards her boat.

Since it was still early spring the approaching evening felt distinctly chilly, but she didn't bother doing up her coat for such a short walk. Soon the bare hedges lining the farmer's field on one side would begin to bud, making them look like a lacy green ribbon. Already the noisy mallard ducks were mating with their usual violence, and before too long the violets would come out, and ducklings would begin to hatch, and winter would become nothing more than a distant memory.

She climbed onto the back of her boat, and using a small key to open the padlock that held the hasps on the two metal doors covering the hatchway together, walked down the steep, short wooden stairs and into her home, automatically ducking her head as did so.

She tossed her coat and bag into the tiny bedroom that was the first of the *Mollern*'s limited rooms, then walked on down through the corridor, no wider than those on a bus, into the small galley at the front of the boat.

She tried not to think of her partner, Steven, who had died a while ago. Missing him still hurt. She went instead to the radio and turned it onto a station that played cheerful 1960s pop, and to the accompaniment of the Tremeloes sang along about how even bad times are good as she opened a can of meatballs and set them to warm on the stove. Cooking had always been more of a chore than a pleasure for her, and leaving the saucepan heating up, she went back to the bedroom to change.

Sitting at the tiny fold-down table ten minutes later and eating her nominal supper, her mind kept straying stubbornly back to Gareth Proctor.

She liked him and admired him, but not long after he'd first started working on her team, she'd discovered him carefully teasing information out of some officers about the murder of a former soldier in Reading — a man called Clyde-Brough.

And it had rung immediate alarm bells with her, not least because Gareth's predecessor had joined the group with a hidden agenda of his own. Luckily, that had all worked out well, but it left her understandably wary.

And as much as she'd tried to convince herself that lightning didn't strike twice, she'd nevertheless called in a favour from someone working the case, and got him to nose around. Specifically, to see if anyone answering Gareth's distinctive description had crossed their radar during their investigations.

She'd been relieved to learn that he hadn't, and that there was no apparent connection between her new boy and the dead soldier, and that had been that.

Or so she'd thought at the time.

But now Hillary couldn't help but wonder if she should have dug a little bit deeper, and not ignored that niggle of instinct that warned her that there was more to the still-unsolved murder of Clyde-Brough — and her latest team member — that needed her attention.

After all, you were only paranoid if somebody *wasn't* out to get you!

Although she had no proof that the phone call to Gareth today had been from one of his former army mates — as opposed to a family member or someone else from civvy street — she would have bet a fair amount of her yearly salary that it had been. There had been something about the way his face had tightened on hearing the identity of the speaker — something that spoke of wariness along with concern.

On the other hand, so what if he *had* been speaking to someone from his former life in the army? Why was she assuming that it meant trouble of some sort? For her, or for him?

She finished her uninspiring supper with a sigh and carried the tomato sauce-smeared plate to the tiny sink. There, she stared out of the small window at the khaki-coloured water of the canal so close and all around her, and ran the hot water tap, using the bare minimum of water needed to do the job. She did so purely out of habit — the same way that she turned off lights as she moved from room to room, to conserve the battery.

Living on a narrowboat taught you to be frugal, if nothing else.

A sooty-coloured moorhen chose that moment to swim past her boat, its distinctive v-shaped white rump cutting a course along the canal, but she barely noticed it.

Was she seeing problems with Gareth Proctor that simply weren't there? Or was she just reluctant to dig deeper because she was worried about what she might find? She not only had high hopes that the former soldier would make a good long-term fit for her team, but she knew that Gareth needed a steady job. One that gave him a feeling of accomplishment and self-worth was vital if he was to make a life for himself outside the army.

The last thing she wanted to do was scupper it for him. And yet the murder of Clyde-Brough was still unsolved. And it just wasn't in her DNA to let something like that lie, if there was even the slightest chance that she could help her colleagues solve it.

'Oh damn and bloody blast it,' she suddenly yelled, angry at herself for prevaricating like an uncertain novice.

The moorhen, rather sensibly, took to its long-toed feet at this unwarranted outburst and, wings flapping, headed for the reed bed on the opposite side of the bank, calling in alarm as it did so.

Hillary watched it and apologized ruefully.

CHAPTER SIX

The next day dawned frosty but bright. Hillary had been going to ask Gareth to do the driving to Headington, where Kevin Philpott still lived, though not any longer with his parents. But after getting to the office and dealing with her emails, she'd noticed that Gareth's limp was particularly bad that day, and changed her mind.

Although he had a fully adapted car and liked to use it, when they crossed the car park at shortly after ten o'clock that morning, she walked determinedly towards Puff, but not quite at her usual speed. Gareth, using his tubular metal walking stick with grim-faced competence, appeared not to notice that she was matching her speed to his, and for this she was grateful.

She unlocked the car doors, and then pretended to fiddle with something in her bag, giving him plenty of time to stow his stick alongside the passenger seat and get settled. Since he had to use both hands to lift and swing his leg up from the ground this took a little longer than usual, but she waited until he was doing up his seatbelt before settling behind the wheel herself.

She'd noticed in the few months that he'd been working with her that some days were better than others for him when it came to his physical problems. The limited strength and movement in his withered left hand and arm didn't seem to vary much, but his walking was a different matter. She wondered if it depended on whether or not he'd slept well — or perhaps slept awkwardly?

She knew from personal experience what it was like when you woke up with a numb arm or cramp in your leg because you'd spent hours in the same position, and could only suppose that you'd have to multiply that feeling by ten if you'd suffered the injuries he had.

'You have his address?' Hillary asked briskly, nothing of her sympathetic thoughts showing in her tone as she turned the ignition. Puff, it seemed, was not in a particularly tragic mood that morning since he started first time.

'Yes, ma'am. Flat 1a, 106 Brighton Terrace Gardens — not far from the Nuffield Hospital, according to the map. He's lived there since 2013.'

'Does he own it?'

'No, ma'am, rented. His family aren't anywhere near as well off as the Becks,' Gareth informed her. 'His father worked for the council in the parks department, and his mother still helps out at a local newsagents part-time.'

Hillary was glad she'd asked him to bone up on all they knew about the witness before arranging to talk to him today, and she planned to take full advantage of it as she drove.

'He married?'

'No, no marriage.'

Hillary nodded. 'You say his family is working class? The boys first met at secondary school, right?'

'Yes, ma'am. They were put in the same form at the age of eleven. A large but well-regarded former comprehensive, now renamed as a college apparently.'

Hillary nodded thoughtfully. 'Which means the Becks didn't send their son to a private school. Interesting. Perhaps they aren't as well off as we'd assumed. The house in Woodeaton could have been inherited from one or the other's own parents. And maybe William's business wasn't as lucrative as all that.'

'Or maybe they have socialist views,' Gareth pointed out, pleasing Hillary that he now felt confident enough to speak freely. When he'd first joined the team, he'd been practically silent until he'd begun to learn that she, Claire and he needed to bounce ideas off each other, and that he was expected to air his thoughts and opinions.

'Yes, that's certainly a possibility,' she agreed. 'I certainly didn't get the feeling when talking to them that they were social snobs. And maybe that liberal attitude wore off on their son too. It didn't stop him from making friends with Kevin, did it?'

It was another fact she added to her mental list of what she knew about the dead man, and the more she learned about him, the more she liked him. On the other hand, what she was learning was bringing her no closer to finding out why someone might have wanted him dead.

Michael Beck seemed, on the face of it, to have been a normal, well-adjusted young man, maybe a little on the quiet side, who'd been doing nothing more controversial with his life than trying to find a job, while indulging his favourite hobby.

As that thought flashed through her mind, Hillary jerked a little in her seat and felt a wave of self-recrimination hit her. 'Damn it,' she muttered.

'Ma'am?'

Hillary shook her head, annoyed at herself. 'I'm slipping. When we talked to his parents, they mentioned Michael had been a keen photographer — and especially keen on wildlife and rural landscapes. And we know that one of the possibilities is that he may have been killed somewhere close to where he was found.'

'So he might have been out in the fields taking pictures?' Gareth said, nodding, following her reasoning. 'The river would have been a favourite spot, ma'am, if he was into wildlife. Kingfishers and things.'

'Yes. But there were no reports in the original investigation about his camera equipment, was there?' she said tersely. 'The fields all around the area were searched — they never found his camera, right?'

While she was sure she'd have remembered reading about it in the files if they had, she still had a moment of doubt. She'd already missed an obvious line of enquiry once — who was to say she wasn't slipping again?

'No, ma'am, there was no mention of his camera being found. He might not have even taken it with him that day,' Gareth pointed out.

'No, it's pure speculation,' Hillary agreed grimly. But it was something that should have occurred to her the moment Martina Beck pointed out her son's photographs with such pride. 'When we get back to HQ, I want you to phone the Becks and ask them if they noticed whether any of his cameras were missing, will you? A keen photographer must have had more than one.'

'Yes, ma'am. Turn left here,' Gareth said, pointing ahead and giving her plenty of time to make the turn. 'I think the place we're looking for must be somewhere up here . . .'

Hillary forced her anger at her lapse to one side, and concentrated on finding the right address. 'I've only got odd numbers my side of the street,' she said, craning her neck for a better view.

'Yes — we're up to number 84 . . .' Gareth informed her.

Once they'd found the right number, there was no parking nearby, naturally, and Hillary had to tour around for a while, turning down various pleasant little cul-de-sacs and other narrow but attractive streets, until she eventually found somewhere not too far away.

Again, she climbed out of the car and took her time looking around to give her companion ample time to get himself out of the car and standing.

'It's up that way, right?' she said, pointing back up the road.

'Yes, ma'am. First right, then second left.'

Hillary's lips twitched. 'Better than a compass, aren't you?' she said dryly.

Gareth Proctor flashed her first an astonished glance, then grinned, then wiped it smartly off his face, and quietly agreed. 'Yes, ma'am.'

* * *

Kevin Philpott's flat turned out to be the ground floor of a large converted Victorian terraced house, built out of yellow brick with fussy white brick trim. Not Hillary's favourite architectural style, but in this area, anything at all was considered valuable property.

A set of steps led down, presumably to the basement flat, while two more floors (the uppermost crammed in under the eaves) provided room for several more residences. Cramped by most people's estimates, in Oxford it was almost the height of luxury.

'Do you think you could afford to rent here?' Hillary asked Gareth, genuinely curious.

'Not quite, ma'am,' he said promptly. He lived above a fish-and-chip shop in Kidlington, and more often than not didn't have much money left over at the end of the month to afford even the comestibles on offer being fried below him.

'Looks as if Michael's friend, while not exactly flying high, is doing more or less all right for himself then,' she mused. 'Let's go and see what he has to tell us.'

Kevin Philpott was expecting them, since Hillary had phoned him before leaving the office last night to make the appointment. She was not surprised when he answered the door within moments of their ringing the bell for Flat 1a.

'Hello — Mrs Greene is it?'

Hillary knew that Philpott had been the same age as their victim ten years ago, so he must now be around thirty-two or so. The man standing in the doorway, however, looked much younger, probably because he was quite fleshy, and had the baby-faced look that went with weight. Not tall, around five feet nine or so, she was looking almost directly into his deep-set brown eyes. He had the colour of hair that was not quite blond, but not quite brown either, and was dressed in faded jeans that did little to disguise his pleasantly rounded pot belly, and a plain white shirt.

Like his dead friend, he was neither handsome nor plain, but when he smiled tentatively at her, it made her want to smile back at him.

'Yes, this is my colleague Gareth Proctor,' Hillary informed him.

Kevin's eyes went over her shoulder and he nodded and stepped back, allowing them to pass into the small communal hall, his gaze skittering a little nervously over Gareth's walking stick. He stalwartly pretended not to notice the other man's awkward, lurching gait as he pointed them to the only door showing. The staircase, right in front of them, was uncarpeted and not very clean, but at least it had a handrail.

'Just push on the door, I left it open,' he called. The space was too small for him to try and push past them, so Hillary, in the lead, obligingly pushed open the door and stepped inside.

The flat wasn't huge, but it impressed Hillary in a way that she hadn't expected it to, and that made her feel slightly discomfited. She must have subconsciously been expecting the overweight man to live in a sloppy or less-than-impressive home, and that was bias, pure and simple. She gave herself a mental ticking off, and looked around with pleasure.

The walls had been painted a silvery mint green, and one two-seater sofa and a matching armchair in black leather didn't crowd or overwhelm the small space. A black-leaded Victorian fireplace — either original to the building, or bought to add ambience — provided a pleasant focal point. Above it, Hillary instantly recognized Michael Beck's work — a large photograph of a spider's web, hanging with dew-drops against a misty autumn background of rust-coloured dock stems gone to seed.

Everywhere was spotlessly clean.

Through the open door in one wall, she could see a small area of the kitchen, which was decorated in tones of primrose lemon and apple green, with sparkling white tops and painted cupboards. Even the chrome taps shone.

On the floor beneath her, an old Turkish carpet covered bare, pale floorboards, which had been lovingly sanded back and varnished. A sideboard from the 1930s, which had been painted and then sanded back to give it that distressed vintage look that was now so fashionable, stood beside the sole bay window. In the window, a plant of some kind thrived in a large, colourful ceramic pot.

A massive and impressive television had been fixed to one wall, the only incongruous note, but she saw Gareth look at it with envy as they both took a seat on the sofa.

Kevin sat on the armchair, leaning forward, looking both nervous but eager to help. 'I was so glad when you phoned last night, saying you were taking another look at Michael's case,' he began, his voice slightly raspy. If he was a smoker, Hillary mused, there was no sign of it in his home — no telltale smell, or slightly yellowed ceiling. Perhaps he was just getting over a cold?

'It's never really sat right with me that nobody was ever caught,' he continued, then immediately flushed. His eyes rounded a little comically and he gulped audibly. 'I didn't mean that to sound as if . . . I wasn't trying to imply that you weren't doing a good job . . .'

'That's all right, Mr Philpott,' Hillary rushed to assure him. The last thing she wanted was for this man to feel defensive or embarrassed. She needed him to feel relaxed and chatty. 'Neither one of us worked on the original case. As I explained on the telephone, I'm a former DI, and I work for the Thames Valley Police Service as a consultant on unsolved cases. And I can assure you, we're going to do everything we can to get justice for your friend.'

Kevin smiled in relief and let out his breath in a slow puff. She was relieved to see him ease back in his chair and nod.

'Sorry,' he said with a wry grin. 'Mike always said I could put my foot in my mouth easier than anyone he'd ever known.'

Hillary grinned. 'Me too,' she lied, and noted the shortened use of Michael Beck's name. It was a timely reminder that this witness probably knew the murder victim as well as anyone. 'So, you were, what, eleven when you first met Mike?'

'That's right. Me, I was no good at school.' Kevin shrugged. 'Too much of a dreamer my dad and teachers always said. Couldn't concentrate for long enough to get anything done! But Mike was different. A real natural at all that learning stuff. He sailed through his exams — well, as you know, he went on to get a degree. I could never understand why he took up with a bit of a dunce like me, to be honest.'

Hillary thought that she could understand it very well. Michael, an only child, studious and perhaps shy, would have been nervous and unsure of himself in a new school. It didn't surprise her at all that he would have instantly been drawn to a much more outgoing, open and comfortable lad, such as Kevin must have been, even back then. And Michael, coming from a small village school, would have found the larger comprehensive one hell of a culture shock, whereas Kevin, who'd always lived in the area, would have been more at ease.

She wouldn't be surprised if Kevin's larger size had also appealed to Michael Beck, assuming the lad had also been big back then. It was far less easy to be bullied if you had a hefty friend to stand up for you. And wondered if the help went both ways.

'Did he help you with your studies?' she asked, happy to ease him gently into the interview, while at the same time learning more about the personality of the dead man. Her old sergeant in training college had always drummed it into her that people were murdered for a reason. And the more you knew about the victim, the more chance you had of finding out what that reason was. And, from that, who had the motive.

'He tried, poor sod,' Kevin laughed, glancing at the photograph on his wall with a smile. 'But even he eventually had to give it up as a bad job. Oh, it wasn't that I was totally thick or anything. I was OK at some things. Reading — loved to read about pirates and adventures and stuff like that. And art — loved painting and drawing. In fact, it was me that got him into photography,' he tacked on proudly. 'But proper academic stuff . . .' Kevin shook his head ruefully. 'Not in me, I'm afraid. I was always thinking outside the box too much to be a teacher's pet.'

'Was Michael a teacher's pet?' Hillary asked, thinking of Dr Durning.

'Oh sure. But not in a smarmy way, you know?' he added hastily. 'He didn't go around trying to butter them up or anything. Mike wasn't like that — there was no side to him at all. Not like some. No, with him, what you saw was what you got. And he was straight with you too. None of this back-biting or constant hustling like you get with some people, you know? But he was quick and interested in his lessons, which is bound to make any teacher happy, right?'

He leaned back in the chair, making it creak a little in protest. 'I mean, I never thought about it at the time — well you don't when you're just a sprat, do you? But now, looking back . . . poor buggers, teaching hundreds of know-it-all little brats. What a life! I'm surprised they ever bothered turning up in the mornings!'

Gareth, who was inconspicuously taking notes, realized that they weren't going to have any trouble getting this garrulous man to open up. He only hoped his pencil was up to the challenge.

'So it's not surprising kids like Mike made their day,' he concluded, finally running out of steam.

Hillary nodded. 'He was especially interested in history though, yes?'

'Wasn't he just!' Kevin let out a burst of laughter. 'I can remember that programme . . . you know, the one where they dug up ancient sites and stuff . . . with that bloke from *Blackadder* in it . . .'

'*Time Team*?' Hillary recalled the television show that featured archaeological digs in sites around the country, which had been popular several years ago.

'Yes, that's the one!' Kevin nodded enthusiastically, making his double chin wobble a little. 'I can remember Mike watched it religiously. And this is when we'd have been about . . . what . . . sixteen or so? It was the sort of show you expected your granny to like! Me, I couldn't see the attraction of digging in the dirt for bits of pottery or hidden walls, or what have you, but Mike loved it. He loved all that kind of stuff. Mind you, he could get "fads", you know, hobbies that he'd really be into for a year or so, then slowly lose interest. Like that,' he nodded at the photograph on the wall. 'For a couple of years he drove me mad, dragging me around places so that he could snap away at rabbits and whatnot. But he was bloody good at it, wasn't he?' he added wistfully.

'Yes, you're lucky to have something of his.'

'Oh, his mum and dad let me pick one,' Kevin said, and swallowed hard. For a moment his eyes shone with unshed tears, and for a moment, Hillary wondered if he was going to hold it together.

But then he shrugged, and forced a smile. 'That was Mike for you. Whatever he was into, he was into it one hundred per cent. And was always good at it. Me, I'd sort of go into things, like collecting comic books, say, but only for fun. You know, more to read and enjoy than to actually *work* at it.'

Kevin gave another engaging grin. 'Bone idle, me, that's what my mum always said! Now Mike, if he'd done the same, he would have researched the subject to death, hunted down rare copies, and wouldn't have let up until he'd got what he wanted. Not that he was into comics, mind, his hobbies were always more high-brow. But history was always the one keeper, for him. He never lost interest in that.'

Hillary nodded. 'So you weren't at all surprised when he chose ancient history to study at uni?'

'Hell no. I probably know more about history than any other subject, just from being around him! But not dates,' he held his hands up. 'Never could remember dates.'

'Me neither!' Hillary lied again, with a grin. 'You never went to uni yourself?'

'Hell no!' he repeated and laughed. 'I couldn't wait to leave to school, set up my own business and earn a bit of cash. And the first thing I bought when I made a bit of lolly was an old transit van! Got it cheap, since it was a bit of a rust-bucket, but at least it was transport, and I felt about ten feet tall riding around in it. Which made me one up on Michael, ironically, who still had to make do with his push bike!' He laughed reminiscently.

'You've always been self-employed?' she asked.

'Yup! Always preferred not having a boss,' Kevin explained with another snort of laughter. 'They can be so unreasonable! Expecting you to be on time and what have you. No, seriously, I have ideas, that's all, and like to see if I can make 'em work. Some do, some don't,' he added ruefully. 'Some earn me a fair bit of money, then I can suddenly crash and burn. But, on the whole, I do OK for myself. I'm not exactly rolling in it, but so long as I make enough to get by, I'm happy enough.' He looked around him with satisfaction. 'Mike would never have been able to live like I do though. Oh, not because his family is well off, don't misunderstand me. Mike never cared that he had more stuff than I did. He was no snob!' he said in earnest, looking at Hillary anxiously. 'I just meant that he was always a planner, you know? He liked to look before he leapt, know where things were going, and weigh up the odds and stuff. He'd have been constantly worrying about making enough to pay the bills and all that. No, he had his whole life mapped out. Get an education, get a good job, meet a nice girl, have a family, all nice and steady . . .'

There was an appalled moment of silence as everyone in the room realized just how much good Michael Beck making a life plan had done him.

'But uni didn't work out well for Michael in all respects, did it?' Hillary said mildly, and saw the other man's rounded, once-cheerful face fall even further.

'That thing with his tutor, you mean? No, that was a bit of a sod, wasn't it?' Kevin drew in a deep breath. 'Oh man, that was ugly. I just don't get it, really. Mike was never gay, never even gave off that vibe, you know?' Kevin shook his head. 'I can't understand why that other guy thought . . . But it really upset Mike, that whole thing, I can tell you. He actually felt guilty about shopping him, did you know that? I told him he'd done the right thing — I mean, what else *could* he have done? But I'm not sure Mike was ever convinced. He blamed himself for not realizing what was happening sooner, before it had the chance to get out of hand, like.'

'You still saw him often then?' Hillary mused, and when Kevin gave her a puzzled look, added, 'Sometimes when school friends leave school they can drift apart.'

'Oh, right, got you. No, we were always meeting up whenever we could. In the holidays, like. Summer, Easter, Christmas, all that,' Kevin nodded. 'I mean, we were close, you know? He was my main friend and I was his. Even though he made other friends at Bristol, and I made friends I met through my various enterprises, we still kept tight. And after he'd got his BA, and had to come home, I tried to help him find a place to rent. I know this area like the back of my hand, and we spent quite a bit of time slogging around. You can't always rely on ads in the paper or online to find a place, can you? They're gone in a flash. We'd go to the newsagents, pubs, places like that, putting the word out. You'd be surprised how often you could get a nibble that way.'

'But not on that particular day — the day he died. You weren't flat-hunting that day?' Hillary asked gently, and saw Kevin's smile instantly vanish.

'No, worse luck,' he agreed quietly. 'Not on that day.'

'You told DI Weston at the time that you didn't know what Michael had been doing that day?'

'No, that's right. We'd arranged to meet up that evening to have a drink in the pub in Islip — the one halfway up the hill, not opposite the river, but . . .' He shook his head.

Hillary wondered if Kevin had heard about his friend's death in good time, or if he hadn't, and had gone to the pub to wait for him — a friend who had consequently never shown up. She hoped that hadn't been the case.

'Do you have any ideas at all about who might have wanted to hurt him?' she asked gently.

Kevin sighed heavily. 'Not really — not unless it was that weird girlfriend that he'd just broken up with.'

'Mia de Salle?'

'Yeah. Her.' Kevin shifted his bulk a little uncomfortably on the sofa. 'Funny, I still see her quite a bit.'

'You *see* her?' Hillary, caught off guard, couldn't keep the surprise from her voice.

Instantly, Kevin coloured. 'No! Hell no. But yes. I mean,' he paused and laughed unsteadily. 'I don't mean *see* her, as in we're dating or anything. Man, that would be just weird. *Seriously* weird. I never even fancied her. She was always sort of odd-looking to my mind anyway. I never quite understood why Mike was so taken with her. No, I just meant every now and then I'll see her around. You know, walking down the street. Coming out of a shop. That kind of thing. I know Oxford isn't exactly London, but it's not *that* small a place either. I suppose it's just one of those weird things that sometimes happen in life, you know? Like, when you see a strange word that you'd never seen before, and then in the next week you see it everywhere? A bit like that.'

Hillary nodded. 'Coincidences happen.'

'Yeah, I suppose. It's just that it always makes me feel a bit uneasy afterwards. I mean, I didn't really know her all that well, considering she was my best mate's girlfriend and all that.'

'Why was that do you think?' Hillary asked, genuinely curious.

Kevin shrugged his well-padded shoulders and sighed. 'I dunno really. Perhaps it was because they were both brain-boxes and I'm not? I mean, when they got talking about intellectual stuff — and that girl liked to show off about how brainy she was, let me tell you — well, I felt right out of it. And I could tell she didn't like me — well, you just know that sort of feeling, don't you? You can feel it. And in her case, she was so possessive of Mike, I got the feeling she was jealous of me, of our friendship.'

Hillary had come across this phenomenon before.

'It got to be a bit . . . I dunno, awkward. It just got to the point where I avoided her. I began to make sure that if I was seeing Mike, it was when he was on his own, you know?'

Hillary nodded. This was the third time she'd heard that Mia de Salle had a strange effect on people. The original investigator, DI Weston, had 'liked' her for the crime. The dead boy's parents hadn't been able to get on with her either. And now Kevin, whom she suspected could get on with almost anybody and everybody, was saying the same thing.

'Do you think she really might have killed Michael?' she asked bluntly.

At this Kevin shifted nervously. 'No. Yes. Maybe. I dunno. Oh hell . . .' he shook his head. 'Sorry. I just don't know. Michael getting murdered . . . I mean *murdered* . . . It just felt so unreal, you know? I mean, even after the shock had worn off. Even now, all these years later, it just doesn't seem *possible* somehow.'

He heaved a massive sigh. 'I know that sounds daft. I mean, he *was* murdered, wasn't he? And I *know* that. But it still seems . . . I dunno. As if the cosmos made a mistake somehow. Why would someone kill him? I mean, he was such a nice, normal, everyday bloke. Like me. He wouldn't hurt anyone, you know?'

Hillary nodded sadly. Yes. She knew.

CHAPTER SEVEN

Six months ago

DI Robin Farrell had just finished eating his supper when he got the call. Divorced from his wife, Diana, five years ago, he'd miraculously managed to hold on to the semi-detached family house in Osney Mead. Mainly, he'd had to admit, because Diana had quickly remarried a big-headed know-it-all Yank with a stock portfolio that kept afloat most of Texas, according to Diana. (And her new husband.)

Thus, having secured such a catch, she'd been less inclined to go for his jugular in the divorce court. Their two grown-up children, Adrianna and Luke, had probably had a lot to do with it too. Not impressed with the Yank, they'd threatened to sever relations with her if she forced the sale of the house out from under him.

Robin was, more than most perhaps, happy just to go home at the end of the day and enjoy the simple pleasures of down time.

The ringing of his mobile phone had found him in the living room, where he'd been watching telly with a micro-waved lasagne in pride of place on a tray.

On answering it, he was not best pleased to hear that he had another call out to a potential murder scene and yet another dead body to deal with. Two in one day was almost unprecedented in Oxford. He'd been inclined to point out that he already had enough on his plate with the murder of Simon Newley, and surely somebody else could take the case instead. But when his superintendent gave him the details of all they had so far, he understood precisely why he was being rousted out of his home on a chilly autumn night.

Now, at just gone ten-thirty, he stood in the lit-up driveway of the home of Lionel Kirklees and watched as his second body of the day was being examined.

This latest victim had been discovered by his next-door neighbour, who'd stepped out to give his dog her usual evening walk. Said dog, a particularly alert and pretty spaniel bitch, had all but dragged him to next-door's gate and commenced to bark so long and so frantically that the dog owner had gone so far as to climb halfway up the gate and peer past the shrubbery.

No doubt the sight of a body lying on the gravel not far from the front door had been enough to get the man scrambling for his phone and reporting it to the police.

A local patrol car had been dispatched, and on finding life to be extinct, the PCs had set in motion the events leading to Robin Farrell barely having time to finish his lasagne.

As he got a closer look at the scene, Robin realized that the medical man was the same doctor who had been called out to Simon Newley earlier that day, which might explain why he'd insisted to Robin's superior that he be informed right away. The similarity in the murder method must have stood out a mile.

Robin waited until the doctor had finished his examination, then nodded at him as he stood up.

'Doctor,' he greeted him cordially.

'Inspector Farrell. Well, somebody besides us has been kept busy today,' the other man said laconically, glancing over his shoulder at the prone body. 'The MO is identical to your other chap. He was hit with a taser, then hit over the head with something rounded, probably metallic. The curvature of the wound is too narrow for something like a baseball bat, but too compact for something like a frying pan or shovel.'

'Have you had a chance to take a closer look at Newley yet?' Robin asked curiously.

'No.'

The shortness of the answer warned Robin not to push it. 'Well, when you've done the autopsies, let me know,' he said equably. 'I take it we can at least assume he was hit with the taser first, then bashed over the head?'

Again, this drew a rather weary smile from the other man. 'Well, technically, I can't say. But I'm damned if I can see why someone would bop him over the head and *then* fire a taser at him, can you?'

Robin grunted. 'Stranger things have been known to happen. My super said you found ID for him?'

'Yes. Kirklees. Lionel. This is his residence apparently,' the doctor said, waving a vague hand at the house behind them.

At this, Robin let out a long, slow breath, and glanced back at the form on the ground. Under the lights set up by the SOCOs he couldn't see much, beyond the fact that the victim was male, lean, lying face down, and well-dressed.

'Someone finally caught up with our Lionel,' he said slowly.

'Known to you then?' the doctor asked, with only vague curiosity.

'Oh yes. We know Lionel all right. Money lender, principally. Nasty sod. Loaned you a thousand quid, and by the time the month was out, you owed him ten times that much. And woe betide you if you didn't pay it.'

'Broken bones?'

'Or worse,' Robin said shortly. 'We've been longing to play host to our Mr Kirklees ever since he came here, but you know what it's like.'

The doctor nodded sympathetically. 'Nobody would testify against him.'

'No.'

The doctor shrugged, with that casual attitude that said that he was glad it wasn't his problem. 'Well, one bright spot. At least it looks as if his poor clients are going to be singing for joy when they read about his demise in tomorrow's papers.'

Robin smiled grimly. 'I wouldn't be so sure. I don't think it'll take a certain person too long to step into his shoes and carry on where he left off. They might be celebrating prematurely.'

The doctor looked at the inspector with a slightly cocked head. 'Do I smell a theory forming?'

Robin grunted. 'It's not exactly rocket science, Doc,' he said. 'Every man and his dog could figure out who's behind this. Let alone my super. It's just proving it that's going to be a bugger.'

And in that, DI Farrell wasn't wrong.

* * *

To get to Beckley from her CRT office was a doddle, so Hillary set Puff off up the A34 for less than a mile before turning off at the Islip turn. She turned and glanced at Claire as she did so.

'So how long has Mia de Salle been working at the reserve?'

'Not long, guv. Less than a year.'

Hillary nodded. When she'd rung Dr de Salle requesting an interview, the woman had been reluctant to talk to her at her home, instead arranging and agreeing to a meeting at her place of work instead. Which had turned out to be the Otmoor wildlife reserve. It specialized in butterflies and certain birds, Hillary knew, but she didn't think it was a particularly large reserve. Nevertheless, being so close to Oxford, naturally it was of great interest to academics, so it wasn't, perhaps, surprising to find one of their main witnesses had a posting there.

'Some coincidence, her working now so close to where our victim used to live, isn't it, guv?' Claire mused, echoing Hillary's own thoughts.

In fact, right at that moment, they were about to drive past the village of Woodeaton.

'Yes,' Hillary agreed thoughtfully, 'but that's all it can be. We were only given Michael's case to look at a few days ago, and since she's already been working there some while, she can't have somehow wangled the position on the spot in order to keep an eye on us. She'd need to be clairvoyant!'

'Got it, guv. Memo to self: don't be paranoid.' Claire grinned.

'I remember going to the Otmoor reserve once as a kid,' Hillary reminisced. 'One of those school day-trip things. I seem to remember lots of walks through swampy-looking ground, and having to draw butterflies and try and find a certain flower. Ragged robins, maybe.'

Claire smiled. 'I used to love school trips out when I was a kid. Anything to get away from the classroom.' But Hillary, Claire supposed, who'd taken an English degree at a non-affiliated Oxford college, wouldn't have minded swotting all that much.

'The entrance has to be somewhere down here,' Hillary muttered, turning her ancient Volkswagen Golf down a small lane and craning her neck to look around. Sure enough, she saw the signage not long later and turned into a half-empty car park.

The weather was cloudy, but it didn't look as if rain was imminent. In the hedges, pussy willow was beginning to flower, exchanging their velvet pearly white/grey buds for lemon, pollen-laden flowers. At least there were still some places for the remaining wild bees to feed, Hillary mused grimly.

As a kid, she seemed to remember all her summers play-ing out to the heavy, pleasant backdrop of the continuous drone of bees. Last year, she'd actually had to make the effort to notice them, and had been relieved whenever she spotted one hovering over the celandines and daisies.

'Do you think these places are going to be enough?' she asked, making Claire, who was walking beside her towards the small shack that guarded the entrance, cast her a puzzled look. 'To save all the bees and butterflies and birds, I mean?' Hillary added helpfully.

Claire shrugged. 'Dunno, guv,' she said indifferently. Her adult life had been more geared to feeding and raising her kids than worrying about saving the creepy crawlies.

Hillary mentally shook her head at this lacklustre response, and reached for her ID as she approached the entrance proper. The friendly staff member in the shack was able to point them in the right direction at once. Apparently, Dr de Salle was down near the reed beds, monitoring something or other to do with caddisfly larvae.

As they walked, keeping strictly to the paths as directed, Hillary wondered what Mia de Salle must think, or feel, working so close to the spot where her former lover had been found murdered. She was intrigued to be meeting this witness and suspect, perhaps more than any other, since she was the one who seemed to arouse the strongest feelings in all the other people involved in Michael Beck's life and death.

But she couldn't let that affect her judgement. The whole point of reviewing a cold case was to go into it with an open mind, a different set of eyes and ears, and no preconceptions.

The wind was picking up, and the resulting susurration in the willows, hazels and other native trees soothed her. The grass paths they were following sometimes merged onto wooden boardwalks that traversed marshy areas, and it was at the end of one of these wooden pathways that they finally found Dr de Salle, squatting down and taking water samples from a small pond.

Hillary knew that Mia had been twenty-five years of age at the time of Michael's death, and would have considered herself a young woman. But at thirty-five, things could have changed radically for her. Some people seemed to gallop towards middle age, while others seemed to be Peter Pans, never really aging at all — physically, mentally or emotionally. And Hillary was intrigued to see how the passing years had affected Michael's lover.

As they approached the scientist, Hillary could see that she was wearing a beige-coloured all-in-one garment, vaguely like dungarees, that looked as if it was made of some hard-wearing material, and was no doubt very practical for someone who worked outdoors all day. She was also wearing less-than-attractive plain black wellingtons — again, very apposite for a job in this place.

She must have caught movement in her peripheral vision because she suddenly turned her head and looked over her shoulder at them. At the sight of the two women approaching her, she slowly stood up — and up, and up. She had to be at least six feet in height, Hillary thought, and in spite of the baggy and ill-fitting outfit, Hillary could also tell that she was whippet-thin.

As they got closer, Hillary began to make out more detail. (She really was going to have to get her eyes tested soon.) Dr de Salle's head looked disproportionately large compared to the rest of her body, but Hillary could now see that this was caused by the immense weight of black hair that she had piled on top of her cranium. Plaited and twisted around and around in a coronet, it must, when it was unwound, reach at least to her waist if not further.

'Dr de Salle?' Hillary said by way of greeting, although she had no real doubt that she had mistaken her for another environmental-studies lecturer.

'Yes.'

She was very striking close up, rather than beautiful, Hillary thought, with prominent cheekbones, a rather large nose and a wide mouth. Hillary's first impression was that such a face belonged in a medieval painting — maybe of some saint or sinner being burned at the stake. She wore no make-up or jewellery, but then, she hardly needed any.

If Michael Beck had been starting to come across as a rather ordinary sort of man, he'd certainly chosen for himself a very extra-ordinary mate, Hillary thought.

'I presume you're the police officer who telephoned me?'

Hillary again took out her ID, introduced herself and Claire and explained her own former DI status, and how she was now working as a consultant to Thames Valley. She then went through the usual speech, about how the cold case team worked, and that Michael's case was currently being reviewed.

The tall woman listened without comment until she'd finished and then nodded, only once and rather abruptly. It was an awkward gesture, but she didn't seem to notice it.

'I see,' she said. 'So, how can I help?' Her voice was curiously flat, with little intonation in it, which gave Hillary an odd, unhappy feeling. Such a voice sounded as if it belonged to some kind of automated machinery rather than a living human being.

She sensed Claire's own unease, and wondered if her colleague was picking up on the same odd vibe.

Mia de Salle watched them from beneath heavy-lidded hazel eyes. She didn't appear hostile, exactly. Nor even impatient, if it came to that. She was not playing the 'I'm busy so let's get on with it' card, but at the same time, Hillary didn't believe she intended to be very cooperative either.

'I'm sorry if this is going to bring up bad memories for you, Dr de Salle,' Hillary began, 'but I'd like to go over your relationship with Michael, from the beginning, if you don't mind.'

She felt oddly exposed at the end of this boardwalk, with water and greenery all around. Which was odd because she'd always felt at home in the countryside. She had to resist the urge to pull her coat closer around her, even though the wind was not particularly cold.

'I met Michael at Bristol. We were both studying there. I was finishing up my PhD and he was doing his BA.'

Hillary nodded. 'So he was younger than you?' she asked, keeping her tone neutral and matter-of-fact, even though she knew the question itself had been slightly provocative. She'd chosen it deliberately for that reason, of course, needing to gauge early on the emotional make-up of her witness.

She knew that the original SIO had found this woman difficult to handle — or get a handle *on* — and so she was expecting some kind of defiance or prickliness at this question. Which left her feeling a little wrong-footed, and maybe a little disappointed, at the distinct lack of a reaction.

'Yes, that's right, by just over three years,' Mia admitted, her voice still flat, even and without expression.

Her eyes suddenly darted quickly to the left, looking past Hillary's shoulder, and before she could stop herself, Hillary shot around to see what had caught her eye. For some reason, she was half-expecting to see some knife-wielding maniac pounding down the boardwalk at her, but there was only a bird — vaguely sparrow-like, hopping around in a nearby stand of sedge.

'Reed warbler?' Hillary guessed, forcing her fight-or-flight reflex back into its box.

'No,' Mia said.

Hillary turned, forcing herself to be calm, and looked at the other woman carefully. Now, nine times out of ten, most people would have been unable to resist adding the actual name of the bird. It was human nature, after all, to feel a certain amount of pleasure in displaying a superior level of knowledge.

Mia de Salle merely continued to watch Hillary patiently.

Again, she felt Claire shift uneasily beside her.

'You and Michael were together for some time?' Hillary carried on, determinedly keeping her own voice calm and pleasant.

'That's right.'

'And when he finished his studies at Bristol, you followed him here to Oxford?'

'Yes.'

According to DI Weston, 'followed' was rather a tame word. More than once he'd used the word 'stalked' when referring to this woman.

'But hadn't you and Michael split up back at Bristol? According to one of his friends down there, you and he broke up just after Michael had finished doing his final exams.'

'That's not true,' Mia denied flatly.

Hillary felt her shoulders becoming more and more tense, and forced herself to relax. She had reread DI Weston's notes thoroughly, and according to one Brian Ormwood, who'd also been studying Ancient History, Michael had told him he'd broken up with his steady girlfriend, and would be returning to Oxfordshire alone — and be relieved to do so. Nor was it only Ormwood who had been left with this impression — a number of his fellow classmates and friends had confirmed that the murdered man had made it clear their relationship was over.

But it obviously hadn't been clear to Mia de Salle. Or else she was incapable of accepting it.

'When you left Bristol and moved to Oxford, where did you live?' Hillary patiently tried a different tack.

'In a small flat not far from Little Clarendon Street.'

'Not with Michael?' she said, making it sound like a fact, not a question.

The hazel eyes flickered for a moment — a minor victory of sorts, Hillary supposed — but otherwise her facial expression didn't change. In fact, Hillary suddenly realized with a bit of a start, her facial expression hadn't changed by so much as a millimetre since the interview began. Which was distinctly unusual. Most people smiled, frowned, and displayed all sorts of expressions without even realizing they were doing it. Human beings had a vast range of body language that provided visual clues as to their feelings; but not *this* woman.

This woman hadn't even shifted her weight on her feet yet. She simply stood, watched, listened, and talked without any of it seeming to touch her. It all felt a bit surreal, and Hillary wasn't finding it at all pleasant.

'Michael had to move in with his parents,' Mia responded to her last statement. 'I didn't think it appropriate to move into his family home with him.'

And from what the Becks had had to say about her, no doubt they'd have felt the same way.

'But Michael *could* have moved into the flat with you, surely?' Hillary pointed out reasonably.

'Michael couldn't afford it. He was looking for a job.'

The unspoken caveat being, presumably, that once he'd found a job, he'd be moving right in with her.

'Did you have a flatmate at the time?' Hillary asked.

'No.'

'And you were paying the rent by yourself?'

'Yes.'

'Michael didn't have any need to pay half the rent then? Not if you could afford to pay for the flat all on your own,' Hillary pointed out, wondering how Mia was going to explain that one away.

'Michael wouldn't have wanted to feel as if he was living off me. He had his pride.'

Hillary nodded, mentally giving her that one. But she was not about to concede defeat. 'Michael told his parents that he'd broken up with you,' Hillary said, careful to keep her tone non-judgemental or argumentative.

'That's not true,' Mia said steadily.

'Then why, do you suppose, he said it?'

For the first time, Mia gave a little sigh. 'They didn't like me. And Michael was a good son. He didn't like to upset them. But he was my boyfriend.'

Hillary was beginning to get a sense of her opponent now. Anything that challenged her view of their relationship, anything that didn't fit with her version of how things had been, was simply going to be flatly denied.

Which meant there was little point in challenging her head on. She would get nowhere.

Instead, Hillary shifted tactics again. 'But even though he was your boyfriend, you told DI Weston at the time that you didn't see him that day — the day he died.'

'That's right. We hadn't made plans to see each other that particular day,' she confirmed.

'And you have no idea what Michael was going to be doing on the day he died?' Hillary persisted.

'No.'

'Do you think he could have been out in the local countryside taking his photographs?' she tried instead.

'No. He wasn't into his photography much by then. It was something he'd been interested in when he was younger, but he'd moved on to different pursuits.'

Hillary wondered if that was true, or if the murdered man had just told her that to stop her pestering him, and asking if she could go for long country walks with him. He might not have wanted to be so isolated and alone with her. According to all the witnesses in the original investigation, this woman hadn't wanted to take 'no' for an answer, and he must have been, by then, very wary of her.

'His parents told me that you called their house often, asking to speak to him. But he'd asked them to tell you he wasn't home.'

Mia gave her second reaction of the interview, with the barest shrug of her thin shoulders. 'They were lying. Like I said, they didn't like me. They were just trying to keep us apart.'

'Do you know why that would be?' Hillary asked, genuinely curious.

'No.'

'You don't sound very upset about that. Surely if you and Michael were together you would want to get on with his parents?'

'His parents didn't matter. Only Michael mattered.'

'You loved him?'

'Yes. Totally.'

At this, Hillary felt the hackles rise on the back of her neck. The words were emphatic, almost chilling in their certainty. And yet the emotion was totally submerged by the toneless voice, the blank, indifferent gaze.

But surely, Hillary thought, struggling to keep a clear head, this woman couldn't have been this . . . odd . . . when

Michael Beck had first met her, could she? Any man, let alone a young and not particularly forceful or experienced man such as Michael Beck had been, would have run a mile if she'd been like this back then.

She could understand, though, why Michael had been physically attracted to her. Although not beautiful by today's standard, to a lover of ancient history her medieval face must have been appealing. And even in her less-than-glamorous clothes, Hillary could see that there was an ageless elegance in the other woman's tall, willowy form. And when she let all that jet-black hair down, well, Hillary had no problem seeing the attraction.

But her demeanour, her personality, must have been different than this, surely? Warmer. More . . . well, *human*.

Was it possible that the death of Michael Beck had broken her? Had she suffered some form of mental illness or breakdown that had left her like this? If so, where had her family been? Or friends? Or even her local GP?

Or had it been a more slow transformation, with her coming to gradually realize that the man she had been so obsessed with was really dead and gone. Irretrievably gone.

For an instant, a half-forgotten line of poetry flashed across Hillary's mind before she could properly get a hold of it. Something that went a bit like . . . '*He is dead and gone, lady, he is dead and gone. At his head a grass green turf, and at his heels a stone.*' Her old English tutor would no doubt be aghast at her for not being able to place it, but right then she had other priorities.

Besides, everyone who had spoken of Mia had said they found her odd, so perhaps she hadn't changed so much after all.

'You told DI Weston that you were in your flat all that day when Michael died, working on some notes?' she said mildly.

'Yes. I was working on my first book.'

'Was it published?'

'Yes.' Again there was no sense of satisfaction, no hint of pride or joy in her achievement. Simply a bare statement of fact.

'And nobody saw you at home that day?'

'No.'

'You didn't speak to anyone? A neighbour? A friend?'

'No. I was working. I like it quiet when I work.'

Again, her hazel eyes moved beyond Hillary, fastening onto something, but this time Hillary was wise to this and didn't turn around to see what it was. If there was a rare marsh tit or a hare doing cartwheels behind her or dancing a can-can, then so be it.

'You must have been devastated when you found out that Michael was dead,' she said, somewhat brutally, but wasn't in the least surprised when Mia de Salle only said calmly, 'Yes.'

All right, Hillary thought. Time to change the direction of attack.

'It's been ten years now. Do you have a current partner?'

At this, Mia turned her hazel gaze back to Hillary. And did she hesitate — just a fraction — before answering? Hillary wasn't sure.

'There's another man in my life, yes.'

'Do you mind telling me who?'

'I can't see how that can have anything to do with Michael's case,' she said, not unreasonably, but for the first time actually challenging her and showing at least some spark of animation.

It was about time, Hillary thought grimly.

'Do you know anyone who had any reason to hurt Michael?' she shot out. Well, you never knew, Hillary told herself. Sometimes a wild card could turn up trumps.

'I have no idea why Michael's dead,' Mia de Salle said flatly. Which was, Hillary thought, a slightly odd way of putting it.

But even though she asked more and more questions, try as she might, Hillary couldn't get the woman to offer any personal insights into either the dead man, or who might have killed him, or why.

'Bloody hell, guv,' Claire gulped later, as they were walking away. 'I've got goosebumps all over.'

'You think she's our killer then?' Hillary asked, lips twitching slightly.

'I think she's definitely got enough bats in her belfry,' Claire said vehemently. 'A whole bloody colony of them, in fact!'

Privately Hillary agreed with her. But all she said, mildly, was, 'Since she's a zoologist, do you suppose they're a rare and endangered species?'

At this, Claire couldn't help but burst out laughing.

CHAPTER EIGHT

Early the next morning, Jason Morley looked about him cautiously before slipping around the corner and walking down a short alleyway. He wasn't often in this part of the city, and although a 'friend of a friend' had given him good directions, even so, he felt unsure and a little uneasy.

He'd be glad when he'd done what he needed to do and got back to his place. It was odd, for although he'd been in foreign parts, where men with guns and booby-traps had definitely been trying to kill him, he felt more alone and vulnerable now than he had then.

Perhaps that was because in the army he'd never been alone, but had his mates to watch his back. Or perhaps because, in the army, his actions had been sanctioned. Right or wrong, he felt happy about what he was doing. Whereas now, he was uncomfortably aware that he was about to break the law. And if he was caught, he, and more importantly his family, would suffer the shame of him being branded a criminal.

For a moment, Jason had to bite back a grim but genuine guffaw of laughter. Wouldn't it be a laugh if it was his old mate Gareth who arrested him? Of course, he knew it couldn't possibly work out that way. Gareth wasn't a proper copper, but only a civilian working for them. Still, Jason found the thought of it rather amusing.

After a few moments the good humour left him as abruptly as it had come, and the usual pall of dull despair seeped back. He straightened up, looked around and, as his instructions had assured him, saw the 'pea-green' paint of a back door. It was, he'd been told, the back door to a betting shop.

He gave a mental nod of recognition then glanced at his watch and waited patiently until it was exactly a quarter past seven. He then tapped on the back door three times, waited and — feeling a bit foolish and rather like some character from a cheesy spy film — tapped three times again.

The door opened at once and a surprisingly short man, barely five feet tall, looked him up and down from the doorway. He was perhaps Jason's own age, with short brown hair and eyes of almost exactly the same colour, set in a surprisingly nondescript but friendly face.

He wasn't what Jason had been expecting somehow.

'Yeah?' he asked casually. He was wearing denim jeans and a grey sweatshirt bearing a logo of some long-ago pop band, now faded into obscurity.

'I'm Jimbo's mate,' Jason said.

'Huh. And how *is* Jimbo?'

'As annoying as ever,' Jason said with a slight twist to his lips. 'Still whinging, and still always on the cadge.'

The man in the doorway gave a brief smile, acknowledging the truth of this assessment, then glanced quickly up and down the deserted alleyway, before stepping back. 'Come on in then.'

Jason, with just a slightly elevated heart rate, stepped into a small, somewhat smelly kitchen. With lime-green linoleum on the floor, standalone stove and units, and tiny lemon Formica worktops, it looked as if it belonged in a 1970s sitcom.

'So, what you after?' the other man said cagily.

'Handgun.'

Jason saw the other man's eyes narrow slightly, and felt the brown eyes quickly run over him. Was he afraid he was wearing a wire? What was he supposed to do, Jason wondered. Strip off? Again, Jason felt slightly ridiculous. And although his heart rate was still operating a little above normal — after all, he was in unknown territory — he wasn't feeling particularly scared.

Apart from anything else, he knew he could take on this pipsqueak with no trouble, if he started to cut up rough. He'd also been careful to keep the door behind him, so if sudden reinforcements appeared he had his exit ready and could always just leg it.

Besides, he had a knife up his sleeve. He wasn't *that* stupid. He was carrying a nice tidy sum of cash on him and, although he trusted the 'friend of a friend', in this day and age you never knew what scammers were out and about.

'Seen enough?' Jason asked sourly. 'You got something for me, or what?'

The other man seemed to suddenly make his mind up that he was OK, and grunted. He then walked over to the sink and opened the cutlery drawer. From it, he brought out a small, old black revolver.

Jason automatically tensed, but the man was already opening it, to reveal that it wasn't loaded.

'That thing belongs in a museum,' Jason grumbled in disgust.

The other man shrugged. 'It still works, that's the point. And it's clean.'

Jason's lips twisted. By 'clean' he supposed that his companion meant that it hadn't been used on any 'job' and so wasn't of interest to the police, because it was certainly in dire need of some maintenance. And actual cleaning.

'You were told the price, yeah?'

Jason nodded and patted his back pocket reassuringly. 'Bullets are extra I take it?'

The other man smiled. 'Naturally. You want some brushes and gun oil?'

Jason sighed heavily. 'Extra, no doubt.'

'Don't grow on trees, do they?'

Jason suspected he was probably being ripped off. But what did it really matter, in the circumstances? 'Fine.'

With mutual caution on both sides, money and gun were exchanged, and a few minutes later Jason was walking quickly back down the alley, carefully checking that nobody followed him from the shop.

Nobody did.

The business had been simple and easy after all, with no complications. Just as he liked it. The right-hand pocket of his windbreaker now weighed down more heavily than his left. But who was there to see? Or care?

He caught the next bus back to Bicester, and sat morosely watching the morning rush-hour traffic streaming past him. At least going from the city and back into the suburbs, the bus was going against the flow.

He was feeling just slightly guilty and ashamed of himself. But not enough to change his course.

It was a pity about Gareth though, Jason thought wearily. But that was life, wasn't it? And of all people, Gareth Proctor was well aware of just how shitty and unfair life could be.

* * *

Three months ago

Superintendent Ross Trenchard looked up as DI Robin Farrell knocked on his door and walked in. He looked wary, as well he might, the superintendent thought. But what he had to say surely wouldn't come as much of a surprise to the DI.

'All right, Robin?'

'Sir,' Farrell said smartly.

'Sit down then, you're making the place look untidy,' the superintendent said tersely. Since he didn't have either the time or the inclination to soft-soap things for his officers, he got straight to the point. 'The Newley and Kirklees cases,' he began, checking the paperwork in front of them. 'We're going to have to power them down, Robin.'

He saw the younger man flush resentfully and immediately open his mouth to argue his case. The superintendent expected nothing less, of course, since nobody liked to fail in any murder case, let alone a double murder. For a start, it didn't look good on the CV, but, to be fair, most officers cared more about getting results for friends and family than in boosting their own status.

And he'd think much less of his DI if he simply shrugged and let it slide without fighting his corner. Nevertheless, before the younger man could say a word, he lifted a hand and cut him short. 'You can't really be surprised, Robin. It's been three months, and let's face it, you have very little to go on, and during the last week, hardly any progress has been made.'

'Sir, I . . .'

'I'm not taking a swipe at you; I know how bloody difficult this case has been. I also know that nobody's talking. You've got no witnesses to either crime — or at least, none that are willing to come forward. Forensics at either site have very little to go on — just a footprint cast of a size ten sneaker, of a brand that sells by the millions, in the front garden at the Kirklees crime scene. But no DNA, no fingerprints, no fibres worth their salt. You've been hitting dead-ends everywhere you turn — sometimes you just don't get the breaks. We've all been there, so don't take it personally.'

'Sir, we know—'

'No CCTV footage worth a damn — only a list as long as the M1 of cars that were seen in the area of either murder site. And you've not managed to link any of the car owners to either victim,' he swept on, giving his junior officer no chance to rally.

'But we know it's Spence, sir,' Robin finally managed to cut in his superintendent's catalogue of woes, his voice tight with frustration and indignation. 'It has to be.'

At this, his superior officer smiled grimly. 'I know how you feel, Robin,' he said, sitting back a little in his chair and regarding his DI with a not unkindly eye. 'And you may well be right, at that,' he conceded.

'I *am* right, sir,' Robin insisted stubbornly.

At this, the superintendent sighed. 'You don't think you might be getting a case of tunnel vision on this case, do you, Robin?' he asked lightly. He'd seen it before, of course. The SIO becoming so convinced that he had the answer that he pursued that one idea to the exclusion of all else.

He didn't really think that was the case here though, to be fair. In fact, he'd always agreed that Robin Farrell's contention that Larry Spence was behind the killings was probably the right one. But it didn't hurt to make sure.

'No, sir,' Robin said, through slightly gritted teeth. 'We've followed up all possible leads and followed them wherever they might have taken us, and kept our initial investigations deliberately broad, as you know. But we couldn't find any personal reasons for either attack. Newley's family were all genuinely cut up about his death. His wife was in pieces. Even his neighbours, who all thought he ran a genuine antiques shop, had nothing but good words to say about the little scrote. We could find no whiff of anyone with a private or personal grudge against him anywhere. And he had no form for violence, so it was unlikely that he got rough with some "customer" with attitude. And as for Kirklees, we had almost the exact opposite problem with *him*. He was an only child and both his parents are deceased. No wife, no kids. He's a loner with no real friends, who came here from the Smoke and didn't exactly surround himself with buddies. The cautious sod never got close enough to anyone to give them a personal motive to kill him. He didn't even have a regular girlfriend, since he preferred the company of prostitutes, so there's not even the chance of a woman scorned in the picture anywhere. Only Spence makes sense in both cases.'

He paused for breath, giving his superintendent the opportunity to hold up his hands again. 'OK, Robin, OK.

I'm not saying I disagree with the direction you've taken, but it's not producing any results, is it?'

At this mild — but damnably true — criticism, Robin sighed heavily. 'That's no big surprise though, sir, is it, with all due respect,' he said bitterly. 'No one's going to grass on Spence, are they? They know they'd end up floating face down in the Cherwell if they did.'

Trenchard snorted in agreement. This was true enough.

Over a year ago now, the city's main criminal kingpin had been put away due to the late Chief-Superintendent Steven Crayle's diligent investigation, creating a vacuum at the top. A vacuum that Larry Spence had been only too happy and quick to fill.

Born and bred on home turf, Spence had begun by taking over the pitiful remnants of the old empire and sucking them into the burgeoning bosom of his own. He'd then set about systematically 'acquiring' other gangs, each with their various and specific criminal areas of expertise, until now he could be found behind most — if not all — of the city's nefarious activities.

'Oh yes, I agree that Spence has to be our prime suspect,' he concurred heavily.

'He hated Kirklees like poison, we've got plenty of anecdotal evidence of that,' Robin said eagerly. 'Kirklees coming up from London and muscling in on his territory really ticked him off. Hit him where it hurt, in his pride. He's been threatening to do something about him for some time. And it fits with his way of doing things too. Nobble the head of whatever gang he's after in no uncertain terms, which puts the wind up the rest of 'em, bringing them nicely in line. And since Kirklees kicked the bucket, guess who's taken over his particular line of business?'

'Yes, yes, Spence,' Trenchard admitted testily. 'But does *Newley* really fit the pattern?' the superintendent put in. 'Newley was strictly a one-man band, with a poxy shop, doing some small-time fencing. Hardly a jewel in anyone's crown, was he?'

'True enough, but Spence *has* taken over Newley's shop too. We got confirmation of that a couple of weeks ago,' Robin said stubbornly. 'His widow was "persuaded" to sell to one of his lieutenants at a very reasonable price, poor cow.'

'Even so, why didn't Spence simply lean on him?' the superintendent pointed out. 'Newley was an old man, and a realist. If Spence really had been interested in hoovering up even the smallest of small fry, he knew that all he had to do was make it clear which way the wind was blowing, and Newley would have been scared stiff! He'd have had enough sense to sell out low and take up an allotment in his retirement. He'd never have had the balls to stand up to someone like Spence, and Spence knew it. Why do something so drastic as killing him? It was bound to bring unwanted attention on him, and not even Spence goes around willy-nilly, knocking off people unnecessarily.'

Even though he knew his superior officer had a point — and it wasn't one that he hadn't also considered himself — Robin was still convinced he'd called this one right.

'Perhaps Spence told one of his goons to lean on the old man, and it got out of hand?' he proffered sullenly.

The superintendent still wasn't convinced. 'But the MO for both Newley and Kirklees doesn't exactly shout "enforcer", does it? Why the taser, for instance? That smacks of someone who needed it to incapacitate his victim first. But Spence could have sent in half a dozen heavies at a time, and they could have overwhelmed their victim in a flash. Especially an old guy like Newley. And let's not forget, blows to the head with an as-yet-unidentified object killed both men. Hasn't Spence's known preference for dispatch always been a long, sharp knife? Administered either in the back, or straight through the heart from the front?'

Robin shifted in his chair. 'Perhaps that's just the point, sir? Spence wanted to mix it up a bit this time in order to divert suspicion?' he argued stubbornly. 'Or maybe he's just got a new man in his heavy squad who likes to bash people over the head? All these thugs have their own favourite ways of going about things.'

'Perhaps, perhaps not. We can discuss the ins and outs all day, Robin, but it doesn't change the facts,' Trenchard said firmly. 'It's been three months now, and I'm afraid the investigation is getting bogged down. You've got no new leads, and the case is in a rut. I'm sorry, but as you know, we simply can't afford to keep it running at the level it is. We don't have the officers, and we sure as hell don't have the budget. Oh, I'm not saying shelve it altogether,' he added, as once more the DI looked about to argue. 'Just put it on the backburner. I've been getting pressure from above for a while now to cut back on it. You know what it's like.'

He felt guilty having to pull the rug from under his junior officer, but Farrell would just have to learn to live with it. As did they all.

'Yes, sir,' Robin finally muttered resentfully.

'All right. You've been given that domestic in Banbury, right?'

'Yes, sir.'

'Well, prioritize that then.'

It was an order, and Robin Farrell heard it loud and clear. He got up stiffly from the chair. 'Yes, sir. Is that all?'

'Yes,' Superintendent Trenchard said, and he watched the younger man stalk stiffly from the room.

He sighed heavily when the door shut — not too quietly — behind him, and glanced out of the window. He knew how Farrell felt of course. He could remember only too well how much he had hated it when, as a young DI himself, he hadn't been able to pursue a case as much as he'd wanted to.

Running a weary hand over his face, Trenchard turned to the latest budget figures, silently cursing all bean-counters everywhere. Within a few minutes, the deaths of Newley and Kirklees slipped from his mind.

* * *

Fuming, and back at his desk, DI Robin Farrell had to give his team the news that the double-murder investigation was being powered down. He'd built up a good team in the last three months, and though, like him, they'd seen the writing on the wall, they too were bitterly disappointed.

But even as Robin began to pack away files, he knew he wasn't going to let this one go. After all, the super had said he didn't have to shelve it altogether, right? So he'd continue to work it, whenever he had a spare moment. Hell, he'd even do unpaid overtime and work on it whenever he had a free weekend, if he had to.

The truth was, Larry Spence had got under his skin. Whenever questioned, he'd stuck to 'no comment' and forced Robin to deal with his smart-arse, super-polite solicitor. His bland smile and elaborately patient attitude had only rubbed it in how clearly he believed himself to be untouchable. That self-satisfied air he had, the way he genuinely never felt even a hint of concern, as if he knew, just *knew*, that Robin would never be able to pin the deaths on him, ate away at the DI like acid.

As far as Robin was concerned, no one should think it was safe to thumb their nose at him and the law — and certainly not the likes of Larry Spence.

Which made DI Robin Farrell utterly determined to bring the murders home to the cocky swine.

One way or another, he *was* going to get Spence. No matter what it took.

* * *

At about the same time that Jason Morley was sitting on the bus and watching the morning rush-hour traffic stream past him, Mia de Salle was sitting at the breakfast bar in her small but detached cottage, eating yoghurt and muesli.

From her window, she could just get a glimpse of part of the grounds of Blenheim Palace, the Duke of Marlborough's huge stately home.

101

She'd been living here for a few years now, having grown tired of Oxford's constant noise and pollution, and preferring the surroundings of a more genteel location. And the very desirable Cotswold stone cottage, set in the outer edges of the very desirable town of Woodstock, suited her perfectly. She adored the thick walls, the wooden window seat, and the sense of being cocooned in a different era.

She'd always thought that she should have been born in Victorian times, when life seemed so much more epic and grand, and when things *meant* so much more than they did now, when Darwin was just challenging the Church, and discoveries of all kinds were there to be made by anyone with an adventurous spirit and the determination to succeed.

She was a great fan of the Bronte sisters and their writings, especially Emily's *Wuthering Heights*, and identified strongly with Cathy. Free-spirited, unconventional, greedy, oh-so-alive-and-in-love Cathy! Within the covers of books, Mia could live vicariously in a way that she couldn't in the drab confines of the modern world.

Looking out of her window now at the passing cars and the dreary, everyday blandness of modern life, she felt that familiar ache, that constant mourning at the lack of romance and the loss of the Gothic. Where, in this day and age, was the magic? Here, computers, dull, pedantic, soulless machines now ruled the world.

It was one of the main reasons why she'd thought Michael Beck had been her soulmate. He too had a deep and abiding love of history, and the romance of times past. He had understood her in a way nobody else ever had. Ever since her late teens, she had been searching for her Heathcliff, or even her Dracula — someone, *anyone*, who stood out from the usual humdrum run of lacklustre twenty-first century humanity.

And then, in her mid-twenties, when she'd all but given up, she found Michael.

Oh, true, in the end, like so many of literature's great heroes, he'd been found flawed and wanting, letting her down because of some malaise in his psyche, some weakness in his soul that wouldn't allow him to love her as wildly as she'd loved him.

But even that, even the heartbreak and the betrayal had, in its own way, been glorious! At least she'd felt alive, as if she existed, as if she *felt*! Even if it was only heartbreak and pain, it had been *something*.

She sighed heavily, and walking to the sink, automatically washed out her now empty bowl and left it to drain. Soon she'd have to go in to work, and do all the things that were required of her.

Michael had found it odd, at first, that she'd been studying sciences, given her real passions. But nature, as she'd explained to him, was timeless and magnificent and worthy of her attention as well. How often did it feature in poetry, art, literature or music? And what was happening to it now? The man-made plagues of technology, overpopulation and pollution were killing even that. Soon there would be nothing beautiful left in the world. No wild orchids, no magnificent bears, no tigers stalking through the hot summer grass . . .

Mia stood for a moment, looking at the vase of beautiful golden daffodils that she'd set in her kitchen window. She always bought cut flowers for herself — fresh, every week. She liked to spend her money freely, but only on things that mattered to her.

The cottage, for instance, which wasn't large but had been built in the late 1790s, suited her admirably. The beams, the inglenook fireplace, the bulging plastered walls. Michael would have loved it here.

She sighed and turned away, gathering her coat and handbag together and heading for the front door.

As she walked to her car, she wondered if she'd see that woman who worked for the police again — Hillary Greene. She hoped not. Mia hadn't liked her. There was something . . . knowing . . . in her eyes and her manner. Something strong. A very clever woman herself, Mia knew when she met another very clever person, and usually she felt drawn to them. As she had with Michael.

But not this time.

Perhaps it was because Hillary Greene had wanted to know all about Michael, Mia thought, climbing in behind the wheel of her Mercedes. And Michael belonged to her. Still. Always. Only to her — even though she now had a new love.

For a minute or so, Mia sat in her car, staring blankly ahead. Of course, even the Victorians had had to acknowledge the dominion of death. If only she *was* Catherine Earnshaw, Mia thought sadly. If only *she* could conquer death. Only, of course, it would have to be the other way around, wouldn't it? This time, Michael's ghost should have come back to seek her out.

How many nights had she sat, in the dark, hoping that he would do just that? Listening, straining her eyes and her ears for any sign.

But nothing.

And, eventually, even she had had to accept her loss, and to look for another.

Mia smiled gently to herself now, thinking of that other. Who would have expected that the answer to her prayers could possibly lay with *him*? Him of all people? He was not a classic Bronte hero, was he? No Mr Rochester, certainly. But he *had* loved Michael too, in his way. More importantly, he had been privileged to spend such precious and momentous moments with Michael — such final, intimate moments, moments that she would have given her soul to have been able to share.

But she had not understood what had been happening until it was too late.

And now she must continue to be patient and pragmatic, like one of the characters in one of Jane Austen's works.

But Mia knew that she was beginning to lose patience recently. How long would it take before he too succumbed to the inevitable and accepted their joint destiny? He was resisting it so far, but that would have to change soon.

Mia de Salle gave a small, grim little shrug, and started her car. She had done her duty — she had pined faithfully for her lost love, and she had waited patiently and for so many years for his replacement to make the first move — as the man should.

But not even *her* patience was infinite.

The police opening Michael's case again had to be a sign of some kind, didn't it? That things were moving once again. A sign that it was time for her to become the catalyst once more in her own love story.

With a serene smile, she sent her sleek car out into the road, feeling more content now that she knew what she must do.

CHAPTER NINE

As Mia de Salle set off for work, Hillary Greene sat beside Claire as she drove them south towards Hampshire and a small market town about ten miles from the coast. It was to this rather nice spot that Dr Timothy Durning had finally settled, working as a private tutor to Oxbridge wannabes.

The sun was shining on and off, and Claire was feeling happy to be out of the office for most of the day. She chatted about her children, her 'better half', the cost of living and the state of her current diet. Hillary, used to her pleasant chatter, let it all flow over her with just the occasional murmur here and there to show willing, and mostly mused on her case so far.

Or rather, the lack of a case so far! As far as she could see, they had unearthed nothing new, let alone earth-shattering, in Michael Beck's case. Gareth had informed her before she set off from the office that the Becks had confirmed that none of their son's cameras had been missing. Which seemed to rule out the idea that he might have been taking some of his wildlife photographs on the day of his death, and been surprised by his killer out in the fields somewhere. It was looking less and less like an opportunist killing.

That, coupled with the fact that his means of transport — his bicycle — had never been recovered, seemed to bolster the theory that he had gone missing either in Oxford, or on his way to or from Oxford. Had he met up with someone somewhere on the road? If so, the original investigation had never found CCTV footage of it, and nobody had come forward to say they'd seen anything odd — like two people struggling on the side of the road.

Mind you, Hillary reminded herself, the first part of his journey, from Woodeaton towards Headington, *did* take him down a fairly lonely stretch of isolated rural road, apart from the rat-run during rush hours, which saw plenty of traffic on that stretch then. Which didn't mean much either way, since Michael had set off from his parents' house a good hour after the morning rush would have passed.

It was possible he'd been snatched, she supposed. Had someone forced him off the road and bundled him and his bicycle into their car? The post mortem had not showed any signs that he'd been hit by a motorcar — but he might have been forced to run off the road onto the grass, which wouldn't necessarily have left any bruises. But then what? Surely he would have put up a fight? He was a young, relatively fit man; he wouldn't have been forced into a car easily. Unless there was more than one killer involved. One to hold him, one to hit him over the head with whatever the instrument used had been, and two of them to sling him and his bike into a capacious boot.

And just what was that blunt instrument? Forensics had tried many comparisons with all sorts of things, but nothing had quite seemed to fit. Could it have been a specialist tool of some kind? Something fairly unique, something the killer needed for their trade, say, or something the killer might habitually carry with him?

The trouble with that scenario was, of course, that until they found out *who* the killer was, they might not find out *what* he or she had used to hit Michael Beck over the head. But speculation of that sort was useless, especially since the killer had in all likelihood long disposed of the murder weapon anyway. Only an idiot would keep the murder weapon on their own premises.

Hillary sighed. Claire, realizing that she'd lost her audience, fiddled with the radio until she found a station playing mainly 80s tunes. Hillary hastily blanked the noise out. She liked 1960s pop, but was not a fan of the New Romantics.

As the miles passed by, Hillary continued to let her mind roam freely, reviewing the case and their slim leads. Nothing that the dead boy's parents had said had rung any particular alarm bells for her. Kevin Philpott, the best friend, hadn't seemed to have anything new to add to the pot either. Which left her with everybody's favourite candidate for the crime — the creepy girlfriend.

As they pulled up at a set of temporary traffic lights at some road works, a newly arrived chiff-chaff sang in a nearby tree and Hillary reflected on Mia de Salle and the interview at the nature reserve.

She could certainly see now just why so many people had failed to warm to Michael Beck's choice of lover. But she could well see how Mia would have appealed to Michael if she'd saved all her energy for him, and him alone. Apart from anything else, he'd have been flattered. And everyone she'd talked to so far had confirmed that her interest in him was whole-hearted to the point of being unhealthy.

And yet, after a while, surely such single-minded devotion would become a burden rather than a pleasure? And when someone like Dr de Salle was rejected, she'd feel it to the very core of her. When you made just one thing or one person your whole world, loss of that one thing or person left you far more vulnerable and devastated than if you had other things to fall back on.

But did any of that necessarily make her more likely to be a killer than anyone else? Hillary wasn't so sure, tempting though it might be to assume so. Oh, she could certainly see that Mia was someone who wouldn't take no for an answer. Who would watch and maybe even stalk her lover, in the hopes of winning him back. But she didn't know enough about mental illness — always supposing Mia *was* mentally ill in the first place — to feel comfortable casting her as the prime suspect simply on the basis that she didn't act like everyone else.

For all Hillary knew, the woman might be excessively shy. Or have some sort of personality disorder that had nothing to do with violence or unpredictable behaviour. It was one thing to cavalierly say 'oh she's not playing with a full deck of cards' and quite another to assume that that made her capable of murder.

On the other hand, there was nothing to say it didn't.

Hillary leaned her head back on the seat as Claire sang along with somebody who didn't want a prayer said for them now, but to save it for the morning after, and sighed again. Eyes closed, she let the warming spring sunshine coming in through the windscreen play across her face, and turned her thoughts from the past to the immediate future, and contemplated instead the business at hand. The interview with the man Michael Beck had accused of molesting him.

Of all the people in Michael Beck's life, only two could be said to have a 'proper' motive for killing him. Mia, out of some twisted love/hate obsession, or Dr Timothy Durning, out of revenge for a career lost and a reputation ruined.

For the next few hours, she had to put everything else aside, and concentrate on the upcoming interview.

'Durning never married, right?' she said, still with her head back and her eyes closed.

At this, Claire instantly turned off the radio, and keeping her eyes on the road said, 'No, guv. He was forty-one at the time, and so is fifty-one now and still single.'

Hillary nodded. 'His background is relatively well-heeled and middle-class?' She already knew this, but sometimes bouncing things around with someone else brought into focus something that she'd otherwise miss.

'Yup. He's got only one sibling, an older brother, now living in Australia. Married with four kids,' Claire confirmed. 'Both parents now deceased. They divvied the family inheritance equally between their two sons though. They didn't leave them a massive fortune, as such, but I still wouldn't have minded my share of it!'

'Hmmm,' Hillary mused. So either they were open-minded about their youngest son's sexuality, or they hadn't known — or guessed — that he was gay.

'I suppose that's how come he can just about afford to live in a nice town in Hampshire on whatever he can earn giving private tuition,' Claire added. 'A private income. Nice for some, innit?'

Hillary smiled, but wondered if Timothy Durning saw it in that light. Did he miss university life? The hustle and bustle, all that communicating with bright young minds and youthful ideologies. Going from a vibrant city like Bristol to a smaller backwater town — no matter how picturesque it probably was — might not have been how he saw the rest of his life playing out.

Had he resented Michael Beck enough to watch and wait for his chance to kill him? Presumably he must have had some feelings for the young man — by Michael's own admission, he'd been his favourite teacher. Which suggested friendship had existed between them, as well as (on the older man's part) physical attraction.

And she knew all about how attraction or affection could quickly turn to hate and rage. Some people — and Hillary had met her share — simply couldn't take rejection — or being thwarted. Some people never seemed to grow up, and could experience rages and tantrums that should have been left behind in childhood. But it was useless speculating about such things until she'd had a chance to meet the man and assess him for herself.

She sighed again and opened her eyes. 'Fancy stopping for a pub meal after we've talked to the good doctor. My treat?'

Claire grinned. 'Are limes green?'

'What about the diet?' she teased.

'What diet?'

* * *

The market town they entered an hour later had everything going for it that a tourist board could wish for. An attractive stone bridge spanning a wide but shallow river, an old Norman church, a photographically appealing high street with a mixture of half-timbered buildings and local stone, and a statue of some bloke who had done something noteworthy at some point in the last three hundred years. Hanging baskets outside several inns and pubs had been newly planted with vibrant spring colours, and daffodils lined the grass verges. In short, it was the kind of place that was either the stuff of dreams, or of nightmares, depending on your point of view.

Dr Timothy Durning lived in a small cul-de-sac not far from the charming church, in a detached stone cottage with a grey-tiled roof and a wisteria climbing up the walls and blooming in all its pale lilac glory.

Claire, having got out from behind the wheel, stood regarding the scene with a wry expression on her face. 'Bloody hell,' was all she said.

Hillary couldn't help but agree. The scene did seem almost too good to be true. It was quiet, with even the town's limited traffic seeming to be muted behind all the cherry and magnolia trees that proliferated in the gardens of the eight houses comprising the little nook. No children played, creating a squeal or a fuss. No dogs roamed, barking or depositing little brown mounds on the pavement. There weren't even any cars parked on the road, causing an obstruction.

'What's that film I saw yonks ago, set in some American place or other. *Stepford Wives*?' Claire said. 'D'you reckon this could be the English version?'

Hillary grinned. Wasn't that the one where all the perfect housewives and mothers turned out to be androids or something? 'Come on. Let's see what Dr Durning has to say for himself.'

'Right, guv. But if smoke starts coming out of his ears, I'm off!' Claire warned her.

* * *

Somewhat disconcertingly, Dr Timothy Durning *did* indeed look rather handsome in a bland way, and *was* impeccably dressed, making him a perfect candidate for a resident of the fictional town of Stepford. But for all that, Hillary was fairly sure that he didn't have robotic sub-routines.

At six foot or so, he was still very lean, with reddish-brown hair (dyed?) and dark brown eyes. His skin looked unlined (nip and tuck?) and was lightly tanned. All of which conspired to make him look years younger than she knew him to be, but that, presumably, was the point. He was also dressed in his trademark waistcoat and bow tie.

'I take it you're the police officers who called yesterday?' he asked. His voice was bland, pleasant, but not, thankfully, robotic.

'Yes, sir.' Hillary and Claire produced their IDs while Hillary went through the standard explanation of who they were and what they did.

At the mention of Michael's name the older man sighed gently, gave a philosophical nod, and invited them in.

The cottage was full of light, and Hillary wasn't surprised when he led them through to a rear extension that had one wall practically made of glass. It revealed a small but lovely back garden, complete with a pond set amid a plethora of native plants. Several bird feeders hung from an apple tree and were currently playing host to a greenfinch, a pair of bluetits and a nervous-looking goldfinch. No doubt Mia de Salle would have approved of the wildlife pond.

'Please, take a seat.' The extension — like the majority of home extensions — had been made into a huge kitchen-diner, with a small seating area near the bi-fold doors. It was to this nest of chairs that he led them. 'Do you want tea or coffee?'

'Coffee, please,' Hillary said instantly. She had an idea this man would make a proper pot, probably of a Brazilian blend, and she was never going to turn her nose up at that sort of offer. Claire opted for tea.

Dr Durning made the beverages in silence and with a neatness and economy of movement that some people seemed to naturally possess. He brought the cafetiere and teapot to the small coffee table on a large tray, upon which also rested small demitasse coffee cups, a Spode teacup and saucer, a silver jug of milk and a matching silver sugar dish. The spoons, naturally, were also silver.

For a moment all three set about making their drinks to suit their own tastes, while a grandfather clock ticked politely against one feature wall. Outside, the goldfinch finally succumbed to its nerves and flew off. A rapacious-looking starling quickly took its place.

A tall, all-glass display cabinet set in the seating area caught Hillary's eye. It contained various small objects, of which she recognized only a lovely ammonite, an ancient flint arrowhead and what looked like a misshapen coin. The other artefacts were much more obscure but mostly seemed to be made out of badly corroded metal, bone or fossilized wood.

Catching her looking at it, the academic smiled. 'That's my collection of historic curios,' he admitted, looking a little wistful. 'I'm fascinated by what time does to everything it touches. We can't easily measure it or display what it does to human beings, of course, but we can see what it does to inanimate things.'

'As a historian, I can understand your fascination,' Hillary agreed, not sure why the contents of the cabinet were making her feel uneasy. 'Which king is on the coin?'

'Emperor,' Timothy Durning corrected her with a smile. 'It's Roman.'

Hillary nodded, but wasn't about to let herself get sidetracked by his hobbyhorse. 'You have a lovely spot here, Dr Durning,' she said instead.

'Thank you. Yes. It suits me. I can write my books here in peace.'

'So you write?'

'Yes — historical non-fiction for people with an interest in history, but who don't want too much academic dryness.'

Hillary nodded. She knew such books sold all right, but she doubted they earned their authors huge royalties. But it probably did his ego a lot of good to be a published author. 'Do you miss the university life at all?' Hillary took a sip — Costa Rican, not Brazilian — and half-closed her eyes in pleasure.

'Not really. At some point I would always have left, I think, in order to do proper research. Teaching had its rewards, but it didn't leave me much time for a proper in-depth study of my passion.'

'What era of history interests you?'

'Roman Britain.'

'Was that Michael's choice too?'

'Michael didn't really confine himself to one specific era. He was interested in the Romans, certainly, but also in the Saxons and the Britons.'

Hillary, now that she'd got him talking, decided to get down to business. 'You were his favourite tutor. Did you know that?'

Timothy Durning crossed one elegantly long leg over the other. He looked a little lost for words suddenly, which surprised Hillary somewhat. She would imagine this man to be very erudite, and seldom socially inept. And he'd known they were coming. Surely he'd rehearsed over and over in his head what he would, and would not say?

Catching her eye, he must have read something of her thoughts, for he smiled wryly. 'I don't quite know how to answer that question. If I say yes I sound big-headed, and I'm worried you'll read more into it than you should. If I say no I run the risk of sounding disingenuous and you'd probably suspect me of lying. You can see my dilemma?'

Hillary nodded. She could, actually. He wanted to show himself in the best light, which was only natural. And not, in itself, suspicious. No doubt he'd been dismayed to hear that a sad and sordid episode from his past was being raked up again, and was too intelligent not to see how the reopening of Michael's case was bound to cause him trouble — regardless of whether he had anything to hide or not.

'Why don't you just be honest and straightforward and let me do the rest?' Hillary advised him with a slight smile and a level look.

For a moment, the academic considered this, and then smiled again. 'Now who's being disingenuous?' he murmured, then gave a weary shrug. 'Well. I'll do my best,' he said.

Beside Hillary, Claire had already got out her notebook, and was unobtrusively taking notes.

'So. *Were* you aware that you were Michael's favourite tutor?' Hillary asked, going straight back to where she'd left off. She was not about to allow this man to get away without answering every question she wanted answering. Well, not without some serious squirming on his part, anyway.

'I knew we had a good rapport, yes,' Dr Durning finally admitted, 'and by that, I mean nothing more and nothing less than the sum of my words. Some students go to university for the experience, rather than to actually study, which is understandable but annoying. Some students aren't particularly gifted, and struggle but work hard, and these need a different sort of attention. And some, like Michael, are just naturally gifted. These, obviously, are like gold dust to tutors such as myself, and are a dream to teach.'

'And it's easier to get to know and build up a rapport with the golden ones?' Hillary mused, careful to keep any hint of censure out of her tone. 'Yes, I can see how that would be. You were drawn to Michael because he was gifted?'

'Not only that. He had a real *passion* for history, the same way that I have. He enjoyed discovery — finding out facts, hunting down little snippets that helped to add to the jigsaw puzzle that is the past. It was in his blood, the same way it's in mine. It's such a fluid, alive, *creative* thing — that's what most people don't understand. They think history is all about dry-as-dust facts, dates, and musty, boring old books.

But that's just where they're wrong! So wrong! It's not like mathematics or physics, where things either are or aren't. History changes all the time, and our understanding of it changes with it. Look at what happened when they found King Richard in that car park!'

He was sitting a little forward on his chair now, his face and voice animated. 'All the debate there'd been for decades about whether he really was a hunchback, or whether it was the result of "bad press" by his enemies! And then they found his skeleton really did have a curvature of the spine! How Michael would have loved all that . . .'

Hillary knew when someone was genuinely fascinated by something and when they were faking it, and there was no doubt in her mind that this man lived and breathed his subject. There was a glow to his face, a force in his words that showed how much he was engaged in his topic. And, from what she knew of Michael Beck, he too had been similarly enthralled by the past. Which was all very interesting, but she needed more meat on the bones.

'But he didn't live to see it, did he?' she slipped in quietly, and saw all the animation drain out of the older man.

'No.' Timothy Durning swallowed hard. 'No, he didn't.' His hand, when he raised his tiny coffee cup, was shaking slightly.

'You must have been very shocked when you heard about his murder,' Hillary said quietly.

'Yes I was. Utterly shocked. I couldn't believe it.'

'By then you'd left Bristol, am I right?'

'Yes.'

'Because of Michael's allegations against you?'

'Yes. But those allegations were never substantiated,' he put in quickly but without any impetus, as if he merely said the words out of force of habit.

Hillary knew that other pupils of this man had come forward to back up Michael's claims, but didn't see the point — yet — of pushing Timothy Durning on the issue.

She contented herself by asking, 'You agreed to resign though?'

'Of course. My position was untenable by then. And I didn't want the university to suffer . . .' His voice wavered slightly and he abruptly put down his cup on the coffee table. 'I'm sorry, but this is very difficult for me. It's a time of my life that I prefer not to dwell on.'

'I can understand that. You must have blamed Michael for what happened to you.' Hillary was careful to make this a statement, rather than a question.

'Not so much as I blamed myself,' Timothy Durning said with a half-laugh.

'Care to enlarge on that?' Hillary tempted.

The older man heaved a sigh. 'Look, I'm not saying I never made a pass at Michael, because I did. But it was a genuine *mistake*, a genuine misunderstanding. I accept that I made a bad error of judgement. I thought . . . but I was wrong.'

'You thought that Michael would welcome an . . . overture . . . from you?' Hillary helped him out.

'Yes. Exactly. But instead he looked shocked and totally surprised. I realized the instant I did it that I'd made a dreadful mistake. I apologized at once. I told him I'd made a mistake, I thought I'd seen signs from him that obviously weren't there.'

'And he accepted this apology? Accepted the explanation?'

'I thought so. At the time,' Dr Durning's voice dropped slightly.

'But after some thought, he pursued a complaint?'

'Yes.'

Hillary nodded. And then said gently, 'That must have hurt.'

'It did, yes.'

'You felt he'd betrayed you?'

'No!' Timothy exploded, then just as quickly deflated again. 'Yes, perhaps a little. I just wish that if he hadn't been satisfied with my explanation that he'd have come to me for more clarification. I think that if he had done, I could have made him see that it was all my fault — entirely. And made him understand that I really was horrified to have caused him . . . Well, that the last thing I'd meant to do was make him feel . . .'

The words trailed helplessly off. The grandfather clock continued to tick impassively. Outside, a blackbird picked a fight with another blackbird, probably over territory. Dr Durning sighed heavily. 'It was all such a mess,' he finished simply.

'Did you see Michael after you agreed to resign?'

'No, of course not. That would have been very inappropriate.'

'Why do you think he decided to make the complaint official?' Hillary asked, genuinely curious.

'I assumed his girlfriend made him do it,' Dr Durning said with a shrug.

'Mia de Salle?'

'Yes.'

'Can I ask,' Hillary knew she needed to be very delicate now, 'if you knew he'd been seeing Mia de Salle for over a year at that point, what made you think he might be open to instigating a relationship with you?'

Timothy Durning smiled gently. 'I was convinced Michael was bisexual. Why else?'

'Do you still think that?'

For a moment, the academic's eyelids flickered. Then he looked out of the window at the flying black feathers as the two blackbirds continued their noisy avian brawl. 'You know, I think I do. I think Michael wasn't really that sure of his own sexuality and what I did scared him because it made him face up to things he'd rather have kept buried deep inside him.'

Hillary glanced at Claire, who raised a thoughtful eyebrow. Either Dr Durning was indulging in a bout of some serious wishful thinking — or he wasn't.

And if he wasn't — did they need to start looking for a possible *boyfriend* who might have played a role in the dead man's final months of life? A secret part, since nobody seemed to know of his existence . . .

* * *

'What did you make of all that, guv?' Claire asked ten minutes later as they sat in a pleasant pub, overlooking the pleasant market square and eating a pleasant meal of chicken and chips with a not-quite-so-pleasant side salad.

'You think our dishy doc was just indulging in so much pie-in-the-sky about our victim being bi?'

Hillary shrugged. 'It's been ten years. Memories have a habit of becoming rose-coloured with age.'

Claire sighed. 'He stuck to his alibi for the time of Michael's murder.'

'Not exactly airtight, was it, as DI Weston found out,' Hillary reminded her. According to Dr Durning, he'd been at home all that day. He'd seen a neighbour at some vague point in the morning, and had done some shopping in a local supermarket in the afternoon.

'Ah, the airtight alibi, so beloved of Agatha Christie fans everywhere,' Claire grinned, spearing a chip. 'In her books, the one who couldn't possibly have done it, always did it. Right?'

'Whereas, back in the real world, the vast majority of suspects have alibis that leak like sieves, and mean exactly nothing,' Hillary said. 'But if Durning *has* been leading us up the garden path, I thought he did it rather well.'

And on this rather morose thought, she speared a chip of her own, and bit into it with pleasure.

Opposite her, Claire eyed the dessert menu.

CHAPTER TEN

Claire and Hillary were unlucky enough to get stuck in a traffic jam on the motorway on the way back to Oxford which ate up practically the rest of the afternoon. When they finally pulled into HQ in Kidlington, neither one of them was in a particularly happy or relaxed frame of mind.

'You get straight off home, Claire,' Hillary said to her relieved colleague as she opened the passenger door of the car. By her watch it was just gone five o'clock anyway. 'I'm going into the office just to check in case something's come in that needs seeing to.'

'Thanks, guv,' Claire accepted happily.

It was as she was walking across the parking lot towards the main entrance that Hillary noticed Gareth Proctor, standing beside his car, with a man opposite him, talking earnestly.

They hadn't seen her, and she found herself instinctively slowing down and moving towards the trunk of a large, flowering horse-chestnut tree. She didn't exactly conceal herself behind it, but she did take advantage of its shade and cover in order to watch the two men closely.

She couldn't have said, at that moment, just what it was about them that had pinged her radar, exactly. They were certainly not arguing. The man with Gareth looked to be around his own age and build, and nothing about his attitude gave her the impression of aggression. If it had, she'd be heading across there now, in case her colleague needed backup.

Something about Gareth's companion — maybe the shortness of his haircut and the erect bearing — told her that, like Gareth, he was more than likely not a former soldier, and she felt herself relax a little, but still didn't move. There was no reason why Gareth shouldn't be chatting to a friend, of course. His workday was over, and he had most likely prearranged for the other man to meet him in the car park so they could go on for a drink somewhere.

At this point, Gareth moved away from the driver's door and moved around the front of the vehicle so that he could stand beside his companion. She wondered if he'd done so because he was worried about them being overheard, for several officers that she recognized from Traffic chose that moment to pour out of the building and swarm vaguely in their direction.

Again, there was nothing particularly suspicious about that. Not everybody liked to have an audience to their conversation. Even so, Hillary found herself observing them even more closely, and after a moment or so, she realized why. There was something very *tense* about the stranger. Although she was too far away to see his facial features clearly (damn, she really was going to have to get her eyes tested soon!) she could tell by his body language that, whatever it was they were discussing, it was no idle chat about football or the weather. And the more she watched, the more she could tell that the stranger's tension was transferring itself to her colleague, for Gareth Proctor was beginning to look distinctly unsettled as well.

At one point, Gareth reached out and put a hand on the other man's shoulder. The other man accepted the gesture, but shook his head at whatever it was Gareth was saying.

A friend in need? Satisfied that whatever had the two men so engrossed was almost certainly none of her business, Hillary finally continued on into the building.

But her mind, as ever, was still stubbornly and actively seeking out answers, and turned almost inevitably to the ex-soldier who'd been murdered in Reading. It annoyed her that her mind kept returning insistently back to that case. It wasn't even *her* case — hell, it wasn't even in her area!

But once she got back to her office it took her a while to drag her mind back to the case that *was* hers. Once she'd managed it however, she diligently typed up her report on the interview with Dr Timothy Durning, then printed off a hard copy and took it through to the communal office to place it in the Murder Book. A quick glance through that document informed her that nothing noteworthy had happened while she and Claire had whiled away the hours stuck in traffic, and with a sigh of relief, she quickly checked her emails, then called it a day.

When she got back out into the car park, Gareth and his intense friend had left. She hoped, whatever the crisis had been, they'd managed to resolve it.

* * *

The next morning, though, Hillary still had the little conundrum stubbornly on her mind, and when she made her way downstairs and saw that Claire had yet to arrive while Gareth was already at his desk, she made a snap decision to try and appease her curiosity. Resolutely ignoring what curiosity was said to have done to the proverbial cat!

'Hello, Gareth, everything all right?' she asked breezily from the doorway.

'Yes thank you, ma'am. I've read your report about Dr Durning.'

Hillary nodded. She was beginning to take for granted his work ethic. 'He's a slippery one all right,' she said. 'We got caught up in that road traffic accident on the motorway on the way back.'

'I thought you might have. I heard about it on the radio on the way home. It sounded bad,' Gareth said sympathetically.

'Yes,' Hillary said grimly. In her early days in uniform she'd done her fair share of attending RTAs. It wasn't something she dwelled on. 'When we got back, I thought I saw you talking to someone in the car park,' she went straight to the point, watching him closely. And saw a definite flicker of unease cross his face.

'Yes, ma'am,' he said promptly. It was, she was sure, a reflex reaction — an obedient response to an officer's question that was nevertheless meaningless and was designed to give nothing away.

'Your friend looked as if he had a lot on his mind,' she said casually.

'Yes, ma'am.'

'He looked as if he might be ex-army too?'

'Yes, ma'am.'

'An old friend then?'

'Yes, ma'am.'

Hillary hid a smile. Gareth Proctor might have had a lot of practice at dumb insolence, but two could play at this game.

'Does he have a name?' she asked bluntly.

'Yes, ma'am,' Gareth said — but didn't quite dare leave it at that. 'Jason Morley, ma'am,' he tacked on reluctantly.

Hillary nodded. Having got what she wanted — a name — she let him off the hook. 'I want to go back to Michael's parents, now that we've met all the main suspects and witnesses in their son's case, and go over things with them again. I want you to come with me this time. It'll give you a chance to observe them, and perhaps pick up on something I miss.'

'Yes, ma'am,' he agreed with far more enthusiasm.

Hillary nodded, smiled, and left.

After she was gone, however, Gareth Proctor watched the space in the doorway where she had been with a slightly troubled frown. Why had his boss been so curious about Jason? Not that he wasn't worried about him as well.

When he'd gone out to the car park yesterday he'd been surprised to see his friend waiting for him by his car, and had expected Jase to ask for a lift to the local. Instead, he'd asked him if he could keep some papers and a few items for him. It was an unusual thing to ask, and naturally he'd wanted to know what they were. His mate had been deliberately vague, saying only that he wanted Gareth to keep them for him for a few weeks. Something about the way Jase refused to look him in the eye rang deep alarm bells, and he'd tried to find out if there was anything wrong.

And somehow Gareth hadn't believed his disclaimers that he was worried about the burglary rate in the area surrounding his new flat.

The result of it all being that he was now in possession of a large padded, sealed envelope back at his flat (which he'd hidden behind the towels under the kitchen sink), and a gnawing feeling that Jase was up to something. And since he hadn't been able to persuade his friend to confide in him, he could only hope that it wasn't something illegal or stupid. Or both.

* * *

In her office Hillary Greene sighed over her inability to just let things go, and phoned an old college friend who was still in the armed forces, and asked her to dig up anything she could on one Jason Morley, Gareth Proctor, and the murdered soldier in Reading. She thanked her and agreed to pay for a meal the next time they met up, and hung up the phone hoping that nothing would come of it.

It wasn't as if she didn't have enough on her plate already.

* * *

Larry Spence looked around the small basement space in a little café just off St Ebbes, his pale blue eyes thoughtful. Down here, there was room only for a trio of tables, each bearing just two chairs. Designed as an over-fill for the bigger, better lit room on street level, he doubted many people came down here by choice. So when he'd stepped in and ordered and paid for his coffee at the till, he knew the waitress had been surprised to see him disappear down the stairs with it.

Even though the breakfast rush had passed, and the morning coffee rush was yet to begin, there had still been the odd customer or two seated at tables upstairs, which was no good for his purposes. He wanted to be sure of a place where he could conduct his bit of business in complete privacy. Which was why he'd chosen the unprepossessing café as a meeting place to begin with.

At six feet tall, the small moulded plastic chair he was sitting on wasn't very comfortable, and if he shifted around he tended to hit his knees on the bottom of the cheap tin table, which was annoying.

In his mid-thirties, he had what one ex-girlfriend had jeeringly described as 'dirty' blond hair, worn long enough to touch his collar. A more delicate shade of blond adorned his lower face in a rather fine beard though, which he wore to disguise what he knew was his worst feature — a weak chin.

He was dressed in Armani. He wore a gold Patek Philippe watch. His cologne was imported from Paris. He looked like a bored businessman, or maybe an academic who was dressed for a job interview.

He certainly didn't look like the now-undisputed criminal kingpin of the city.

He glanced at the pricey timepiece on his right wrist and absently noted that his guest had two minutes to go before becoming officially late.

Larry wasn't particularly worried that he might be wasting his time. When he'd 'bought out' Simon Newley's business from his grieving but subservient widow, he had been slightly surprised by some of the more exotic and esoteric items that the old codger had handled. He had also been alternately amused and annoyed by the old man's habit of referring to his regular clients only by a nickname.

Consequently, the only thing that he currently knew about 'Teddy Bear' was that Newley had been dealing with him for over ten years, on an irregular basis, and that Teddy Bear only dealt in gold items. Very old gold items.

Which had been more than enough to pique his interest. For although the vast majority of his wealth came from his stable of girls, drug-runners, car thieves and extortionists, Larry liked to think of himself as a man of some refinement. He might have grown up in Oxford's seedy underbelly, but he prided himself on having crawled out of it. He now lived in a very nice white-painted mansion in the north of the city, overlooking the golf club. He drove a very fine Aston Martin.

And acquiring a punter who dealt in a very niche line of old and golden artefacts appealed to his sense of self-worth and vanity.

When he'd heard on the grapevine that tentative inquiries were being made about who had taken over Newley's business and had finally received an anonymous phone call asking if he was interested in 'specialized' gold items, he had instantly arranged a meeting.

Although Larry knew from Newley's impeccable records that Teddy Bear's business was never spectacular — usually involving sums of around ten thousand or so every time they did business — over the decade or so, that had added up.

And, besides, it intrigued him. For, try as he might (and he'd put the word out everywhere on the street), nobody seemed to know just who this Teddy Bear was, let alone what his game was. Unlike the vast majority of Newley's clients, whose identities (and dodgy dealings) had been far easier to discern.

The caller had used a pay-as-you-go mobile when contacting him (Larry had, of course, checked) and had been distinctly wary during their negotiations to meet up today, so as he sipped a surprisingly good cup of no-nonsense black coffee, Larry was half-prepared for Teddy Bear to be a no-show.

But even as he mused on the thought of a wasted journey, he heard feet coming down the wooden stairs, and a moment later a man appeared at the bottom, looking around carefully.

Since Larry was the only one there, the stranger's eyes rested on him and stayed. For a long moment there was one of those strange periods of time when everything but nothing happened simultaneously. Neither of them spoke, or moved, or made any indications of any kind. And yet judgements were made, various thoughts chased each other around, and by some kind of tacit, mysterious process, decisions were being made.

On Larry Spence's part, he decided at once that he was indeed dealing with Simon Newley's long-term client, Teddy Bear. And that Teddy Bear was not an undercover cop, someone working for a rival gang, or someone from the criminal classes. Nor did he suspect he was armed, either with a concealed knife or anything else of interest — which was always good to know, especially since he'd left his regular 'minder' with the car.

On the whole, Larry was pleased. It meant that his prospects for sealing a lucrative bit of business within the next ten minutes were pretty high.

On the part of Teddy Bear, he decided that Larry Spence was indeed the same Larry Spence that he'd been busy researching for the last few days. Namely, an Oxford born-and-bred criminal, who had fingers in most of the nasty pies that proliferated in the city. He was probably armed with a shank of some kind, slipped up that pristine sleeve of his, but didn't look as if he intended to use it. And he didn't have any of his usual bully boys concealed in the small basement area.

All of which meant that his prospects of continuing to do a nice bit of business now that Newley was no longer available looked promising.

Larry Spence watched as the stranger slowly approached the table and smiled diffidently. 'Do you mind if I join you?' he asked politely.

Larry affably waved at the chair opposite him. 'Feel free.'

Teddy Bear sat down. He appeared slightly nervous, but that didn't worry Larry. Most people who knew who and what he was were nervous when around him.

'Didn't we speak on the telephone yesterday?' Teddy Bear made the opening gambit. He was wearing a well-cut suit in navy blue with a plain white shirt. Not Armani though, Larry noticed with a satisfied inner smirk. He was freshly shaven, and to Larry Spence looked distinctly 'soft'.

As a thug who'd grown up fighting and clawing for everything he wanted, he knew a man who'd become used to the finer things in life when he saw one. What's more, Teddy Bear definitely struck him as belonging to that smug, privileged breed who were used to living the good life and not doing much work to earn their life of ease.

But while he might instinctively despise the other man on that basis, he also scented opportunity, and was careful to allow nothing of his feelings to show on his face.

Just where and how did Teddy Bear come by his nice little golden trinkets? That was what he most wanted to know. And if he was a middleman for someone else, he wanted to know the name of his client. The geese that laid the golden eggs were always his favourite kind.

'I believe we did speak on the phone, yes,' Larry agreed casually. 'A matter of gold, wasn't it?'

His potential new income source nodded vaguely, and looked around. The room was still reassuringly empty.

Teddy Bear, aware that he'd asked the waitress in the room upstairs for a coffee, and that she might come down with it at any moment, leaned back slightly in his chair. 'You inherited Mr Newley's . . . er . . . business, I take it?'

'I did,' Larry acknowledged, all at once feeling rather amused by the situation. The more time that passed, the more certain he became that he was dealing with a total amateur. A so-called 'respectable' citizen who, for some reason, found himself being forced to take a bit of a walk on the wild side in pursuit of that most desirable of all things — money.

And he was even more intrigued than ever. How was it that this rather insignificant specimen had gained access to such a store of precious gold items? According to old Newley's books, Teddy Bear's transactions always followed the same pattern. He would turn up at Newley's shop with a small variety of ancient gold artefacts for sale to a 'specialist' buyer. Meaning, of course, a collector.

And Larry, since taking over Newley's business, was learning more and more about collectors. They were an odd breed — absolutely obsessed with whatever it was that they coveted, and prepared to go to extraordinary lengths to add to their collection. It had somewhat surprised him just how big a network of greedy collectors Newley had acquired over the years. And all of them desperate to pay Newley for all sorts of guff.

Who'd have thought that silly old geezer Newley to have had such nous?

In Teddy Bear's case, he had always insisted that who-ever Newley sold to, they had to agree that the items would not be put on display (even in a private residence) or — nat-urally — appear as an asset in their tax audits. Which led Larry to believe the items had been stolen, and would appear on police lists as being hot.

This, of course, hadn't worried the various collectors Newley had approached in his role as agent for Teddy Bear one little bit. They only cared about adding to their hoards.

Newley had dealt with coin collectors, sometimes with jewellery aficionados, even collectors of ancient weapons, on Teddy Bear's behalf.

All of which suggested to him that this unlikely and distinctly soft specimen now seated opposite him was either a very canny thief or — far more likely in Larry's opinion — had inherited a collection of stolen items. A collection that he had got into the habit of selling off in bits and pieces in order to live the good life.

Larry took it for granted that part of Teddy Bear's rea-son for doing business this way was to avoid coming to the attention of the police's art and antiquities squad, while also depriving the tax man his rightful share.

One thing was for sure — Larry was going to find out just where this ripe pigeon stashed his treasure. While that old plodder Newley might have been content to sell on bits and pieces and take his cut, Larry wasn't. He smelt money — gold in fact — and he was damned well going to have it all.

But he had to be careful. First, he must lull this punter into a false sense of security. Sell on one or two pieces for him maybe, let him think that everything was fine, and that things could go on as they had before in Newley's day.

But he'd make arrangements to have the mug followed and put a proper name to him. Then he'd have him watched. It shouldn't take that long. And then, one dark night he'd have his boys snatch him and persuade him to give up his secrets. His boys were good at that. And who could Teddy Bear complain to? The police? Hardly!

Larry smiled amiably. 'So, do you have something for sale?' he asked indifferently.

'Yes. Not on me, of course.'

Larry shrugged. 'Of course not!' he said, his tone indicating that such a thought would never have crossed his mind. 'Perhaps you might just be able to give me a description of what you want passed on though, so that I can contact the right people?'

Teddy Bear nodded. 'We'll start with a ring — about a thousand years old.'

'Gold, of course?'

'Yes. Gold.'

Larry nodded. 'I don't see any problem with finding a buyer for that,' he promised.

'I want a good price,' Teddy Bear said flatly — and with a certain amount of bite that Larry hadn't expected.

Then both men stiffened as they heard footsteps coming down the stairs. The two exchanged mutual, speculative looks of mistrust, but it was only the waitress with Teddy

Bear's order of coffee. She placed it on the table in front of him, and cast Larry a speculative look.

But she wasn't pretty enough for him to respond, and she left with a bland wish that they enjoyed their coffee and that cakes were available if they should feel peckish.

When she was gone, Larry drained his coffee cup. 'I always get good prices for my merchandise,' he said equally flatly. He hadn't quite liked the way Teddy Bear had just spoken to him. He had expected a little more deference from a pigeon like this; that he would show a little more gratifying fear.

Perhaps it was time to make the stranger aware just who was the boss in this relationship. Nothing too much — not enough to frighten him away before Larry could get a handle on him — just enough to put him in his place. 'People tend to want to please me,' he said blandly.

The stranger nodded but didn't look at all impressed, and to Larry's surprise, abruptly changed the subject. 'I take it the police are still involved with Newley's death? I can't have them finding out about my arrangement with him — and now with you.'

At this, Larry laughed caustically. 'Oh, don't you worry about them. Inspector Farrell is in charge, and he can't tell his arse from his elbow.'

At first Larry had been amused by Farrell's pathetic efforts to pin Newley's — and Lionel Kirklees's — murders on him. Now he was beginning to get weary of it. The man was like a terrier with a rat. Still, eventually even Farrell would have to run out of steam and stop harassing him. Sometimes he dreamt of dealing with the DI as he would with some drug pusher who tried to scam some profit for himself. But much as he might like to, even Larry knew better than to kill a copper. It just wasn't worth the hassle that inevitably followed.

'Really?' Teddy Bear said, looking interested. 'Are they not making any progress then?'

Larry laughed. 'No, and they won't, not now,' he assured him. 'Everyone knows if they can't solve a murder in the first week or two, then they hardly ever do.'

Teddy Bear digested this thoughtfully and nodded.

'Don't worry about them,' Larry said softly. 'It's not them you need to keep in mind, but me.'

Teddy Bear looked at him without expression.

Larry felt a little shaft of annoyance at the punter's obtuseness. 'I'm not like Newley, Mr Teddy Bear. I'm not an old has-been. And while I don't see any reason why we shouldn't have a long and profitable relationship,' he lied blithely, 'if you don't play straight with me, you'll find yourself regretting it.' Larry spread his hands and said genially, 'I can be a very dangerous man when crossed.'

When it was clear that Teddy Bear was going to make no response to this (the rabbit was probably too shit-scared to speak), he got up, nodded, and left.

Teddy Bear waited for a short while, until the other man's tread couldn't be heard, then reached slowly for his cooling cup of coffee. And said quietly, to the empty room, 'And so can I, Mr Spence. So can I.'

CHAPTER ELEVEN

Mia de Salle loved driving her classic E-type Jaguar. Although she used a more environmentally friendly and economical car for work and general use, every now and then she liked to indulge herself and take her pride and joy out for a spin. It had been expensive, but so worth it.

Mia, like most people would, enjoyed having and spending money, but she was very particular in what she chose to splurge on. Not for her anything so mundane as holidays abroad or flashy modern jewellery or fancy gizmos and pricey gadgets. For her, it had to be all about romance, or maintaining her own sense of style and — most of all — not letting the blandness of modern-day life win. She was determined to rise above the mundane and flout the dreariness of this ugly time she'd been born into.

And to her, the E-type was the equivalent of her fiery steed, her dragon!

That morning, she was driving through the greening countryside, her heartbeat skipping, as it always did, when she knew she was going to see *him*. And her racing-car green steed, with its cream leather interior and powerful, growling engine, all added to the thrill and the sense of adventure.

The admiring glances the car got as it ate up the miles to her destination only added to her satisfaction. She let the window down, even though the spring air was still rather too cool for comfort, and thought about her day ahead.

She had to go to work later on, of course, but she was more or less her own boss, and could dictate the flexi-hours she worked. But she did not want to contemplate all the tame and uninteresting daily chores that waited in the wings for her right now. Now all she wanted to think about was seeing him again.

They had to be discreet, of course; she knew that, and accepted it. Nobody must ever see them together, although it was all so very tiresome. Sneaking around, never letting on that they were a couple, always having to be careful because of what had happened to Michael, which might set people to begin asking awkward questions . . . Although she understood it, she still longed for the time when they could be properly together.

Oh, he was not everybody's idea of a great man, a handsome, romantic hero in the Jane Austen or Emily Bronte sense, but that didn't matter to her. What did physical beauty, either male or female, really have to do with true, timeless love anyway? What did age matter, or impressive muscle or young, toned flesh? She herself was no vision of the romanticized feminine ideal — no blonde-haired, blue-eyed beauty — as a single glance in the mirror told her only too well.

But what did any of that matter to them? They were classic, star-crossed lovers, victims of fate and death and tragic separation.

But while her suffering was satisfying, it sometimes wore thin, and she was desperate to feed herself on him. To remind herself of the reward that awaited her for all her long-suffering patience and loyalty.

Nearing her destination, Mia began to slow her beautiful car and began the tedious task of leaving the glorious open countryside behind and instead navigating the increasingly frustrating, suffocating banality that was the twenty-first century urban environment.

Finally, she pulled into one of her favourite waiting spots, not far from where he lived, and turned off the purring engine.

Her heart was now beating so fast that she could hear it pounding in her ears. How soon before he came by and she could watch him approach?

As she waited with the patience of a spider in the car, with the people passing by still casting admiring and envious glances at the Jaguar as they did so, she thought how funny life could be sometimes.

When she'd been younger and far more foolish than today, she'd been so in love with Michael that she thought it might kill her. But in the end, he'd let her down, leaving her broken-hearted and bewildered. Why had he abandoned her? Why hadn't her love been enough? How many weeks after he'd broken up with her did she torment herself with such questions? How long had she watched him, trailing after him in her less-conspicuous car, wanting and willing him to relent and take her back?

Looking back on herself at that point in time, she could feel only pity and perhaps a little scorn for her old self. But she could forgive herself too. She'd been desperately, crazily, whole-heartedly in love with him, and love made fools of everyone, didn't it?

Odd to think, now, that if she hadn't met Michael, she'd never have met the man who was destined to be her *real* love, her one true soulmate. Even more astonishing to realize that, when she'd first met him, she hadn't been able to *stand* him!

Mia shook her head now in remembrance of her own folly. To think, in the beginning, she'd been so blind that she had endured him only for Michael's sake! Resenting their closeness and never understanding what Michael had seen in him and wishing only that he'd just disappear from their lives for ever. So utterly unaware of what should have been staring her in the face.

That *he* was so much greater than Michael had ever been. So much stronger, braver, so much *more* than Michael had ever been. Even given the fact that he could seem so unassuming, so everyday, his greatness perfectly camouflaged in an ordinary exterior, it was still almost beyond her understanding that she could have made such a mistake.

All the while she'd been thinking that Michael had been the one with the old soul, Michael who had the extraordinary character and strength of will to become her ideal and worthy mate. When all the time it had been the other one.

And it wasn't until that day when everything had changed for ever, and she'd finally seen *him* in his true colours, that the scales finally fell from her eyes. Leaving her hopelessly dazzled, stunned, and bewildered.

It had taken her a little time to realize just what *had* happened, of course. To piece it all together and realize the true extent of her new love's cleverness and bravery, his extraordinary abilities to present one face to the world, while hiding the almost unimaginable glory of his real face. To take charge, to be unafraid of taking action, to risk everything! To be a real man! A real man in this world of wimps and dullards.

Michael, and the memory of Michael, had faded into nothing beside him. What had Michael been but a young, callow man whose passion for history had been his one redeeming feature?

She shifted restlessly in the bucket seat of her car and glanced at her watch. Surely he would come by soon? Her outlaw, her unlikely Heathcliff, her secret and guilty love. Surely he would come into sight anytime now?

She needed to see him. She'd die if she didn't see him . . .

There was a fluttering feeling racing around her body, an almost unbearable excitement washing over her, making her tremble. Maybe this time, this day, this hour, would be the one when he finally told her they could be together forever?

She couldn't bear this much longer otherwise . . .

* * *

Hillary drove Puff carefully through the narrow and hilly village of Islip, then up over the humped bridge over the river, towards the now familiar route towards Woodeaton.

Beside her, Gareth Proctor sat silent and thoughtful. He was still brooding about Jason, and what, if anything, he should do. He felt instinctively that his friend was nearing some sort of crisis or other, and that giving him the mysterious package to look after was a cry for help of some kind.

Was he supposed to open it and see what it contained? Or was *not* opening it the test that he needed to pass?

He unknowingly sighed, earning him a quick, sharp-eyed look from his boss. Perhaps he should have a word with Jase's mum and dad? But they already knew he was suffering from depression. His GP had given him pills. Jase's sister looked in on him regularly. So what more could he or they do?

Apart from helping put his own mind at rest that he'd 'done something' — at the expense of disturbing *their* peace of mind — what would that realistically achieve? What did he expect them to do? Commit their son to a mental ward?

No. He could only try and find out what was bothering Jase and promise to help and be there. After work, he'd go over and . . .

'Here we are.' Hillary Greene's crisp voice startled him out of his contemplation, and he saw they'd arrived at a smart-looking, large country cottage without any real memory of getting there.

He caught his boss watching him knowingly, and hoped he didn't look as guilty as he felt. 'Yes, ma'am,' he said smartly. 'Do you want me to take notes?'

'I think you'd better,' Hillary said. 'I was going to ask you if you wanted to start the interview and get in some practice, but I have a feeling your mind isn't on the job.'

Hillary saw him flinch a little. Having made her point, she relented and sighed. 'Come on then,' she said briskly. 'Clear your head and pay attention. You're no use to anyone unless your mind is on the job at hand.'

'Yes, ma'am!' he said and firmly put all thoughts of friends in need onto the mental backburner.

* * *

It was Martina Beck who let Hillary into the house. She seemed surprised to see her arrive with a different officer, and looked even more disconcerted when Gareth limped past her once they were in the hall. Hillary saw her eyes fall to his misshapen left hand and look quickly away again.

She wondered if Gareth Proctor ever got fed up of people being too scrupulously polite to notice his injuries.

Martina showed them into a large and pleasant light-filled study-cum-library, decorated in tones of green and cream, where her husband was seated in a green leather armchair reading a PG Wodehouse novel.

Hillary introduced Gareth to them, and they all took a seat. William instantly put down the book and leaned forward attentively in his chair. He too noticed Gareth's somewhat awkward handling of his notebook and pen, but like his wife, looked quickly away again. Hillary wondered, vaguely, why it irritated her so much.

Perhaps she was just getting cantankerous in her old age!

'Have you made any progress?' William asked, looking at her hopefully.

Hillary smiled slightly, expecting the question, but knowing it wasn't one she could ever answer, even if they had made a significant breakthrough. The sad fact was, not even the families of the bereaved could be made privy to meaningful evidence in case it might taint or prejudice any subsequent court case.

So she stated the usual platitudes. 'It's early days yet, Mr Beck. We're still in the collating stage, but now we've had a chance to interview all those closest to your son, I just have a few more questions. I think I mentioned before that we might need to come back to you — perhaps several times — in order to clarify some points.'

'You've seen Mia de Salle? And Dr Durning?' Martina said eagerly. 'What do you think of them? She's weird, right? And he's a creep.'

Hillary understood her bitterness, but right now she didn't need their anger. She needed them calm and quiet and thinking rationally.

So she said softly, 'They were only preliminary interviews, Mrs Beck. I'm still trying to get a clearer picture of your son, his personality, his life, and more details about the last time you saw him.'

She deliberately brought out her own notebook, where earlier this morning she'd made a short list of questions she wanted to ask, and made a show of consulting them. It wasn't necessary, of course, but she knew that helping to focus their minds would reduce the emotion and tension in the room.

Sure enough, Martina nodded and sat back a little more in her chair. 'Ask us anything you like,' she said, rubbing her hands nervously together in her lap. 'We want to do all we can to help.'

Hillary smiled again. 'Thank you. Now, let's start with his friend Kevin Philpott. Something he said when we talked to him about Michael made me think,' she began, but then instantly paused as she caught Martina rolling her eyes at her husband.

She saw William notice that she'd caught the by-play, and he smiled a little wryly and leaned even further forward in his chair. 'Oh, don't mind us, Inspector Greene. It's just that we always rather wished that Michael had chosen his friends more wisely, that's all. Especially his best friend.'

'Oh? You don't like Kevin?' Hillary asked, intrigued, her radar instantly twitching.

'Oh, we liked him well enough in a way, I suppose,' Martina said with a brief shrug. 'He was a friendly enough lad, I'll give him that. And he always seemed to be able to make Michael laugh. But Michael always saw the best in people. He wasn't always . . . He didn't always have much discernment.'

Hillary nodded slowly. 'You saw faults where he didn't?'

'Yes, I suppose so,' William said. 'Of course, we're older and wiser, and aren't so easily taken in. And like my wife said, Kevin was a nice enough lad, but he was a bit of a *cadger*, if you know what I mean?' He looked at her hopefully, one grey eyebrow raised.

'Can you give me an example?' Hillary asked gently.

'Oh, you know . . . just general stuff. If Michael got a Christmas or a birthday present that he didn't really like or want, it would inevitably find its way to Kevin. Oh, he'd never outright ask for it, but even so . . .' William gave another wry smile and spread his hands.

Martina Beck helped him out. 'Whenever they went somewhere that required money — an entrance fee to the zoo or something, or going to see a film at the cinema — it was always our son who paid for the both of them out of his pocket money. You know, that sort of thing.'

Hillary nodded but said nothing.

William frowned slightly. 'Don't get us wrong, Inspector Greene, we're not snobs. We know Kevin's family isn't well off. And although we never over-indulged Michael with really expensive things, we were well aware that he never had to worry about money on a daily basis. And that not all kids were so lucky — like Kevin. It was just that we didn't like to see him being taken advantage of.'

'And you think his best friend did that?'

'Oh not intentionally, perhaps. Not knowingly,' William said hastily. 'And you know what kids are like — they don't see things the way adults do. To Kevin and Michael, they probably just grew up taking it for granted, you know, what was Michael's was also Kevin's. And Michael never minded sharing.'

Hillary thought she had it now. 'But Kevin took Michael's largesse a bit too much for granted?'

'Yes. Like I said,' William said dryly, 'He was a nice enough lad, but he wasn't really . . . I don't know how to say this without sounding awful, and I don't mean to, but . . .'

He broke off, clearly lacking the courage to actually say what he wanted to say.

Luckily for Hillary, his wife was made of sterner stuff. 'He was never as bright as Michael, for one thing. And no, I'm not blaming him for that either,' she added hastily, flushing slightly. 'We're all born with our own strengths and weaknesses, aren't we? But whereas Michael was industrious and curious, Kevin was lackadaisical and idle. Even Kevin's dad thought him a bit of a dreamer who'd never amount to much in life. Of course, I don't know what happened to him since Michael died . . .' she trailed off and sighed. 'I just wish our son had made friends with boys more like himself. Do you see?'

Hillary thought she did. For people like the Becks, academic achievement meant getting into a good university and getting a good degree, which in turn led to the setting up of a good career. And from there, a good marriage to a suitable partner and grandchildren, who must be encouraged to do well at school, and so the cycle continued.

So kids who were not on the same path were seen as potential problems. But of course, that was a distinctly adult and parental point of view. Kids did indeed see things differently. To Michael Beck, Kevin had probably been a friendly face in a new and perhaps intimidating environment when they'd first met at secondary school. To him, a pal that he could joke around with, confide in, maybe even feel superior to, had probably been well worth the handing over of his old bicycle when he got an upgrade, or paying for the odd cinema ticket, or covering their rounds at the pub.

'Is he doing OK? Kevin, I mean?' Martina asked diffidently, and Hillary wondered if she was feeling guilty about not knowing how her son's best friend was doing in life.

Hillary thought back to Kevin Philpott in his unassuming but pleasant enough place in Headington, the suburb where he'd grown up. Kevin with his hit-and-miss schemes that sometimes paid off and sometimes didn't. He certainly hadn't made a name for himself, moved far away from home, or even earned enough to buy his own place.

So would his own father feel justified in his prediction that his son would never amount to much?

But on the other hand, he'd seemed happy and content enough. Would that count for anything in the Becks' philosophy?

She shrugged and said brightly, 'He seems to be doing all right, Mrs Beck. But it's something he said that I'd really like to discuss with you.'

She noticed both the Becks straighten up slightly and turn alert and intelligent eyes her way. 'He said that Michael was the type of person who didn't do things by half. That when he did something, he really worked at it. Would you say that he was right?'

'Oh yes,' Martina said, her hands stopping their restless twitching. Perhaps she'd been expecting her son's old friend to have said something uncomplimentary about him, but she suddenly looked relieved that Hillary's question was so prosaic. 'Michael was always like that. Put his heart and soul into whatever it was he was doing.'

Hillary nodded. In her experience, people who had one-track minds could often be blind to any harm they might cause others. They got so caught up in what they were currently fixated on that they didn't pick up on the more subtle things going on around them. Bulls in china shops, her gran would have said.

'Kevin also said that although he really got into things and did them thoroughly, that didn't mean that he didn't get bored and move on to other things. And that only his love of history remained really constant.'

As both parents nodded in agreement with this, she swept on, 'So I was just wondering — do you know what your son was concentrating on around the time of his death? Was he still taking wildlife photographs for instance?'

'No, now you mention it, he wasn't taking as many as he used to,' it was William who spoke first. 'But I don't quite see what this has to do with things? How can any of this help you find out who killed him?'

He was sounding a little impatient and disillusioned now. Perhaps he had expected them to arrive and say they'd caught his son's killer. Or report they had a strong lead, or a new clue. The general public, as Hillary knew only too well, was often inclined to be unrealistic. So this seemingly aimless line of questioning must appear disappointingly tame.

Hillary reminded herself to be patient. 'It's possible that something Michael was doing or involved with around the time of his death might have contributed to the reason why he was killed, Mr Beck. So if he wasn't taking photographs any more, had he moved on to another hobby? Another interest perhaps?'

'His metal detector,' Martina said at once.

Instantly Hillary turned to her and felt a slight prickle of excitement. 'He had a metal detector?'

'Yes, he'd had one for quite a while,' his mother said. 'He was so interested in history, and that television programme, *Time Team*, really opened his eyes to the possibilities of archaeology. So he got a metal detector and took to going out in the farmers' fields and seeing what was around. Oh, I don't think he found much — rusty nails and whatnot. He'd often come home disgusted with all the metal junk people threw away, but he wouldn't give up.' She smiled at the memory, and then her lower lip trembled as she realized her son would never complain about metal junk again. 'He'd got the fever, you see.'

'The fever?' Hillary prompted.

'Yes. You know — the lure of making a significant find,' the boy's mother said with a smile. 'He was a bit like a little kid looking for pirate treasure.'

'Oh it was a lot more grown-up and technical than that, Marty,' her husband broke in gently. And turning to Hillary, he smiled. 'You see, he was convinced that there was a big find to be had in Oxfordshire somewhere,' William explained. 'Don't forget, he was a historian through and through, and he'd done his research. Really looked into it. So it wasn't just some pie-in-the-sky wishful thinking,' he added, as if Hillary had voiced scepticism. 'He really knew what he was talking about.'

'I'm sure he did, Mr Beck,' Hillary said softly. To her, the likelihood of Michael Beck finding a treasure trove seemed about as statistically possibly as winning the lottery. But she had no wish to antagonize them by pouring cold water onto their dead son's dreams.

To her surprise, however, the older man stood up, crossed over to a desk set against one wall and rifled quickly through some papers. Then he came back to his seat and handed over a small buff-coloured file to her.

'We found these in his room. His research. Go on, take a look,' he demanded.

Obediently, Hillary did so, glancing through the dead man's selection of hand-drawn maps, the printed references from various textbooks and historical manuscripts that he'd collated, and finally the neat handwriting in his personal notebooks detailing his reasons for his belief of hidden treasure.

It was methodical, meticulously researched, and to her — the non-historian she was — it all sounded plausible enough. Michael Beck had certainly known his stuff.

'I can see what Kevin meant when he said Michael took things seriously,' she said. 'Your son would have made a great historian.'

'You're damned right he would,' William said gruffly. 'And that's not just a proud father talking. Take a look at the newspaper article at the back of the file. I added that to it just five years after Michael died.' His voice resonated with both pride and pain, and something in the air made Hillary's heart beat just a shade faster.

She quickly shuffled through the papers and found the newspaper article. She read it rapidly, and gave a silent whistle. No wonder Michael's proud parents had wanted her to see it.

'It says that a market executive called James Mather found a hoard of Anglo-Saxon coins and jewellery in 2015.'

She read aloud mainly for Gareth's benefit, so that he could update his notes. 'Seven items of jewellery, two hundred coins, fifteen silver ingots, and many coins of Alfred the Great. The TVC — that is, the Treasure Valuation Committee — valued the find at 1.35 million pounds. It's on display at the Ashmolean Museum.'

She folded the papers neatly and thoughtfully.

'That could have been our Michael who found that,' Martina Beck said sadly. 'He specialised in the Anglo-Saxon period. He'd done the work, both the paperwork and the research, and nearly every day he was out with the metal detector. He could have found it, had he lived. I'm sure he could,' she whispered. 'It would have meant so much to him . . .'

Again her lower lip began to tremble.

'Yes. I can see how it would have,' Hillary agreed, her mind beginning to race.

'Don't misunderstand him, Inspector Greene,' William Beck said sharply. 'He was no night-hawk! He didn't want to find things so that he could quietly dig them up at night and sell them on to rapacious collectors who only wanted to line their own pockets, or hoard treasure for their own greedy pleasure. He *hated* people like that. No, if our son had found anything significant, he would have called the coroner instantly, and notified the local university's archaeological unit at once so that the finds could be removed, handled, and documented properly. He'd have been fascinated to see a proper dig in action.'

'I'm sure he would,' Hillary acknowledged, but even as she said the words she wasn't sure how much she actually meant them. So far, she'd been thinking of Michael Beck as one of the 'good guys', mainly because he was the murder victim, and so far she'd never met anyone who hadn't liked him, or could provide her with any reason to think otherwise.

But what if Michael Beck wasn't a particularly good guy? What if he'd been a bad guy?

But William Beck was speaking again, and she forced herself to concentrate on what he was saying. She could always save her speculations for later, when she was alone and had time to indulge them.

'Michael only wanted to find things to advance historical knowledge,' the boy's father insisted firmly. 'He wanted to discover finds that would help historians understand things like commerce at the time of King Alfred, the true role the Vikings played, how kings and peasants alike lived back then . . .'

He suddenly stopped and took a deep, slightly shaken breath. 'I'm sorry. I'm ranting a bit now, aren't I?' he admitted sheepishly. He ran a slightly shaking hand over his lower jaw. 'But all that sort of thing meant so much to Michael. And he was just beginning on his career. There was so much he could have done, so much for him to look forward to. That find, for instance,' he nodded at the folder she still held in her hand, 'he'd have loved to have seen it for himself. And now he never will.'

'I'm sorry,' Hillary said inadequately. She understood all too well their grief, and the gall that all that wasted potential represented.

But her mind was still busy racing with questions. What if Michael Beck *had* found something? Oh, nothing as spectacular as the Mather hoard perhaps, but nonetheless something valuable. What if all his research had paid off, and he'd made a discovery of his own? In spite of what his parents thought, it was perfectly possible that he would have kept the news to himself.

Even giving the dead lad the benefit of the doubt — that he didn't intend to sell the stuff on the black market — as a historian, he might have wanted to study his finds in detail. Maybe write a paper on them, before letting the world in on his discovery? Hillary knew the world of academics could be a vicious one, and Michael had been planning on becoming one himself. What historian-in-the-making would pass up a chance to steal a march on his rivals, and publish a definitive book on previously unknown, undiscovered material?

And if someone had found out about it . . . was it really possible that Michael Beck had been murdered for a hidden cache of Saxon gold?

Wryly, she told herself to calm down. She was getting way ahead of herself. Not long ago she'd been mentally shaking her head over the image of a young man foolishly searching for treasure, and now here she was, getting excited about hidden treasure herself!

'Did Michael seem especially excited about anything in the days before he died? Was he especially cheerful perhaps?' she asked, striving to keep her tone casual.

'No, I don't think so,' William said, shooting a questioning glance at his wife, who also shook her head.

'Do you know if he took the metal detector with him that morning?'

'No, I don't think he could have done. He was on his bicycle,' Martina said. 'It would have been too cumbersome for him to balance it, and it wouldn't have been safe in traffic, sticking out like it would have done. Michael was always safety-conscious on his bike.'

Hillary nodded. So the lad hadn't been looking for buried gold on the day he died then. 'Did DI Weston and the original team know about Michael's hobby? The metal detector?'

Husband and wife swapped quizzical glances. 'I don't think so,' Martina finally said. 'I don't think anybody ever asked us about it, did they?'

William shook his head. 'I don't remember talking about it. Why? Do you think it could have been significant?' he asked, sounding worried.

Instantly, Hillary leapt in to reassure him. 'Oh, it's probably not relevant at all, Mr Beck,' she said gently. And meant it. It was one thing to have the beginnings of a possible avenue of investigation not hitherto explored, and another thing altogether to give the Becks false hope that it would lead somewhere.

After all, the chances that Michael had come to grief over his latest hobby had to be a thousand to one, right? If not slimmer!

'Do you mind if I keep this for now?' Hillary asked nevertheless, waving Michael's research file. 'I'd like to copy the contents. I'll get it back to you within a few days, and I'll write a receipt for it, of course.'

William Beck, who looked as if he might have been about to object, sighed and sank back against his chair. He looked suddenly deflated, all his previous animation now gone. He also looked like his seventy-plus years. 'Of course, if you think it will help. I only showed it to you because I wanted you to understand the sort of boy our son was. How much we lost when he was taken from us.'

Hillary nodded. 'I understand. Thank you. I think that's all for now,' she added gently. 'We'll see ourselves out.'

She motioned to Gareth, who rose, murmured some polite but slightly awkward goodbyes, and limped after Hillary as she made her way to the front door.

CHAPTER TWELVE

Once back behind the wheel, Hillary sat for a while, her eyes narrowed in thought as she tried to analyse just what she did — and didn't — have. She wasn't aware of how long she'd been sitting there though, just thinking things through, until she noticed Gareth shifting restlessly on the seat beside her.

Taking the hint, she put the key in the ignition. Puff sputtered, coughed, swore under his breath and went silent.

Hillary tried again. This time, the tragic wagon consented to run, and she drove him slowly back to HQ. Again, her companion was silent on the way back, but Hillary didn't mind his habit of hardly ever speaking unless spoken to first. Given Claire's sometimes non-stop approach to conversation, she found it restful rather than unnerving.

Just before they arrived at the Kidlington roundabout, however, Gareth Proctor roused himself and said, 'So do you think this is a possible lead, ma'am? The victim's new hobby, I mean. It was something the original investigation never knew about.'

Hillary nodded. 'Yes,' she said with satisfaction. 'It is.'

'Do you think it's really significant though?' he prompted. 'Something as simple as that?'

Hillary smiled grimly. 'Now there's the sixty-four-thousand-pound question. Maybe quite literally! But until we start digging into it — sorry, no pun intended, honest — we have no way of knowing. It could be a significant new lead, or just another dead end.'

But something in her bones was fizzing, and an old, welcome, familiar feeling whispered to her that she was finally onto something at last.

* * *

The first thing she did once she was back at the office was to get her team to hit the computers and start researching all they could find on or about the treasure trove. She gave herself the task of researching the Mather hoard more fully, as well as any other historical finds in or around the area. She also set Claire and Gareth the more general task of finding any links that might exist in the database between murder, violent crime, and the involvement of ancient and historical artefacts.

'Oh, and, Claire, see what you can find out about the financial status of Dr Durning and Mia de Salle,' she added in parting. 'I want to know if either of them are living way beyond their means.'

That, she knew, would keep them busy for some time.

She spent an hour or so trying to educate herself about buried treasure in Great Britain, and quickly learned that discoveries of ancient artefacts were far more common than she might have thought. But that truly spectacular hoards such as those discovered by James Mather were few and far between.

But even a small stash of coins (most of which would have been hidden by ancient merchants or noblemen in times of war or unrest) was well worth finding, being worth hundreds of pounds per coin.

But before she could settle down to some really serious screen time, she knew that she should update her boss on how things were progressing.

* * *

Roland 'Rollo' Sale listened appreciatively as Hillary filled him in on their new information, but when she tested out her tentative speculations about what it might mean, he frowned thoughtfully.

'I don't know. It's all a bit far-fetched isn't it, Hillary?' he complained mildly when she'd finished. 'You said it yourself, there's no proof that the lad actually found *anything* aside from soda cans, rusty horseshoes and bits off old ploughs.'

'No, sir, there isn't,' Hillary assented readily enough. 'And while I agree that it has to be a billion-to-one chance or whatever that he actually found another Mather hoard, smaller finds aren't quite so rare. And I've just got a feeling in my bones that the answer to the boy's murder lies somewhere in this metal-detecting lark.'

At this, Rollo's eyes twinkled. 'A feeling in the bones, hey? A detective's best friend, they are! But you and I both know that you can also put them down to nothing more than a touch of rheumatism or arthritis.'

Hillary grinned. 'Always a distinct possibility, sir.'

But when she left the office a little while later, Rollo had given her permission to do things her own way.

When had he ever done otherwise, he mused to himself, as he watched her leave. And if he secretly thought that she was, for once, in danger of barking up the wrong tree, he had enough sense not to voice his doubts out loud!

Because when it came to Hillary Greene, you just never knew when she was going to pull a rabbit from even the most dodgy-looking of hats.

* * *

Jason Morley sat on the sofa of his small, empty and utterly silent flat, and looked at the gun in his hand. It was a piece of junk as far as firearms went, but it was deadly enough to do the job.

He had a can of lager that he'd just opened in the other hand, and slowly drank from it. When it was empty, it would be time to act. He knew that. He'd promised himself that — no more wavering.

But it wasn't empty yet. Not quite yet. He still had time.

He sighed and stared out of the window. It wasn't raining, but the sky had that cold, overcast look that made a mockery of the fact that it was supposed to be spring. If he went to the window and looked around the dismal housing estate, he would feel no warm, golden sunshine on his face. There were no bluebells to see, or daffodils growing in the surrounding concrete gardens. There would be no birds singing. If he opened the window, only cold, damp air would seep in.

Cold, damp air . . .

He let his mind drift back to that other time of cold, damp air, when he'd carefully and faithfully trailed that bastard Corporal Francis Clyde-Brough through the narrow back streets of Reading. Until, satisfied they were at last alone, and that there was no CCTV to capture his image, he finally closed in and gave the sod what he deserved.

Funny, when he thought about it now, he felt nothing, nothing at all. Not remorse, or guilt, but no sense of justice or satisfaction either.

Jason took another gulp of lager. The can was just under half-full now. But he still had a few minutes until it was empty. Still had time to think.

As a soldier he had killed before, of course, but that had always seemed to him to be more of an exercise, an abstract concept rather than a visceral, human thing. What's more, it had always been done at one remove. In a war zone, you didn't see the people killed by mortars, or ground-to-air-missiles — or even by automated gunfire, if you were keeping your head down at the same time that you were spraying bullets about.

But killing Clyde-Brough had been up close and personal.

It had had to be done, and he'd done it. Simple as that. Oh, he'd got drunk afterwards, when he was safely away from Reading, and safe.

Safe.

Jason smiled at this odd, bizarre concept, and took another sip out of the can. Just one more mouthful left. He looked at the flimsy can, gave it a contemplative little shake, and almost laughed.

Down to his last gulp. He'd better be careful how he used it.

He leaned his head against the backrest of the cheap sofa and sighed again.

Of course, 'safe' could mean so many things to different people. And it could mean nothing at all. Was anybody ever safe? When you could just drop dead of a stroke or a heart attack at any time? Or walk out to get a pint of milk and get wiped out by a drunk driver?

Would he be safe from his old mate Gareth Proctor — as good a pal as anybody could ever ask for — if Gareth found out what he'd done in Reading?

Maybe. Maybe not. It was hard to tell any more. Jason exhaled noisily. He felt rather tired. When they'd both been serving army officers he would have trusted Gareth Proctor with his life, and without hesitation. Because he knew that clever, careful, and gutsy Gareth Proctor would always have his back. And he knew that Gareth would have felt the same way about him.

But they weren't in the army any more.

Everything was different now.

Slowly, deliberately, Jason raised the can of lager to his lips and drained it. Then he leaned forward and set it carefully on the floor.

Then he reached for his mobile and began to write a text.

* * *

At the moment that Jason hit the 'send' button on his mobile, the telephone on Hillary Greene's desk began to ring. She was still reading about archaeological finds (specifically about how much some rare Roman gold and silver work had fetched) and absently reached out to pick up the receiver.

'Hello?'

'Hillary? Sophie here. I've been asking around about that little matter you were interested in.'

Hillary dragged her eyes away from the screen and leaned back in her chair, mentally switching gears. 'Hello, Soph, and how's the army treating you nowadays?'

'Like it always has,' her old friend said, with the usual bite to her voice. 'If I wasn't a colonel I'd bloody retire.'

'You've been saying that for years.'

'And if I didn't think it would please them all so much to see the back of me, I'd retire tomorrow.'

Hillary laughed. 'You've been saying that for years too.'

Her old college friend finally laughed. 'Do you want the info you asked me for or not? Unlike ex-coppers, I don't have all day.'

Hillary reached for her notebook and grabbed a pen. 'Shoot. If you'll forgive the expression.'

Again, she heard familiar laughter, then an exaggerated groan, then she got quickly down to business. 'OK, I've managed to find some things out about your dead soldier in Reading.'

'He's not mine,' Hillary interrupted.

'Nor mine either, I'm pleased to say,' her friend shot back. 'The sod was kicked out a while ago and good riddance. He's strictly a civilian matter now.'

Hillary could feel her spirits start to sink. 'I take it he was a bad 'un?' she sighed.

'Yup.'

'How bad?' Hillary prompted. 'And before you say it, yes I know you can't give me details or you'll end up getting court-martialled or put up against a wall and shot or whatever it is they do to you nowadays. Just the general gist will do.'

'Good, because that's all I could get myself without anyone wondering what I was up to. So — in no particular

154

order, he was lazy, stupid, cowardly, but probably not actually corrupt. Not to your copper's way of thinking anyway.'

'You mean he wasn't bent? Wasn't flogging off stolen guns or whatnot?'

'Can't say.'

Hillary paused, pen hovering over the paper. 'Can't say, or won't say?'

'Bit of both,' her friend admitted. 'You know the army — no, scratch that — you don't, do you? Let's just say that we're good at covering our arses when things go wrong. We don't advertise it. We just hide it or flush it out of the system like so much sewage.'

'Charming image,' Hillary said dryly.

'Right. Well, in the case of Clyde-Brough, I naturally couldn't find out specific details, but then I didn't go asking for them. The last thing I need is my CO asking me why I'm being so curious. I just asked a someone who knew a someone, who knew the general gossip in this particular case.'

'Which was?'

'That some of the men in a certain unit, in a certain part of the war zone, died when they needn't have because Clyde-Brough didn't do his job properly.'

Hillary took a long, slow breath. 'Did the name Gareth Proctor feature anywhere in this . . . er . . . cock-up?'

'Just a minute . . .'

Hillary waited while there was a rustling sound as her friend checked her notes.

'Nope, no Proctor.'

Hillary wasn't aware that she'd been holding her breath until she suddenly had to let it out in a whoosh. Then the sense of relief washed away. 'How about Jason Morley?'

'Don't want much, do you?' Sophie grumbled. 'Hold on . . . ah.'

Hillary's heart sank. 'I don't like the sound of that "ah".'

'No. Do you know this Morley character?' her friend asked cautiously.

'Never met him,' Hillary said truthfully.

'Hmmm. OK. Well in that case . . . Morley was involved in the cock-up as you call it, but he and several others were on the receiving end of it. Mind you, he was lucky. He got out alive. Let me see . . . huh. Yeah, he got out without any physical injuries, but his psych eval wasn't good. He was given an honourable discharge. But reading between the lines, in his case I think PTSD had risen its ugly head.'

Hillary closed her eyes for a moment, then sighed. 'So would I be right in thinking that Jason Morley would *not* have been a big fan of Clyde-Brough?'

'Oh I think you can most positively say that,' Sophie agreed dryly.

'Thanks. Next time we meet up, the Chardonnay's on me,' Hillary promised.

'So is the three-course meal that goes with it,' the army colonel said with a laugh, and hung up.

For a moment, Hillary sat in her chair and thought. She was almost certain that her colleagues investigating the Reading murder case wouldn't have had access to this information. As her friend had said, the army didn't air its dirty washing in public.

And they definitely needed to know.

But she couldn't ring Reading without telling Gareth she was going to do it first. He deserved to know, and besides she didn't like to do things behind people's backs unless she couldn't avoid it. They had to work together, and for that to be productive, he had to trust her.

Besides, if Jason Morley was suffering from PTSD, he'd need a friend to help him cope with police scrutiny, and once Gareth knew it was going to happen, he could be there for him.

So she got up and walked the short distance down the corridor to the small communal office. As she looked in, however, she was surprised to see the former soldier's chair empty.

'Where's Gareth?' she asked Claire, who was frowning intently at her computer screen. Whatever she was doing, it was obviously engrossing, because she looked up only vaguely, then glanced at the empty chair opposite her, and gave a brief shrug.

'Oh, yeah, guv. He got a text about five minutes ago — he said it was urgent. He looked a bit upset. I asked him if it was bad news, but he said he just needed to go and see a friend. He said to tell you he'd make up the time tonight, like he did the last time.'

'OK,' Hillary said and went back to her office.

In the modern computer age it didn't take her more than a minute or two to find out the current address of Jason Morley.

Grabbing her bag, she left the office at a run. She might be worrying over nothing, but she didn't like the way things were shaping up.

Why had Gareth been so interested in the Clyde-Brough case to begin with unless he suspected something? And if he knew that Jason had good reason to bitterly resent Clyde-Brough, he might not have been able to hide his worries — or his suspicions — when the man was murdered months later.

And his friend, Jason Morley, might well have noticed his unease. And with Gareth then getting a new job working for the police . . .

The desk sergeant watched her charge through the lobby, bolt out the door and then run across the car park, and grinned. Somebody looked like they were about to get it in the neck. Because when Hillary Greene went after you with a look like *that* on her face, somebody was definitely in for the high jump!

* * *

Puff the Tragic Wagon started first go and responded at once to her unusually heavy touch on the accelerator, as if he understood her sense of urgency. As she drove towards the ever-expanding market town of Bicester at just a touch over the speed limit, she tried to convince herself that she was overreacting.

For a start, there was nothing to say that the text Gareth had received had even been from Morley. Her colleague must have more than one friend after all. And even if it *had* been from Morley, there was no reason to suppose there was a crisis looming. She knew she was still feeling a little off-kilter after talking to Sophie, and that might be affecting her judgement.

Nevertheless she kept her speed up and a wary lookout for her colleagues in Traffic. The last thing she needed was to get pulled over. Taking time to explain would strain her already tight nerves to breaking point.

Plus it would be a real pain to get a speeding fine.

But she made it to Bicester in good time and without incident, only to have to wait in a long queue at the roundabout that led to the shopping mecca that was Bicester Village. Traffic was always heavy around the world-famous shopping precinct so beloved of foreigners and domestic shoppers alike, and as the minutes ticked away she drummed her fingers impatiently on Puff's steering wheel. From time to time she checked her phone, where the map showing Jason Morley's exact address was displayed.

Just her luck, it was on the far side of Bicester in an area known as Glory Farm. In her experience of urban sprawl, she doubted if there would be a farm in sight, and that the area would prove to be anything but glorious.

Her cynicism was vindicated when, nearly ten minutes later, she turned into a maze of narrow, uninspiring streets that were a mix of low-rise commercial estates and 'affordable housing'.

Trusting the satnav, she followed the directions to a three-storey block of perhaps twenty small flats, with grey pebble-dashed walls and newish-looking white PVC doors and windows. Unfortunately the parking spaces in front of it were all taken, and she scanned the vehicles anxiously for Gareth's car. She couldn't see it, but that didn't mean he hadn't been forced, as she was doing, into cruising around and trying to find a space on the streets somewhere.

Eventually she found a free spot and moved quickly back towards the building, all but running by the time that she spotted the entrance. When she reached it, the door turned out to be unlocked, with not even an entry-phone system to provide minimum security.

A little breathless, she walked through a totally empty and cold hallway with dirty black-and-red tiled flooring, a single lift, and a set of concrete stairs leading off to her right.

She guessed from the number of Jason Morley's flat that his would be one of those on the top floor, and not fancying the look of the lift, went to the stairs and began to climb.

As she did so, she mentally rehearsed what she was going to do.

If she knocked on the door, and Jason Morley turned out to be alone, she'd have to pretend to be a market researcher or something.

If Gareth answered, then she was going to take the bull by the horns and insist on speaking to both of them and explaining that the Reading police would need to interview Jason. She'd have to be careful to make it clear that it would be just a matter of routine — that Jason wasn't even a person of interest yet, and that there was no cause for alarm. The last thing she wanted to do was alienate . . .

The sound of a gunshot suddenly filled the narrow staircase, the flat, ugly and unmistakable sound of it echoing off all the empty spaces and hard concrete surfaces.

Her heart seemed to leap into her throat and then commenced to do a wild jig in her chest, leaving her momentarily unable to take a breath.

She was just passing the door leading to the second floor and instantly she began to run up the final flight. Once there, she erupted onto a small concrete landing, with seven or eight doors leading off it.

But even as she began to move cautiously forward, a door to her right began to open and she instinctively froze, experiencing the atavistic fight-or-flight mode that sent her adrenaline levels soaring.

A woman, aged about forty, looked gingerly out. She looked wary, a little puzzled, a little frightened, and her eyes instantly fastened on Hillary and widened. 'Did you hear that bang . . . ?'

'Get back inside,' Hillary said quickly. 'Lock the door, just in case. Don't worry, I'll call the police, in case it's something serious. I don't think it is,' she lied with a comforting smile. 'Probably someone just put an aerosol can in the woodburner or something! But I wouldn't open the door to anybody for a while unless they can post police identification through your letterbox, to be on the safe side.'

She hoped the woman was reassured. The last thing she needed was to have panic-stricken civilians running around. Then she thought of something else. 'Wait!' she said, as the woman began to close the door. 'Do you know which door belongs to someone called Jason Morley?'

'The new tenant? Right at the end, on the left,' the woman said helpfully.

Cautiously, Hillary crept along the corridor. Her eyes constantly moved around, alert to any movement, but also registering her surroundings. Here, the same dirty black-and-red tiles lined the floor, and magnolia-coloured woodchip wallpaper covered the walls.

Her heart was still racing, but at least nobody else came to the doors to look out and nearly give her a heart attack. She could only hope that the vast majority of the building's occupants were out at work.

As she moved, she fumbled around in her bag for her mobile phone. Retrieving it, she speed-dialled Rollo Sale's number and put the phone to her ear. She was aware that her hand was shaking slightly and tried to control it.

'Sale,' a voice said cheerfully in her ear.

Hillary went to speak, realized her mouth was bone dry, and swallowed hard to work up some saliva. 'Sir, it's Hillary,' she whispered.

'Speak up, Hillary, I can barely hear you.'

'Sir, I can't,' she whispered. 'I'm in a block of flats in Bicester,' she rattled off the address details, 'and I've just heard a shot fired. I'm on the top floor, and I think the origin of the gunshot is a flat at the end. I'm outside it now, but there's no sign of a gunman.'

For a moment there was a profound silence, then Rollo's voice again, firm and clear but sharp with anxiety. 'Get out. At once. I'll call for an armed response unit.'

'Sir, I have reason to believe Gareth Proctor may be in one of the flats — and probably the one where the gunshot was fired,' she said urgently.

There was another moment of profound silence, then, 'My orders stand. Make sure you get everyone out that you find in the public areas, and don't let anyone else in. You need to secure the scene and prevent any casualties if possible.'

'Sir, Gareth might be injured and in need of assistance,' she argued.

'Assistance is on the way. I'll notify the armed response team to that effect and send for an ambulance. But no medical personnel can attend until given the all-clear by us. Do you have any information about the suspected gunman?'

'Gunman might be Jason Morley,' Hillary whispered. 'I believe it likely the gunshot came from his flat. But that's not confirmed.'

'Understood. Now get out, Hillary, that's an order. Understand?'

'Yes, sir,' Hillary said and hung up. She put the mobile back in her bag.

And stood.

And thought.

But didn't move.

Rollo Sale was thinking and acting like the senior police officer that he was, and he knew the rules and protocols as well as she did. His police officers didn't run willy-nilly into danger. Especially unspecified, unknown and ongoing danger. To do so would be reckless, hardly ever effective, and often resulted in others getting hurt. Usually innocent bystanders.

So what you did was back off, assess the situation, wait for backup and try to control the damage.

Hillary looked around. Nobody else had come to their doors to investigate the loud bang, which meant that the other flats were probably unoccupied, as she'd surmised. Either that, or they simply weren't curious enough to investigate the source of the noise. And the woman who had responded was now safely locked behind her door.

She couldn't hear any sounds coming from the floors below, or in the stairwell, and suspected that anybody at home down there would be unlikely to come looking for the source of the noise, since it hadn't yet been repeated.

So — unless whoever had fired that shot had gone berserk and come out looking for other victims to shoot, then everybody was safe, for a while.

And, though she might be wrong, this didn't have a lone, mad gunman vibe about it to her.

The UK, like so many other countries in the world, had suffered its fair share of such incidents and they usually followed a similar pattern. A man (and it usually *was* a man) finally flipped his lid and decided to go on a killing spree. He was usually a loner and a gun-fanatic. They often (but not always) started with the gunman shooting family members or those in the same residence as himself, before taking his weapons out onto the street, just randomly killing any poor soul who happened to cross his path.

But so far, nobody had emerged from Jason Morley's flat.

So — as far as damage limitation went, Hillary couldn't see that she could do anything to make the inhabitants of the building any safer than they were at this moment. And once the armed response team arrived, civilian safety would be their pigeon.

She felt slightly sick and shaky, and leant against the wall for support, taking deep breaths. Her legs felt a little numb, and she knew she was going to have to be very careful now. She was frightened, and frightened people didn't always make the best decisions. Logically, she knew that Rollo Sale was right. She was getting too damned old for this sort of thing, and there was no shame in looking after your own skin. She should just get out and wait for the armed response team to arrive.

They were the experts in situations like this, after all.

But how long until they got here? They were a rapid-response unit, but even so . . . ten minutes? Probably more? And when they arrived, they wouldn't just rush in. They would need to assess the situation thoroughly, and all that took more time. Would they evacuate the building first, going door to door and getting anybody at home out to safety before tackling the prospect of a gunman holed up in a good defensive position? By now, they'd have the details of Jason Morley's flat in respect of the general layout, and she thought it highly likely that they would. A top-floor corner flat — if you were going to have a shoot-out — was the ideal place to have it from a containment point of view.

And in the meantime, for all she, Rollo, or they knew, Gareth Proctor could be dead, or — in some ways, even worse — seriously injured and bleeding to death right now.

This minute.

If he was dead, then logically there was nothing that could be done to help him, and she would be risking her life for nothing. But if he wasn't dead . . . She had to do something to help him. When it came down to it, it was as plain and simple as that.

A long time ago she'd gone on a course about how to talk down the hostile party in a hostage situation. How much of it could she now remember?

She took a few more slow, deep breaths. Her mind was jumping about like a flea on a hotplate, and she needed to remain calm and think clearly.

OK, Hillary, she thought. First things first — was she going to follow orders, do the 'correct' thing, and leave?

No.

She wasn't.

She knew it, almost before she'd formed the words in her head. She knew that if she left and it later turned out that Gareth *had* been injured by that shot, and then subsequently died when he might have been saved if he'd been extracted and been taken to a hospital in time, she'd never forgive herself.

Saving her own skin might feel like a mighty good idea right now — and she wasn't fooling herself, her instincts *were* screaming at her to do just that. But she would then have to live with herself afterwards.

OK, so standing here doing nothing wasn't helping Gareth either. She needed more facts. What's more, the armed response team would need them too, when they arrived.

OK, so gather more facts, she told herself.

And to do that she had to stop clinging to the wall like a wilting terrified violet and get closer to the scene of the action.

CHAPTER THIRTEEN

Forcing herself to approach the end door took her a little more effort than her self-esteem would have liked, but slowly, patiently, and most importantly of all, silently, she persuaded her limbs to move and tentatively edged closer.

As she got nearer, she began to see that the door to Jason Morley's flat wasn't latched properly, and that a wafer-thin strip of daylight was visible, coming through it in a straight, vertical line. Which meant that gaining access wasn't going to be a problem. That was a definitive plus. If the door had been closed and locked, her options would have been severely limited.

A definite minus, however, was that sound travelled further and easier through an ajar door than a firmly shut one. So she couldn't afford to make even the tiniest of sounds, and alert whoever was in that room that she was out here.

She swallowed hard again and kept edging forward, then abruptly stopped. A small voice was screaming some kind of a warning at her from the back of her mind. But through all the tension, fear, anxiety and stress, it wasn't getting through. She forced herself to try and calm down. What? What was it she hadn't done? Or needed to do? What . . . Her phone!

She quickly scrambled in her bag and turned it off. The last thing she wanted was for Rollo to call her for an update and have the bloody thing ring! She might just as well draw a set of crosshairs on her back and write 'shoot here' on it.

She realized she was grinning like a loon, and knew she had to fight back imminent hysteria. She also felt as if she wanted to be thoroughly sick.

After a few more deep breaths she had control of herself again. The nausea caused by fright passed.

And now came the next hurdle.

At the moment, she was pressed flat against the wall, with the door beside her, hinges closest to her. In order to be able to push it open a little further in order to see inside, she needed to cross in front of it and gain access to the door-handle side.

Of course, she could reach her arm out and try and push the door open that way — but she would be doing that blind. What if someone was stood right in front of the door, watching it opening? No, she'd rather try to get a tiny peep at what was happening inside first, before she committed herself to any course of action.

And now she wished she hadn't watched all those thrillers, where the hero of the piece did exactly that, and the villain inside opened up, missing the hero by a whisker.

Telling herself that things like that only happened on the television, Hillary forced herself to take three swift steps across the door, a cold shiver crawling up her spine every step of the way.

There was no hail of gunfire, but now she stopped and listened hard.

Although the door was almost in the frame, she thought that she should be able to hear something — especially if someone inside was moving about, or maybe even having a whispered conversation.

But she could hear exactly nothing.

She reached out and slowly, very slowly, nudged the door open a fraction of an inch.

Nothing.

Her mouth bone dry, her knees feeling decidedly wobbly, she nudged it open another fraction of an inch.

Nothing.

Of course, as she'd already speculated, whoever had fired that shot could be just standing there, watching the door slowly move with a big ugly smile on their face, just waiting for some idiot to give them a target.

Or the gunshot might have come from another room in the flat altogether.

Hillary, with one bent knuckle, nudged the door just wide enough to take the width of a human eye, and put *her* eye in the now wider crack and looked inside.

And in that tiny vertical line of vision she saw the end of a sofa, and a pair of boots, lying on the floor, sticking out from one side of the piece of furniture. They were not lying flat, with the soles to the ground, as they would have been placed if they were empty and waiting to be worn, but were instead lying with the toes downwards to the floor.

And inside them, just disappearing behind the sofa, were unmistakably a pair of black socks. Which meant that someone was lying flat on the floor, face downwards; somebody who was wearing a sturdy pair of boots.

And try as she might, she could not remember what footwear Gareth Proctor had worn to work that morning.

Hillary stared blankly at the footwear, and then, very slowly, nudged the door open further. And as the rest of the sofa slowly came into her vision, so too did the shape of the head of the man who was sitting on it.

Gareth Proctor's head. She recognized his short fair hairstyle at once.

She let out a wavering breath of relief and gratitude, and cautiously pushed the door open a little more. She remained careful to make no sound though, for until she could be positive of just what had gone on here, she had to acknowledge that Gareth must still be regarded as a possible suspect in a shooting. She didn't really believe that her colleague was guilty of such a thing, but in a situation such as this, she knew that she could take no risks.

She could smell the cordite in the air, that unmistakable scent of recent gunfire, and quickly surveyed the rest of the room.

The living room was compact, with a small single window that was firmly shut. The carpet was of the grey hard-wearing type, and the walls painted blank off-white. And it was empty of any other human being, save her colleague, sitting on the sofa.

Slowly, her heart rate began to return to normal. She was wondering how best to go about announcing her arrival without giving him too much of a jolt, when she heard a slight sound coming from the sofa. She recognized it for what it was — a stifled sob.

She began to move forward, and as she did so, got a better look at the man on the ground.

She didn't look for long. It was not a sight that she wanted to burn into her retinas. When you put a gun in your mouth and pulled the trigger it left one hell of a mess behind. Most of that mess had been hidden by the presence of the sofa, and Hillary quickly turned her gaze to the gun, which was still clasped in the dead man's right hand. It looked old, and she didn't recognize the make — but then she was no expert on firearms.

A soft rustling sound had her eye swinging back to the sofa — and as she drew ever closer, and thus got a better view of him, she could see that Gareth Proctor was hunched over and reading something.

A suicide note was her instant thought, and a rather long and detailed one at that. She felt instantly relieved. Once SOCO got here, she was fairly sure they would confirm that they were dealing with a self-inflicted gunshot wound, but the presence of a suicide note written in the deceased's handwriting confirming that conclusion was always a welcome bonus. Coroner's juries usually liked having more than one indicator as to the cause of death.

She was just about to softly call his name, but something about the intensity with which Gareth was looking through the pages suddenly changed her mind.

Her colleague, who was still totally unaware of her presence, looked from one page to the other, holding one in his left hand and the other in the right, and then made a small sound. Not quite a word, not quite a sob, not quite a sigh, it defied interpretation.

But what Gareth Proctor did next most definitely didn't, and it made her freeze on the spot. He took one of the pieces of paper and carefully folded it, and reaching behind him, shoved it into the back pocket of his trousers.

Hillary swore silently to herself and began to back away. Once at the now open door behind her, she withdrew, then tiptoed down the corridor and out onto the top of the stairs. There she put on her mobile phone, careful to switch it to vibrate, not ring, and saw that she'd missed a number of (probably frantic) calls from Rollo Sale.

Of course he'd have called her back for an update more or less at once, and on discovering that her phone had been switched off, it wouldn't have taken him long to figure out why. After all, who would turn off their mobile in a crisis, when lines of communication meant everything, unless they had a good reason for wanting to go silent?

And the only reason she'd want to go silent is because she'd put herself in a position where a giveaway noise could be very costly indeed.

It was only then, as she stood looking at the missed calls from her boss, that she realized that in disobeying his direct orders and breaking protocol, she might well lose her job over this.

But she couldn't worry about that right now. It wasn't *her* job that was uppermost in her mind. Gareth was trying to interfere in an investigation, and a really nasty prosecutor could argue that he was attempting to pervert the course of justice as well. Hillary had a pretty good idea what that page of the suicide note would contain, and why Gareth was trying to suppress it. But if Jason Morley *had* confessed to killing Francis Clyde-Brough, her colleagues in Reading needed to know it. And much as she admired Gareth's loyalty to his dead friend, right now, it presented her with a massive problem.

For while she couldn't let it pass or let him destroy the evidence, she didn't want to see him lose his job over it, or even worse, get a criminal record. Who the hell would hire him then?

The problem was, she wasn't entirely sure that if she marched in there and demanded he put it back where it belonged, that he would obey her. And if he didn't, what then? He might try to destroy it and she would have to try and stop him. But could she? Yes, his left side was weaker than his right, but he was a trained soldier, male, fitter and younger than herself. Could she take him, if it came to it? She wasn't sure.

But she sure as hell didn't want it to come to that! Because if it came down to a physical struggle between them, then Gareth Proctor was finished in his new career before it had hardly even begun. Oh, she wouldn't press charges, but how could they ever work together after something like that? He'd resign, and she'd have to let him go.

She thought desperately for an answer to her predicament, and as she did so, felt the phone vibrate in her hand. Checking it, she saw that it was yet another call from Superintendent Sale. Grimly, she ignored it.

Rollo Sale couldn't help her right now. In fact, she realized, there was only one person who *could*.

Hillary Greene sighed heavily and began punching out the number that very few people at Thames Valley HQ had access to — the private number that would put her directly through to one Commander Marcus Donleavy.

Hillary knew that a lot of people at Kidlington HQ speculated gleefully over the exact nature of her relationship with Donleavy, which wasn't surprising. Coppers were notoriously curious and total gossips. For a while, with human nature being what it was, she knew that they'd speculated on a possible affair between them, but that rumour, over the years, had slowly died a total death, with absolutely no corroborating evidence supporting it. Then it was conjectured that Hillary was Donleavy's in-house spy, but that rumour too withered on the vine as it became obvious that that wasn't the case. Some said that she was Donleavy's 'golden girl' because of her solve rate, but they'd clashed often enough for them to realize that she was no teacher's pet either. In the end, they'd had to settle for simply not knowing why Donleavy and Hillary Greene were so close.

Sometimes Hillary wondered herself, but the fact was, Donleavy and the powers-that-be tended to regard her as a safe pair of hands when it came to sorting out certain problems that needed discretion.

And this, Hillary thought grimly, was definitely something that needed discretion. If it came out that a civilian consultant had been allowed to tamper in an ongoing murder investigation, then the odorous brown stuff would hit the fan in no uncertain terms.

In her ear, she heard the phone connect and ring, and then his voice. 'Commander Donleavy.'

'Sir, it's Hillary Greene.'

'Hillary. I've just had Rollo Sale on the line. He seems to think that you're in imminent danger of getting yourself shot,' the commander said, his voice sounding less alarmed than amused. 'Do you, by any chance, have a loaded gun pointed at your head right now?'

'No, sir. But *we* might,' she didn't need to clarify that by 'we' she meant the police force as a whole, 'if something isn't done PDQ.'

A long-suffering sigh came down the line. 'What do you need?'

'First, inform Rollo and the team he's dispatched that we're almost certainly dealing with a suicide here. We have one man dead at the scene, and two of us on site. And the likelihood of any more gunfire is minimal to none.'

'The two on the scene, that's you and this ex-soldier member of your team, right?'

'Yes, sir. And I need you to send over Sergeant Nick Rawson right away.'

There was nothing wrong with the commander's memory, as he knew who she meant right away. 'The one who looks about eighteen and is always going undercover and infiltrating youth gangs?'

'That's the one, sir,' she confirmed. 'I need his pickpocketing skills.' A year ago, she knew that a reformed pickpocket had taught Rawson all the tricks of the trade. This was so that Rawson could go in and successfully find out who was the mastermind behind a well-organized pickpocketing gang that was getting far too big for its boots.

'All right. I'll find him and send him over. What exactly do I tell him?'

'Tell him to report to me and follow my orders. And, sir, it's vital he comes in *before* anyone from either the rapid-response team, or whichever regular SIO is given this case, is allowed on scene. And he needs to keep his mouth very firmly shut, and when I tell him to, skedaddle without logging his name anywhere. There must be no official record that he was ever on site.'

There was a moment's silence at this, and Hillary understood why. Going against protocol was never something anyone did without thinking about it. Especially an ambitious survivor like Marcus Donleavy.

'And if he doesn't?' Marcus asked cautiously.

Hillary smiled grimly. 'Then, sir, I'm probably going to have to involve myself in a very undignified physical struggle, which I might well end up losing, the result of which will cause embarrassment all around, and muck up what should otherwise be a very straightforward suicide case here. Oh, and negatively affect an active, unsolved murder case that's out of our manor.'

It was this last warning, she knew, that would force the commander to accede to her wishes. Nobody liked to cause a stink that would earn you the animus or derision of another police service.

'Do I want to know what this is all about?' he asked grimly.

'Not if all goes well here, sir,' she said, hoping fervently that it would. She didn't want Rollo Sale to have to take any of the flack if it turned out that she couldn't keep Gareth — and by association, the CRT — out of the mire.

'So you'd better see to it that it does then,' he warned her.

'Yes, sir, thanks for that,' Hillary said bitterly, and hung up. It wasn't often you got to hang up on the likes of a commander, but it sure felt good when you did!

Then she took a deep breath and went back to Jason Morley's flat. She was relieved to see that Gareth hadn't moved from his position on the sofa. While she'd had to take the risk that he might have torn up the page from the suicide note and flushed it down the toilet while she'd been making her phone call, she thought it unlikely. He wouldn't want to risk even a trace of it being found at the scene, for one thing. He'd learned enough in all his training courses to know that pieces of paper could be retrieved from u-bends.

'Gareth,' she finally said quietly, and saw him jump and look around. His eyes were red-rimmed, and he looked awful. She held out her hands in a 'peace' gesture. 'Are you all right?' she asked. What she meant was, did he have himself all together.

'Ma'am, what are you doing here?' Gareth croaked.

'When Claire told me that you'd got a text that seemed to upset you, I thought it might be something to do with your friend again. Jason Morley, right?' She glanced quickly at the dead man, then away again. 'Is that him?'

'Yes, ma'am,' he said, swallowing hard.

'Were you here when he . . . ?'

'Sort of, ma'am.'

'Tell me what happened. I've already called for a team to come out, so you might as well get your thoughts in order

173

by practising on me first. Whoever they assign SIO will want your detailed statement.'

'Yes, ma'am,' he muttered, visibly pulling himself together. 'As you know, Jase — sorry, Jason — texted me, about an hour ago it must be now, saying that he needed to see me urgently. He's been really depressed lately, so I thought I'd better come.'

Hillary nodded. 'You'll have the text on your phone? The SIO will want to see it.'

'Yes, ma'am. When I arrived, I rang his bell and then immediately heard a gunshot. The door wasn't locked, so I rushed in and found him . . .' He waved a hand in the direction of his dead friend but didn't look at him.

Hillary nodded. So Gareth must have arrived barely a minute or two before she did. He'd have taken the lift, given his weaker leg and the amount of stairs to climb, which is how they must have missed each other in the lobby.

'Had he given any indication of being suicidal?' she asked gently. She needed to play for time now, to give Rawson time to arrive. If she remembered rightly, he was actually stationed at Bicester, so with a bit of luck he could be here within minutes.

Gareth hesitated. Then sighed. 'Yes and no. He was depressed and angry and couldn't seem to hold down a job. He moved flats recently because he couldn't seem to settle. But he'd been like that for a while. Today . . . I suppose it just all got too much for him.' He swallowed hard.

No doubt, Hillary thought grimly, the poor sod was now thinking back, trying to see if he'd missed signs, and giving himself hell for not being a better friend. In her experience, the family and friends of suicide victims often blamed themselves unnecessarily.

'Any idea why he waited for you to ring the bell before . . . seeing it through?' she asked delicately.

Gareth winced. 'I suppose he wanted to be sure that I would be the one to find him, ma'am. Spare any civilians the trauma of discovering him, I mean, or even a member of his family.'

Hillary nodded. She supposed that made some sort of macabre sense.

She spent the next five minutes gently coaxing him to talk about Jason Morley, all the while listening out for the arrival of Rawson. It wasn't his footsteps coming along the corridor that announced his arrival though, but the vibration of her phone.

She brought it out and saw an unknown number on the screen. She punched the button. 'Hillary Greene,' she said.

'Guv, it's Sergeant Rawson. Commander Donleavy asked me to make contact?'

'Where are you?'

'Downstairs.'

'Come to the top floor. I'll meet you not far from the open door to the flat at the far end of the corridor.'

'Guv.'

The click in her ear had her rising slowly to her feet. She'd never met Rawson in person, but she knew that she'd have no trouble with him, even if he were aware that as a former DI, she didn't have any official standing any more. Getting a phone call from a commander and being given direct orders tended to focus the mind very speedily on what was, and was not, relevant!

Gareth looked too washed out and miserable to move, and when she heard the outer door from the stairwell open, she felt safe enough nipping out for a few moments to give Rawson his orders.

The sergeant did indeed look to be in his late teens, though she knew him to be somewhere in his late twenties. Slim, with fair hair and a pale face, he was dressed in jeans, sneakers and a faded T-shirt.

He watched her approach with interested eyes. He knew who she was of course — everyone knew about DI Greene, station-house legend, winner of a medal for bravery, and with a solve rate second to none. And when he knew he'd finally be meeting her, he knew it was going to be something good.

'Sergeant,' she said briefly, keeping her voice low. 'I take it Commander Donleavy has briefed you?'

'Not really, guv. He just said I was to get myself here double-quick and do whatever you told me then make myself scarce, like.'

Hillary's lips twisted. Nice wording on Donleavy's part, she mused. If, later, things went belly up, he could always deny giving any specific orders. Which left her very neatly holding the poisoned chalice. But she didn't mind that. They both knew how things worked, and she didn't need her hand holding.

'Right. Here it is — in there,' she indicated the far flat, 'we've got one male dead from a self-inflicted gunshot wound. Also present is Gareth Proctor, a former soldier and now a member of my team in CRT. He sustained injuries to the left side of his body in the army. It's his best friend lying dead on the floor so he's not in the best of shape. An armed response unit is on the way but has been informed there is no immediate danger of further gunfire. Commander Donleavy will have ordered them to wait for me to give the go-ahead before coming in. With me so far?'

Nick Rawson's eyes had slowly widened, but although his mind must have been racing with questions, that was the only indication on his face that he was in any way affected. 'Yes, guv.'

'Gareth Proctor has a piece of paper in the back right-hand pocket of his trousers. I want you to extract it from him, without his knowledge, at the first opportunity that presents itself, and give it to me, without him seeing you do it. I'll try and get him on his feet quickly, and with his back to you. All right?'

Apart from an even further widening of the sergeant's eyes, there was again no other sign that Nick Rawson found the situation in any way out of the normal. He'd go far, this boy, Hillary thought happily. 'Yes, guv,' he said.

Hillary nodded and jerked her head. 'Put some gloves on and follow me then,' she said softly, reaching into her bag and pulling on a pair of gloves herself.

They went in, and Gareth looked up. Even to someone who didn't know him, it was clear that he'd just had an almighty shock.

'Gareth, this is Sergeant Rawson. I need to phone Superintendent Sale,' she said, somewhat dryly, 'and let him know we're safe.'

She took a deep breath and punched in Rollo's number, mentally preparing herself for a well-deserved rollicking.

CHAPTER FOURTEEN

For once, luck was on Hillary's side. After meekly accepting her tongue-lashing from her highly relieved superintendent, she gave him a succinct briefing and promised to hold the fort until reinforcements arrived.

She managed to get Gareth up and out of the flat by simply ordering him to follow her outside into the corridor, without explaining herself. She figured that, as a former soldier, this was probably the best approach. He was still visibly shaken, but was already beginning to rally somewhat. And having an order to follow would probably help him to feel as if things were beginning to get back to some kind of normal.

Once outside, she noticed that Rawson casually positioned himself behind Gareth, who was leaning heavily on his walking stick, and try as she might — and even though she knew what was about to happen — could not detect the moment when he artfully lifted the page from Gareth's back pocket.

It was only when he moved slightly to one side and gave her the briefest of nods that she knew he'd done it.

Facing Gareth, she said gently, 'You look all done in. I think you'd be better off outside in the fresh air.' Seeing that he was about to argue, she added, 'You can't help your friend by staying in there,' jerking her head to indicate the flat behind them, 'but you *can* make yourself useful by briefing the next attending officer and directing them up here to me.'

Gareth drew in a slow breath and straightened his spine. 'Yes, ma'am,' he said.

'Sergeant Rawson will go down with you,' she added, giving the young officer a quick look to see if he'd got the message. He had. He gave a brief nod of understanding. Once he'd seen Gareth outside, he'd be off before he had to give his name and appear in any official log.

As all three waited by the lift, Hillary felt something touch her hand and realized it was the piece of paper. Without looking down, she closed her gloved hand around it, and making sure that Gareth was unaware of what she was doing, slid her hand down to her side, keeping it out of sight.

When the two men got in the lift, she nodded at Rawson. He nodded back.

Once the lift door closed behind them, she moved quickly back to the flat and reached down to pick up the other two pages of the suicide note that Gareth had left in situ on the coffee table to one side of the sofa. She hoped that it was in the same place where he'd first noticed it.

She slipped the sheet of paper back into place, smoothing out the creases, and quickly read the entire thing through. It was, as she'd thought, a suicide note, and was thankfully unambiguous. The first sheet began with an apology to Gareth for choosing him to be the first on the scene and leaving him with the initial problem of starting to clean up his mess and telling him the envelope he'd left with him contained his will, and funeral preferences. As well as a slim, expensive watch, which he wanted Gareth to keep in remembrance of him.

The second page stated simply and factually that he'd 'done for' Clyde-Brough, who had deserved everything he got, and gave enough details of the killing to satisfy her colleagues in Reading.

The final page was a lament to his parents, and a brief word for the coroner, stating that nobody had helped or aided him in his efforts to kill himself.

Although the segue from first to third page (without benefit of the second) was a bit clumsy, she doubted that it would have been unduly commented on by either the SIO or coroner, if it had been logged into evidence without the middle page. After all, nobody expected somebody about to blow their brains out to be overly concerned with their syntax.

Leaving the now-intact note on the table, Hillary breathed a sigh of relief and then nearly jumped out of her skin when her phone vibrated in her bag. She switched it back to ringer mode and answered it. She kept her eyes firmly away from the still, damaged figure lying on the floor.

'Hillary Greene' she said simply.

It was Rollo, with news that Inspector Sam Waterstone would be arriving on the scene shortly, and was SIO on the suicide case. Also en route was the armed response team, who would still have to assess the situation, given that there had been a discharge of a firearm.

Hillary thanked him and hung up. She and Sam Waterstone were good mates of long standing, and she knew the big, rugby-playing inspector wouldn't question her with any great suspicion or give her or Gareth a hard time. Which made her feel guilty. Abusing the trust of a friend was not something that sat well with her.

She tried to comfort herself with the knowledge that Jason *had* committed suicide, and her actions had kept all the evidence intact for him, but it still left a bad taste in her mouth.

And could she detect the subtle hand of one Commander Donleavy in ensuring that it was Sam who'd been assigned this particular case?

She smiled wryly. Trust the commander not to miss a trick.

* * *

As she'd surmised, when Sam joined her outside the door to the flat about twenty minutes or so later, he listened to her evidence without questioning any of it. She told him about Gareth's worry over his friend, and her worry over Gareth, and how she'd arrived mere moments after him, the gun having gone off as Gareth rang Jason Morley's doorbell.

It took a good hour for Sam and his team to get both her and Gareth's witness statements down. The only bad moment came when Sam asked her about Rawson. In all her rush to get things sorted, she'd simply failed to plan for this obvious oversight. It made her mad at herself for overlooking it. Of course Gareth was bound to mention Rawson's presence when giving his statement.

It was scant comfort to her to realize that, even if she *had* anticipated this, she could have done little to mitigate it. She couldn't have asked Gareth not to mention Rawson without him getting suspicious and demanding to know why. And the last thing she needed was for Gareth to get antsy or bolshie, thus undoing all her good work on his behalf by making Sam Waterstone wary.

She shrugged at her old friend and said that she knew Rawson from before, and that he was stationed very nearby, and so she'd called and asked him to come by, in case she needed an official and serving police officer on the scene. Until the arrival of the tactical team, she pointed out, there'd been no official representation at the crime scene. When it became clear that he wasn't needed, he'd left.

And as soon as she had a moment, she quickly found and called Rawson and told him what story he should stick to, if asked.

When they were finally finished, she walked with Gareth towards the side street where he'd parked his car. He looked tired, and dragged his left leg visibly.

'You should go home,' she said quietly. 'You've had a hell of a shock.'

'I'd rather go back to HQ, ma'am, if it's all the same to you,' he said flatly.

Hillary nodded. She understood his reluctance to go back to his quiet and empty flat all too well. Sometimes, when you'd had your world rocked, you needed people, noise, and normalcy around you. Left alone in a quiet space, there was nothing to distract you, allowing things to grow and magnify in your mind.

'All right. But I'm going to ask the police doctor to give you a going-over.'

'Ma'am, I'm fine,' he protested.

'Good. Then the doctor won't have much work to do on you, will he?' she said with a gentle smile.

As they reached his car, she looked at him closely. 'I think we'll take my car. I'll drive. Give me your keys, and I'll have someone drive your car back to your place.'

'Ma'am,' he said, too tired to argue. He reached into his right jacket pocket and handed them over.

They walked on in silence to where she'd left Puff, and went back to HQ in even more silence.

One thing was for certain, Hillary mused, he'd not yet checked his back pocket. But when he did, things would get very interesting indeed.

At first, he'd think he must have lost it somewhere. But when he stopped and realized it couldn't have easily fallen out of his tight pocket, his quick mind would soon put one and one together.

And then there'd be fireworks.

As she drove, Hillary was already mentally rehearsing just how she was going to respond to the flare-up when it inevitably came.

* * *

While Hillary Greene contemplated her immediate future, Mia de Salle was contemplating her distant past.

The churchyard where Michael Beck was buried was looking at its best in a ray of spring sunshine. In one corner, a white-flowering cherry tree looked heartbreakingly lovely, and in it a jenny wren was singing its little heart out.

Mia walked the familiar route through the graves, although she hadn't been there for some time now and stopped in front of the white gravestone. She had a bunch of colourful and sweet-smelling freesias in her hand, and bending down, was glad to see there was room (and water) for them in the small pot recessed into the bottom of the plinth.

His parents had chosen the wording for him, of course, so she found it plain and uninspiring. No lines of poetry, or even a personal comment, to make it unique. Just his name, date of birth and death, and the usual, pious claim that he had been a 'beloved son', as a final insult to her.

Why didn't gravestones habitually say lover or soulmate of such-and-such?

Of course, she thought fairly, she couldn't claim to be either of those things now. She sighed and stood looking around the deserted country churchyard with wistful eyes and a slowly burgeoning resentment.

She didn't deserve this, any of it. She was lonely and alone. Her first faithless love was dead, and her new love wouldn't acknowledge her. Although it was romantic and all very fine to 'pine away' with a broken heart, she was getting seriously fed up with all of it. Now that Michael's case had been reopened, he should have come to her. Asked her to lie for him, or to simply run away somewhere so that they could be together and safe. But no — still he wouldn't trust her. Still he was reluctant to love her like he should.

Why should she have to put up with it? All her life, men had misused and mistreated her and let her down, and failed to live up to even the lowest of expectations. But she knew there was no answer for her here. Michael was long and safely dead. Nothing could touch him anymore. It was she who was alive and suffering.

She reached down and snatched the gorgeous freesias from the small pot and tossed them angrily onto the quiet green turf. Then, deliberately, she put out her foot and ground their beautiful, fragrant petals into the ground. Wasn't that, after all, what the two men in her life had done to her — each in their own separate ways?

She'd been patient, but his refusal to come to her now was one betrayal too far.

And she would suffer in silence no longer.

It was time she had vengeance.

* * *

As Mia stalked from the mockingly empty and quiet country churchyard, Gareth Proctor was sitting at his desk, sipping from a mug of hot, sweet tea. It was Claire who had provided it, on learning from Hillary what had been happening, and it was Claire who watched him surreptitiously as he drank it. Her motherly eyes were anxious and concerned, and she found it hard to concentrate on her own work. Though she did remember to fill Hillary in briefly on what she'd come up with on some of her assignments.

'About the financial status of Dr Durning and Mia de Salle, guv,' she said. 'Both of them live in houses that they own outright, as opposed to renting. Neither of them has a current mortgage, although Dr Durning had one but has now paid it off. Dr Durning doesn't earn much salary as a private tutor, and so far hasn't published any books that could be said to have earned him a decent living. But he owns a nice car, and holidays abroad at least twice a year. Mia de Salle bought a very nice place in Woodstock as a cash buyer, about eight years ago.'

Hillary frowned. 'Does her family have money?'

Claire lifted a hand, palm flat, and rocked it from side to side. 'They're not poor, guv, but they aren't rolling in it either.'

'Hmm. Interesting,' Hillary said. Then, seeing that Gareth was now settled down in the main office, she left them both to it, and, straightening her shoulders, went to report to Rollo Sale.

From the superintendent's reception of her, she realized two things. One, now that the tension and anxiety had passed and she and Gareth were both safely back at HQ, a fair amount of his worry and anger had had time to dissipate. And two, at some point, Commander Marcus Donleavy must have made it clear that she was not to be officially disciplined for disobeying his orders.

Since she couldn't expect Rollo Sale to be happy about the powers-that-be going over his head when it came to how he handled his personnel, she stood stiffly in front of his desk and let him make it clear just how displeased he was, and didn't take it personally.

Afterwards, she apologized, explained her thinking, and promised never to do it again. Thus, with honour satisfied on both sides, Hillary left, with both of them giving and receiving a mutually strained smile. Nevertheless, they both knew that she was in his bad books, and probably would be for some time.

Letting out a long sigh as she walked back down the corridor, she paused in the doorway and glanced in. Claire shot her a quick look with a raised eyebrow. Gareth was staring blankly at his computer screen.

'Gareth. Do you have someone we can call?' Hillary asked. And when he transferred his blank gaze to her, added, 'It might be a good idea if you had someone stay with you overnight. A parent? A friend, perhaps?'

'Thank you, ma'am, but I'll be fine.'

Hillary looked at him thoughtfully for a moment, then sighed. 'All right. But if you want to get off early, go ahead.' A quick glance at the cheap, battery-operated white plastic clock on the wall showed her that it was nearly four o'clock anyway. 'Claire can drive you home. Your car should be parked by your front door by now.'

'Sure thing,' Claire said brightly.

Gareth forced a smile.

Hillary went back to her office. After a few moments, she reached for her notebook and checked the next item on her to-do list.

She reached for the phone and dialled the Becks' home phone number. William answered.

'Mr Beck, it's Hillary Greene. A quick question I forgot to ask before. You said that last time you saw Michael, he was on his bike, and so didn't have his metal detector with him. Is that right?'

'Yes, that's right.'

'Can you just confirm then that the detector is, or was, still at your place? I mean, when it came time to sort out Michael's belongings, did you find the metal detector in his room, or the shed perhaps, or wherever it was that he usually kept it?'

'Oh, now you're asking me,' William said. 'I'm not sure, off hand. It was ten years ago now.'

'Yes, I can appreciate that, but it *is* something I need to know,' she pressed gently.

'Hold on a moment, I'll get my wife. She dealt with most of that sort of thing,' he said.

Hillary heard a little click, and then a moment or two of silence, then the muffled sound of voices, and a little while later, Martina's voice.

'Hello? William says you're asking about Michael's metal detector?'

'Yes, Mrs Beck, sorry to bother you again. I just wanted to know what happened to it after Michael's death. Did you give it away to someone, or donate it to charity perhaps?'

'No. No, I don't think so,' Martina said, after a moment's puzzled silence. 'I remember giving his clothes to Oxfam, and his books to Sue Ryder. We kept his watch and St Christopher, of course. But his metal detector . . . I'm sorry, I don't remember seeing it . . .'

'Did he keep it in his room?'

'No, in the shed with his bicycle and other stuff.'

'Try and picture it in your mind,' Hillary said helpfully. 'What other things of his were kept in there?'

'Well, his bicycle, but we never got that back, as you know. He kept his wellingtons and dirty sneakers and stuff in there. An old dog lead and bowl of Tizer's that he couldn't bear to get rid of.' She heard Martina Beck's voice catch a little as she recalled the obviously long-gone family pet. 'Michael was heartbroken when he died. There's a spare freezer in there . . . You know, I really don't think I've seen his metal detector at all since . . . since he left us.'

Hillary, who'd been feeling a growing sense of being on to something at last, tried not to get ahead of herself. 'Do you know of anyone else in your circle of family or friends who might have had a use for it? It's possible you gave it away when you were still feeling below par and just simply can't remember it now. As your husband said, it was ten years ago.'

'I suppose so,' Martina said, but didn't sound particularly convinced. 'Do you want me to see if I can find it? Although I don't think it can be in the shed . . .'

'If you wouldn't mind, Mrs Beck. And if you could call me back and let me know?'

'Yes, I will,' she promised, sounding a little distracted, and abruptly hung up.

So did Hillary. And she had the distinct feeling that when Martina Beck called her back, it would be to report that the metal detector was nowhere to be found.

Which meant . . .

Which meant she now had a fairly good working theory as to who had killed Michael Beck, and why.

But proving it was going to be a real challenge . . .

It was at that moment that the door to her office flew open so hard that it hit the inner wall with a sound like a gunshot, and started to ricochet back. Hillary's nerves, which had just begun to settle down, went abruptly into overdrive again and she only just prevented herself from letting out a little scream.

In the doorway, looking at her with a face pale and tight with fury, was Gareth Proctor. Hovering behind him, looking upset and bewildered, was Claire.

'What the hell did you do?' Gareth thundered at her. He was breathing hard, as if he'd just run a marathon, and was sweating slightly with tension.

Hillary looked at him calmly, then let her eyes drift casually over his shoulder. 'Claire, why don't you go home early. I'll drive Gareth back to his flat.'

'Yes, guv,' Claire said uncertainly. She looked at Hillary closely, to see if she was signalling for her to go and get help, but Hillary merely stared flatly back at her.

Claire nodded and backed away. When Gareth had stood up, checked his back pocket and suddenly started acting really weirdly, she had instinctively followed him when he blundered out of the room. But she knew when it was wise to beat a retreat. Whatever it was that was happening between Hillary Greene and the newest member of the team, she intended to keep out of it.

For a moment both Gareth and Hillary remained perfectly still and quiet, listening to Claire's retreating footsteps.

'You needn't bother to drive me home. I'll call a taxi,' Gareth grated.

'Fine. Come in and close the door. There's no chair in here so you're going to have to stand.'

'I prefer to stand, ma'am,' he said, his voice hard.

'Good. Because I prefer you to stand as well,' Hillary said, her own voice just as hard. She saw his eyes flicker, just a little, in surprise at her clearly unexpected response, but he was still too obsessed with one thing to really take heed of the warning.

'You stole something from me, didn't you?' he immediately went on the attack. His right hand was clenched into an angry fist, and he had his weight settled firmly on his right leg. He was leaning just slightly forward, everything about his body language screaming that this was a man in a combative mood. She, however, was sitting with a desk between them, in a tight space where he'd have no room to manoeuvre, and with backup from the technical boffins in the office down the corridor just a shout away.

This time she had no doubts about who would come off best if things got physical.

But she wouldn't — couldn't — let it come to that.

'Incorrect,' she snapped back instantly. '*You* stole something from *me*, and I merely took steps to retrieve it.'

She again saw his eyes flicker uncertainly as, yet again, things didn't seem to be playing out as he'd expected. Maybe he thought she'd bluster or deny things or try and bluff it out. Or maybe he thought she'd be submissive and placatory and try to explain herself.

Now, with just a few crisp sentences, he was beginning to sense that he'd read the situation — and her — all wrong. But he was still too angry and too shocked from his friend's brutal death to make the mental adjustment needed. He was still too focused on trying to do right by his dead friend to realize the danger he was in.

But by the time she was finished with him, he would fully understand the danger he was in.

'You read his suicide note, didn't you, once you'd fobbed me off with Sergeant Rawson,' he went back on the attack.

'Of course I did,' Hillary said flatly. Perhaps he had expected her to feel guilty about that, because her uncompromising statement seemed to wrongfoot him for a third time. But he quickly rallied, still so sure that he held the moral high ground.

'Then you know it was meant for *me* to find and deal with.' His eyes flashed. 'You had no right to interfere. It was nothing to do with *you!*'

Hillary slowly leaned back in her chair and cocked her head slightly to one side. She let her eyes narrow a little. '*Nothing . . . to . . . do . . . with . . . me*,' she said, deliberately elongating the spacing, her tone utterly disbelieving. 'Let me see. I've been a police officer for all my adult life.' She ticked the points off ostentatiously on her fingers as she spoke. 'I'm still working for the police force as an investigator. And the murder of a man in Reading, of which I now have direct evidence and knowledge, is nothing to do with me?' She smiled gently. 'Hmm, an interesting hypothesis,' she said sardonically. 'Now let me just sit and think about that for a moment.'

She was relieved to see that a slightly guilty flush had now crept over his face, that some of his surety was being eroded. He opened his mouth to speak, and she instantly held up a hand.

'Be quiet, Mr Proctor,' she said, the words a clear and unambiguous order. 'You are going to listen to what I say next very carefully and without interruption. And I suggest you bury your anger and your burning sense of righteous indignation and engage your brain. Because your future is going to depend on it.'

Gareth instinctively stiffened to attention at the voice of command, but then began to look almost instantly mulish again. No doubt he was beginning to remember that he was no longer actually in the army. And that Hillary was not his superior officer.

Before he could begin to get his head properly around that, she began to speak.

'What you did today was a criminal offence,' she began, her words crisp and clear. 'For which you could be charged, and, if found guilty, be sentenced to jail time. You would have to serve your sentence, and come out with a criminal record at the end of it. And if you found getting a job hard before, just how hard do you think you'd find it then?'

Gareth swallowed hard, but said nothing.

'I understand you have an ex-wife and a daughter who, presumably, rely on your financial help?'

'Now wait a minute . . .'

'And your actions today could have far-reaching consequences for them,' Hillary steamrollered over him.

It shut him up, as she knew it would. No doubt, during the heat of the moment and then the awful numbing aftermath of his friend's suicide, all his thoughts had been with Jason Morley.

Now she needed to make him see that he had other commitments.

'When you stole that piece of evidence, you were also becoming an accessory after the fact to the murder of Francis Clyde-Brough,' she informed him coldly.

'That bastard deserved everything he got,' Gareth said hotly, unable to control himself any longer.

Hillary had no doubt that he was gearing himself up to explain just what awful thing it was that the murdered soldier had done overseas which had resulted in Jason Morley and probably several others wanting him dead. And that he fully expected her to be as outraged as himself. And she probably would be too.

But again, she ruthlessly cut across him. 'You may well be right about that, Mr Proctor,' she said briskly, 'but right now, that's irrelevant.'

'No, ma'am,' Gareth snapped out, 'it isn't! Jason only did what his friends couldn't because they were dead. Killed hundreds of miles from home because of that stupid bastard's incompetence and cowardice. Clyde-Brough might as well have killed Jason as well, because he was never right afterwards. Oh yes, he was one of the lucky ones who came home, but he couldn't forget. Couldn't settle. He became depressed, had terrible nightmares. He just kept spiralling down and down until he did what he did out of sheer desperation. You can't judge him. You don't have the right.'

He paused for a much-needed breath, which came rasping in and out noisily from his throat. 'Jase doesn't deserve to be remembered as a killer. His *family* doesn't deserve to have his memory dishonoured. Don't you get it?' Gareth's righteous anger turned to appeal. 'He texted *me*, and waited for *me* to come, at the darkest moment of his life. And then he shot himself when I was at his door, so that *I* would be on hand to make sure everything went as he would have wanted it. Because I was his *mate*, and he knew he could trust me. *Trust me!* And now you've made me let him down!'

Hillary sighed heavily, but wasn't all that convinced by Gareth's scenario. To make your best friend part of your suicide sounded more like an act of aggression to her, rather than a matter of trust. She wasn't surprised that Gareth was seeing things from only one side, but she would be willing to bet a fair amount that, friend or not, Jason Morley had probably harboured some resentment towards his friend. Maybe subconscious and unacknowledged, but there nevertheless. Gareth obviously hadn't been part of whatever it was that Clyde-Brough had got so drastically wrong. And Gareth, although suffering the results of his own disaster, had still come through it and was managing to cope. He'd got a new flat, a new job, a new life. Friend or no, Jason Morley's feelings towards his mate must have been mixed, to say the least.

But she knew it was no good saying any of this to Gareth now. He wouldn't want to hear it. He'd probably never want to hear it.

She nodded slowly, giving him time to calm down. 'I understand how you feel,' she said quietly.

Gareth snorted insultingly.

Hillary's eyes hardened again. 'Do you think you're the only one who understands loyalty to a colleague, Mr Proctor?' she asked him, her voice dangerously quiet now.

And suddenly Gareth remembered Hillary's résumé — and her award for bravery, for taking a bullet for a friend. 'Ma'am, I didn't mean to suggest . . .'

'When I watched you tampering with a crime scene, do you know what I *should* have done, Mr Proctor?' she asked, again cutting across him, but careful this time to keep her tone casual. 'I should have backed out, called Superintendent Sale, told him what I'd seen, and have Sergeant Rawson come over to arrest you on the spot. I'd then have retrieved Jason's confession to the killing of Clyde-Brough, when it would have been used not only to clear the Reading murder off the books, but also at your own trial. That's what I *should* have done. That's what my duty as someone working for the police dictated I *should* have done,' she emphasized.

She let that hang in the air for a moment and was glad to see that he was having difficulty looking her in the eye now. 'But is that what I did?'

When he remained silent, she repeated gently, '*Is that what I did, Mr Proctor?*'

'No, ma'am,' he said reluctantly.

'No, I didn't, did I? Instead, I called in a favour and got Sergeant Rawson — who in case you were wondering, was taught the tricks of the trade by a very successful pickpocket — to come and retrieve the evidence without any fuss. And then leave, making no report of it anywhere, and agreeing to keep his mouth firmly shut. Thus putting his own professional neck on the line to save yours.'

This direct hit made Gareth flinch. Good. He was beginning to realize that he — and more importantly, Jason Morley — were not the only ones he needed to think of now.

'I then returned the now-intact suicide note to the coffee table, compounding the irregularities, thus putting *my* neck on the block too, and what's more, never said a word to the SIO who'd been given the case. And by the way, just in case you're interested, Sam Waterstone is a good mate of *mine*,' she said flatly, 'and lying to him didn't sit with me. At all.'

Gareth shook his head. 'I never asked you to do any of that,' he said stubbornly, but without much force now.

'No, you didn't,' Hillary agreed, suddenly feeling very tired. Something of her weariness must have shown on her face, for his fierce gaze started to soften.

'I did it because, in spite of the spectacular evidence to the contrary given your actions today, I think you're a good man,' she carried on. 'I think you have good brains and I think, given time, you'd make a good fit with my team and be a real asset to the CRT.'

She ran a hand over her face and sighed. 'Now, I want you to go home and instead of thinking about your friend, who is now dead and thus beyond your help, I want you to think instead about all the people who are not.' She shifted in her chair and shook her head. 'Gareth, you've been with us long enough now to know and fully grasp the importance of what the CRT does. It finds killers. It brings the truth out into the open, delivers justice for the dead, and hopefully brings some kind of peace and closure to the loved ones of the victims. People like the Becks. And you need to make a

193

decision now. Perhaps one of the more important ones of your life. Do you want to stay a part of that? Do you want to spend the next ten, fifteen or even twenty years working on behalf of the dead, the forgotten, the mourned? Or are you going to let your friend's tragedy ruin your own life too?'

'Ma'am, I—'

'Shut up,' Hillary said brutally, but in truth she really was beginning to feel wrung out. It had been a hell of a day. She'd had to deal with a devastating suicide, receive a rollicking from a man she both liked and respected, done Marcus Donleavy's dirty work for him yet again, and had been forced to make ethical decisions that she felt totally unequal to making.

She was tired and she wanted nothing more than to go back to the *Mollern* and the peace and quiet of the canal, and just curl up on her bed and go to sleep.

'I simply don't have the energy or the patience to deal with you anymore right now,' she added flatly. 'So go home. Think about everything I've said. Then come in to work tomorrow and either hand in your resignation, or be prepared to do your bloody job. I have a feeling things will be moving in the Michael Beck case very soon and we're going to have to be on the top of our game. Go on.' She waved to the door behind him. 'Get out of my sight.'

He stiffened, looking about as tired and beat as she felt, but turned to go. When he was halfway out of the door, she said laconically, 'And by the way, Mr Proctor, if you *do* decide to stay on and do a worthwhile job, don't ever expect me to pull your fat from the fire again. If I can't trust you, you're of no use to me.'

For answer to that warning, he slammed the door behind him.

Hillary sighed and closed her eyes for a few moments, then gave a weary half-snort, half-laugh. Well, she'd either got through to him or she hadn't.

By now, Sam Waterstone would have read Jason Morley's suicide note, bagged it in evidence, and been in contact with the Reading murder squad, who would no doubt greet his news with open arms.

There would be no scandal or newspaper headlines tearing into Thames Valley's performance over the mishandling of a suicide, and Commander Marcus Donleavy and Superintendent Rollo Sale could rest easy in their beds tonight.

And Hillary Greene?

She suddenly grinned. Hillary Greene was going to go back to her boat and have a bloody stiff drink. That's what Hillary Greene was going to do.

And then tomorrow she was going to close the Michael Beck case.

With a bit of luck, and supposing the universe wasn't still feeling in a bloody-minded mood, that is.

CHAPTER FIFTEEN

Hillary drove into work not knowing if Gareth Proctor was going to be at his desk or not. But she didn't go straight to the small communal office as she would normally have done, or even her own, but made straight for Rollo Sale's office instead.

She tapped on the door, uncomfortably aware that, for the first time in their working relationship, there might be awkwardness between them. It made her sad, but it didn't deter her.

After zonking out and getting about four solid hours of deep sleep, she'd spent the rest of the night tossing and turning, not thinking about Jason Morley or Gareth Proctor, but about the state of her latest case.

And although she thought she could now take a pretty good guess on the identity of Michael Beck's killer, as well as the motivation behind it, she knew, right now, that was all it was: a guess. And if she was going to successfully close the case, she needed help. Initially, her boss's help and maybe that of DI Robin Farrell as well.

She tapped on the superintendent's door, waited for the summons to come in, and stepped inside, searching his face for signs of annoyance.

There were none. He looked up from behind his desk, and a brief, professional smile lit his face. 'Hillary, come in.'

'Sir. Do you have time to discuss the Beck case?'

'I've a meeting in an hour.'

'That should be fine.'

She took a seat, and then began to talk. She started at the beginning, going through all that they'd done so far, and why she'd come to the conclusions she had. Rollo, as was his habit, let her talk without interruption, occasionally making notes. When she was finished there was a long moment of silence.

'It's very thin,' Rollo finally said.

'Yes, sir. Paper thin.'

'You have no forensic evidence at all?'

'No, sir, not after all this time. And with no witnesses and no corroborating evidence — yet — the CPS won't touch it with a barge pole.'

'In other words, we're going to have to rely heavily on a confession. Always supposing we can get one, and always supposing that's enough for the CPS.'

'Yes, sir,' Hillary said. Then said cautiously, 'Of course, the murders that DI Farrell is investigating might hold out better hope of a result.'

'Hmm. This idea you have that Michael's murder and those of Newley and Kirklees are connected, and share the same killer, is somewhat thin, Hillary,' Rollo pointed out.

Hillary nodded, utterly agreeing with him. 'Yes, sir. But I think our best way forward is to concentrate on those now. The fact that all three appear to have been murdered with a similar, unusually shaped weapon has to count for something.'

'DI Farrell won't like it,' Rollo predicted with a smile. 'He's convinced Larry Spence killed them to expand his empire.'

'Yes, and he may well be right,' Hillary said mildly.

'But you don't think so?'

'No. But as of this moment, I have nothing to go on but instinct and years of experience.'

'Ah. That good old feeling in your bones you mentioned.' Rollo smiled.

'Which might well turn out to be rheumatism,' Hillary put in, with a smile of her own. Not that she had much to smile about. The Beck case was proving to be far more complicated than she'd initially thought, and was going to be a real hard nut to crack. Plus, she was not at all sanguine that she *could* crack it.

Although the idea that Michael Beck's killer would never be brought to account was a hard one to stomach, she knew that the chances had to be pretty high that she might just have to deal with exactly that scenario.

'We need to get DI Farrell on board,' Rollo mused. 'I've been keeping an ear out for news about that, and I'm pretty certain that the Newley/Kirklees case stalled and Farrell's guv'nor had powered it down. So it might just be that Farrell will jump at any chance to keep it active, even if it doesn't align with his own thinking on it. Let me get him down here anyway, and see what he thinks. What, exactly, do you want done?'

Hillary felt some of the tension drain out of her. 'Well, sir, as you know, here in CRT we can't really do surveillance — we don't have the manpower or the training for it. If DI Farrell and his team can be persuaded to keep a watch on our target, we might get lucky. If I'm right, and Michael Beck found treasure trove all those years ago — and was killed because of it — at some point, the killer will want to offload some of the items. I think that, over the years, that's what had been happening, with Newley acting as go-between.'

'So you're assuming, what, that for some reason that relationship went stale, with our target being forced for whatever reason to get rid of his fence?'

'Yes.'

'And Kirklees? Why would our target kill him?'

Hillary spread her hands helplessly. 'I don't have all the answers yet. At this stage, we're still in the dark about some things. But with the MO being so precise, whoever killed Newley had to have killed Kirklees too. The timing, with both men being killed the same day, with what appears to be the same unusual weapon, makes it virtually certain as well. We just don't know why yet.'

Rollo sighed heavily. 'Even if you're right about the recent murders being tied up with our cold case, there's no telling when the target will approach a new fence in order to sell off an item.'

'No, sir. It could be days, weeks or even months,' she admitted grimly.

'No way we can afford to keep the target under surveillance for that long! Even a few days will be stretching the budget,' Rollo told her in no uncertain terms.

'Yes, sir. But we might get lucky. And it's a start. Like you said, we really need to know more about why Newley and Kirklees were killed, and make the connection. Ideally, I'd like to take a look at DI Farrell's files, but I know he won't wear that.'

'Neither will the top brass,' Rollo agreed. 'Cold cases are our remit — not ongoing ones.'

'Yes sir, I know. It's a pity we don't have enough to get a court order to check on whether the target has a safety deposit box or not. Let alone get permission to look inside it.'

'You think whatever Michael Beck found is lodged in a bank somewhere?' Rollo asked sceptically.

Hillary laughed. 'Well, sir, if *you* found a fortune in ancient gold by digging it up out of the ground, where, presumably, someone had once hidden it for safe-keeping, would *you* feel safe re-hiding it?'

Rollo grunted. 'No, I suppose not. No, it's not human nature, is it? You'd want to keep it somewhere you knew *nobody* could stumble on to it. And you're right, that probably means a safety deposit box. And it's certainly safe enough if that's where it is, because right now no judge in the country would say we had grounds to have access to it.'

For a moment the two of them looked at one another with the same, grim thought. 'This is turning out to be a real sod of a case, isn't it?' Rollo eventually said.

Hillary couldn't disagree.

'All right.' Rollo glanced at his watch. 'I'll ask DI Farrell to come down and see if he's willing to put a watch on the target. Like I said, I think he'll be desperate enough to agree to that. But I don't think he'll be overly impressed with our reasoning.'

Hillary didn't think he would be either. But it's not as if they were awash with other options.

'In the meantime, you'll keep digging on the Michael Beck end of the case, right?' Rollo Sale prompted.

'Yes, sir. There are still things we can do there. We need to identify the murder weapon if possible. Now we know that Michael Beck must have been using specialist equipment for his hobby, we might be able to ascertain what might have been used to kill him. That's something the original team never had a chance to do.'

'Right.'

'And then there's the detector. If, as I suspect, Mrs Beck rings me back today to say that she can't find it, then my theory as to what happened the day Michael was killed is looking better and better. It's always possible that avenue might provide some physical evidence at last.'

Rollo snorted. 'I can't see our target being stupid enough to keep either the detector or the murder weapon, can you?'

But here Hillary surprised him. 'Normally I'd say no, sir. But in this case . . . I'm not so sure.'

But on that she wouldn't be drawn further. She didn't want to look like a complete idiot if she was getting everything really, really wrong.

When she left Rollo's office, she had to pass the door to the communal office, and heard the unmistakable sounds of human voices — one male, one female.

She didn't pause at the doorway however as she might otherwise have done, but carried on to her stationery cupboard. There she found her desk clear of any unstamped envelopes containing a resignation letter. Which was promising.

But the day was still young.

She settled down at her desk, went through her emails, then started looking at archaeology websites, concentrating on the tools used by excavators. Michael Beck, Simon Newley and Lionel Kirklees had been killed by blows to the head with an oddly shaped, rounded metal object. And although there were a few things that looked vaguely promising for use as an impromptu murder weapon, nothing was totally ideal.

It wasn't until she left the professional sites, and started looking at more amateur posts, usually set up by how-to-get-rich-quick merchants peddling the idea that anyone could find hidden treasure, that she finally found what she was looking for.

Not surprisingly, amateurs out on the hunt for easy pickings were more inventive (and more budget-strapped) than most, and one self-confessed 'guru' of metal detectors and treasure-seeking on the cheap offered quite a range of 'useful' if unconventional kit that could help out your average night-hawk.

One of which was a simple spud planter.

And on finding more information on this humble gardening accessory, Hillary began to feel as if she was earning her salary at last.

A spud planter was exactly what its name suggested. It was an implement for people who wanted to plant potatoes — or anything of similar size or shape, one presumed — which saved the gardener or allotment owner the need to dig a trench.

Some of these were long-handled, with a round metal tube or cone shape on the end, with a bar just above it, allowing the user to apply the weight of their foot — a bit as you would with a normal spade. The idea being that you stuck it in the ground, pressed down and pulled up — removing a deep, round piece of sod. You then dropped the spud in, and by releasing the handle, popped the divot back on top.

Great for planting a row of spuds. Or, if you'd just had a beep on your metal detector and didn't fancy digging a bloody great hole with a regular spade, pushing it into the ground directly over the 'ping' in the hope of pulling up something very interesting in your divot of turf.

Rounded, metallic, hefty, but probably not commonly used as a murder weapon.

Just then her phone rang. It was Rollo Sale, telling her that DI Farrell had just reluctantly permitted two of his greenest constables get some surveillance practice on the target, starting immediately. Which, they both concurred, was no more than they could reasonably have hoped for.

She had just hung up and found the original forensic pathologist's file (which to her relief *did* confirm that spud planters hadn't been looked at as a potential murder weapon) when the phone rang again.

This time it was Martina Beck, confirming that her son's metal detector was nowhere to be found. And that she could not recall seeing it after her son's murder.

Hillary thanked her, assured her she'd been very helpful, and hung up.

Things were beginning to fall into place, but they were only minor things. Just little pats on the back here and there to reassure her that she was on the right track. But there was nothing yet that she could say was going to light a fire under her case.

And yet, for once, Hillary's pessimism was uncalled for. Perhaps she'd just had her quota of bad luck for a while, or perhaps the random whims of fate had turned once again capriciously in her favour. But barely four hours later, when DI Farrell's green constables had been watching the target for less than two hours, they hit pay dirt.

The first indication she had that things were moving, and moving in quite a spectacular fashion, was when Rollo called and asked her to come to his office pronto.

Once she'd hot-footed it to his door and answered his summons to come in, the first face she saw was not that of her boss, but that of Robin Farrell.

And he was grinning from ear to ear.

'You're not going to believe this,' he said, eyes glowing with satisfaction.

* * *

One hour before Hillary Greene was summoned to Rollo's office, Teddy Bear walked into the park and found one particular bench under a large cedar tree, just as Larry Spence had described it.

Less than five minutes later, Larry himself came strolling along and casually took the seat beside him. 'Pity there isn't a pond,' he muttered laconically. 'We could have fed some ducks.'

Teddy Bear smiled thinly and glanced around. There were the usual number of students scattered around, skiving off their studies, and the almost obligatory old geezer sitting on the bench further down the path, reading the *Oxford Times*. All were ignoring them.

Teddy Bear took no notice as two more students, a lanky lad and an equally lanky girl, lay out on the grass a little bit away from them and instantly got out their mobile phones. The sight of youths messing about with mobile phones was so commonplace as to be invisible. But mobile phones had cameras in them, and not all the young people in Oxford's parks were students. Some of them were excited constables, let out of uniform and given a 'fun' assignment.

Teddy Bear, unaware of having been followed for the last half-hour, reached into a jacket pocket and withdrew a small gold item and passed it across to Spence.

Casually turning to roll onto one arm, the lanky female student propped up her phone and took photographs.

'This the ring then?' Larry Spence said, rather redundantly, as he took the item from his client and looked at it curiously. He'd never seen ancient jewellery before, and didn't know whether to be impressed or not. It was rather crude, by modern jewellery standards and design, the actual loop of the ring itself a little uneven in thickness, and it had a distinct dent in it, making it far from circular. Perhaps at some point, a farmer had driven over it with a plough or something. The beaten gold top disc was also chunky and uneven, but it had been carved at some point with some design that meant nothing to him.

But it was reassuringly heavy, and the colour of the metal was undeniably lovely — a rich buttery gold. Some punter obsessed with Saxons, or Britons, or whoever the hell had made this, was going to pay a fortune for it, he was sure.

'Very nice,' Larry said, grinning obligingly for the lanky young man who took his photograph while pretending to take a selfie.

'Can you get a good price for it?' Teddy Bear asked flatly.

'Oh yes. Much better than that loser Simon Newley would ever have got for it,' he boasted. 'Whoever topped him did you a favour, I reckon.'

Teddy Bear shrugged. But then just had to ask, 'How are the cops coming with that, by the way? Last time we spoke, you seemed to think they had you in the frame for it.'

'What? Oh, yeah.' Larry laughed. 'I told you — that DI Farrell's got no chance of pinning it on me. 'Specially now they've got the station hotshot in on it.'

'What?' Teddy Bear asked sharply. 'What do you mean?'

Oxford's premiere crook looked at his client and grinned. 'I've got eyes and ears in his investigation, right? First thing I did. I'm no mug. And it seems that they've got someone else working the case with him now. And she could be a problem,' he added more thoughtfully.

'Who?'

'Former DI called Hillary Greene. Whereas Farrell couldn't find his own backside in a blackout, she's a different proposition all together.'

Teddy Bear went very still. 'Good, is she?'

'One of the best, so my source reckons. When she was a regular DI she had a solve rate second to none. They always gave her murder cases too, whenever they came up. Now, apparently, she's retired, but working on cold cases. And lo and behold, the same thing! She's closed more unsolved murders than you've had hot dinners.'

Teddy Bear said nothing.

Larry Spence pocketed the gold ring with a sense of immense satisfaction. If this soppy client of his had more of this good stuff stashed away, he was on to a real winner. 'Well, best be off. Got to see a man about a dog, and all of that.'

Teddy Bear vaguely smiled, then watched as Larry Spence walked away.

Over on the grass, the female constable said quietly to her colleague, 'The target doesn't look very happy!'

'Nope,' her companion agreed. 'But I can tell you who *is* going to be happy. Our guv'nor. He's been longing to get something on Larry Spence for months! And here we've got him receiving dodgy goods! Let's send him our photos and make his day!'

* * *

A little while after this, Hillary listened keenly as DI Farrell filled her in on what had been happening and looked at the uploaded photos on his mobile.

'You think we can get a warrant to search for any safety deposit box the target may have now?' she asked Rollo, who nodded.

'I've already got that underway,' the superintendent said happily. 'So what next?'

'We bring the target in and question him,' DI Farrell said at once.

Hillary frowned. 'That might be a bit premature. We don't want to spook—'

She wasn't allowed to finish the sentence however. Already Robin Farrell was talking over her. 'We need to get him to roll over on Spence. This is the first real evidence we've got of criminal activity on his part. I know it's not a murder rap yet, but it's something to hold him on. And if we get him for fencing, it'll give us probable cause to start poking around in other things as well. Once the smaller sharks scent blood in the water, they'll start to turn on him! All we need is one greedy lieutenant of his scenting an opportunity and all sorts of stuff might come pouring out of the woodwork. If the boss goes away for life, career opportunities open up for everyone else.'

'Actually, unless we can prove that the gold ring in the photos is part of the undeclared treasure trove, you don't have anything on him,' Hillary pointed out gently. She knew a detective who had blinkers on when she saw one. And although she understood what it felt like to have tunnel vision when it came to nabbing a particular nemesis, she couldn't let Robin Farrell's burning need to see Larry Spence behind bars scupper her investigation.

'All the more reason to bring your target in,' Farrell persisted stubbornly. 'The superintendent tells me you have no forensics on your cold case, no witness, and nothing tying your suspect to Beck's death. But the Newley/Kirklees case is still current. We know Spence killed *them* in order to expand his empire, and if we can break the target with these photos, I'll finally have a thread that I can pull on! If we make the target a deal if he rolls on Spence, we can kill two birds with one stone.'

'Hold on,' Hillary said firmly. 'I'm not offering the killer of Michael Beck any damned deal! And we don't know that Spence *did* kill Newley and Kirklees.'

Robin Farrell looked at her impatiently, then turned to Rollo Sale. 'We both know that my open and current case takes priority. I'm going to recommend to my super that we pull in the target and put the squeeze on. The only question is — do you want in on it or not?'

Hillary too turned to look at Rollo Sale. But even as she did so, she knew his hands were tied. One sympathetic glance from him confirmed it.

She sighed heavily. 'OK. But I want to be the one to bring the target in.' She didn't trust the gung-ho Farrell not to blow what might be a rather delicate undertaking.

Robin, having got his way on the major issue, was happy to agree to the minor one, and shrugged. 'Fine. But I'll tag along. You don't have the authority to make an actual arrest, right?'

Silently Hillary cursed the fact that he was right. 'Fine, but only as a backup. *I'll* do the talking.'

'Suits me,' Robin agreed happily. To him, Hillary's suspect was small fry.

'And I want to take Gareth Proctor with me,' she added.

At this Rollo shot her a quick, surprised look. 'Do you think that's wise? After the shock he had yesterday . . .'

Robin looked curiously from one to the other, realizing that there was some subtext going on here that he wasn't aware of, but he wasn't interested enough to ask for details. Now that things were finally moving on his case, he was anxious to get going.

Hillary held her superintendent's gaze firmly. 'He needs to get back on the horse, sir,' she said.

Also, she thought pensively, he needed to make his mind up whether or not his job meant anything to him anymore. And if being thrust into the heart of the action just when the Beck case was heating up didn't help him make up his mind, then nothing would!

She left the now ebullient Robin Farrell in Rollo's office and walked to the community office. Claire was rummaging in the biscuit tin. Gareth was staring morosely at his computer screen.

'Gareth, we need to bring someone in for questioning. Get your coat.'

Claire looked up, glanced at Hillary's set face, and returned her concentration to acquiring a custard cream.

Without a word, Gareth rose and followed her out.

Outside the superintendent's office she introduced him to DI Robin Farrell who noted the former soldier's physical injuries with a quick interested glance and briskly shook his hand. They decided to go in DI Farrell's car, which was a newer, roomier, and more reliable car than Puff.

All three of them made the journey to the target's residence in a rather strained silence.

* * *

When Teddy Bear opened the door and saw Hillary Greene and Gareth Proctor, he smiled automatically and stepped aside to let them in.

They'd agreed on the drive over that Robin would stay in the car, unless called on for help. In her bag, Hillary's mobile phone was on, and she'd dialled Robin's number before approaching the door, leaving the line open. Now he could listen in on how things progressed.

'Hello again,' Teddy Bear said amiably. 'Please, come in. How are things going? Are you making any progress on Michael's case?'

'Yes, sir, I believe we are,' Hillary said. 'In fact, we'd like you to come with us to Kidlington to answer some further questions, if you wouldn't mind?'

At that point, Hillary fully expected him to agree. Oh, he might demur, might be a little difficult, but she could see no reason why he would refuse. As far as he knew, things might have taken a rather ominous turn, but he had no reason to worry too much yet. The reasonable, logical course of action was for him to go with them, answer their questions carefully and see if they could gauge the lay of the land.

And if her suspect hadn't just got back from hearing from one of the city's top crooks just how good Hillary Greene was at catching killers, that was probably what he'd have done.

Instead, Teddy Bear panicked. It wasn't totally out of character for him, because he was never as confident on the inside as the image he liked to project to the world. And rash action wasn't new to him either. Killing those that threatened him, in the form of Simon Newley and Lionel Kirklees, proved that. And yet it had definitely taken a toll on his nerves. After a decade of feeling safe and comfortable, the events of the last six months had shaken him.

And now this! The tension ratcheted up, and a nervous voice at the back of his mind screamed at him that his luck had run out at last, and that if he wanted to avoid jail time — and he did, the very thought of it *terrified* him — then it was time to run!

If he'd had time to think, to swallow down his intense fear, to make some sort of a rational plan, then the killer of Michael Beck might have acted differently than he did.

Instead, he acted instinctively.

He smiled, said mildly, 'Of course. Anything I can do to help. Just let me get my phone,' and walked away to a sideboard, where he pulled open a drawer and reached inside. When he turned around, however, he didn't have a mobile phone in his hand, but a taser.

Hillary recognized it at once, and yelled, 'Weapon!' at the top of her lungs. At this, Gareth reacted instantly, leaping towards the target. The target turned and at that point Gareth's weak leg buckled suddenly beneath him with the abrupt pressure being put on it, and he felt himself lurch sideways and slightly forward.

Hillary, seeing his peril, instinctively went to his aid and stepped forward, putting herself between him and the man with the taser, thus making herself the most obvious and most immediate danger.

At which point, Kevin Philpott turned the taser in her direction, and fired it.

CHAPTER SIXTEEN

Hillary's world became an instant jumble of shock, pain and weirdness. She thought she heard a buzzing sound. Thought she could smell burning. But the most distressing thing was that she totally lost control of her body. She could feel herself jerking, and realized she was on the floor.

She thought she was making some sort of a sound, but didn't know what it was. She couldn't seem to think in a straight line. Thoughts passed through her mind too quickly for her to grasp them. But she was aware of a sense of urgency.

Danger.

Someone was in danger. Herself. Someone else?

For no discernible reason, the galley of the *Mollern* flashed into and out of her mind.

Then she heard other sounds. Swearing. Male voices. Something bumped into her painfully, bruising her ribs. But she couldn't curl up to protect herself. Her limbs were splayed. And through one eye, she got a really good close-up, side-on view of her right hand. It was lying on a carpet, palm uppermost, and her knuckles were doing an odd little jig, up and down against the floor.

What the hell?

Then she heard a hard sharp sound, like a gunshot. But it wasn't a gunshot. Or at least, she didn't think so. What was it? She was sure she'd heard it before, not so long ago . . . Then she was back in her office, and Gareth Proctor, looking good and mad, was standing there, having just opened the door so hard and fast it . . .

Gareth. Gareth was in danger, not her. That was right, wasn't it?

Something or someone landed beside her heavily, with a groan and a thump. And then someone was leaning over who or whatever had joined her on the floor.

Yes. Floor. She was lying on the floor.

She tried to turn her head, but couldn't. But her peripheral vision was all right, and she could see that, lying a little way down from her, was Kevin Philpott, one side of his cheek squished to the carpet. The chubby man was writhing, swearing, and then crying, big fat tears running down his face.

She should help him.

No.

Hillary blinked. Her teeth chattered.

But the male voices she could hear were beginning to make sense now.

One of them said, 'My cuffs are in my back pocket . . .'

A moment — or was it much later? — the same voice said, 'We need an ambulance for your guv'nor.'

Ambulance? That meant someone was hurt. Hillary knew she needed to get up. She must help. Obviously a police officer was down . . . Who . . . Robin Farrell?

Or . . . what had she just been thinking? She sighed.

Slowly, her hand stopped dancing its weird tattoo against the floor and her teeth stopped chattering. At some point, the sweating, frightened face of Kevin Philpott disappeared, just yanked upwards and out of her view.

She tried to move, and found, to her relief, that she could.

'Don't try and move, ma'am,' she recognized Gareth Proctor's voice now. 'You've been hit with a taser, but you're going to be all right. A paramedic is on the way. Everything's all right. We've got the suspect in custody. Everything's fine.'

Hillary nodded. Her head actually moved. And she could think again. More or less.

So that's what it's like to be hit by a taser, Hillary thought blearily.

All in all, she concluded, it was not a particularly edifying experience.

* * *

The paramedics arrived a few minutes later, by which time Hillary had persuaded Gareth that she could move far enough to allow her to prop her back up against a chair. She was still sitting on the floor, but she felt a bit more dignified now that she was sitting, rather than lying.

Also, the shakes had stopped, and her mind felt clearer. The paramedics, a young girl with a soft smile and silky hair, and an older man with a cheerful personality that could be either reassuring or annoying, depending on your own state of mind, did their thing with kind but brisk efficiency.

Hillary let them get on with taking her blood pressure, listening to her heart and all the rest of it, and patiently answering their questions. She answered 'No' to having double vision, shortness of breath, chest pain or any numbness in her extremities.

She was being only fifty per cent truthful however. She *did* have pins and needles in her hands, and her chest *did* hurt. But her chest felt sore, as opposed to sharp pains, and she was convinced that it was due to the taser strike rather than anything more serious. And the pins and needles would wear off with time. She hoped.

Luckily, they had been able to remove the taser wires without too much trouble, and Hillary had watched as Gareth sombrely put them and the rest of the weapon into an evidence bag.

Gareth had, at some point, reported back to Rollo, because he'd sent Claire out to the scene. She arrived just as the paramedics were packing up their equipment.

'Hello, guv, you've been having fun I hear,' she said with that false cheerfulness that worried people often adopted, and sensibly watched the proceedings without getting in the way. 'The superintendent wants you to get checked out at A&E.'

'That's not necessary,' Hillary said firmly, turning to get her knees under her, then using her arms — which still felt decidedly weak and made of jelly — to lever herself properly into the chair.

The paramedics watched this with interested, professional eyes. 'As you can see, I'm fine,' she insisted.

'Boss's orders,' Claire argued.

'A&E are busy enough without me adding to the backlog,' Hillary said flatly. 'If I start to feel worse rather than better, I can always change my mind,' she added, her eyes on the paramedics.

In the end, they agreed that her vital signs were fine, she'd received no head injury when she'd ended up on the floor, but that if she started to get a bad headache, chest pains, severe nausea, double vision or dizziness she must get herself to the John Radcliffe right away.

Claire, quickly realizing that she wasn't going to win the argument, assured them that Hillary wouldn't be left alone for the next twenty-four hours, and they all watched the medical professionals leave.

Hillary leaned back in the chair and sighed.

'I take it that DI Farrell came crashing in like the cavalry?' she said to Gareth, who was also sitting down now, looking quiet and composed.

'Ma'am, I owe you my thanks.'

'Do you?' she said, vaguely surprised.

'Yes, ma'am. Philpott was about to shoot me with the taser, but you distracted him and took the hit instead. My leg gave way . . . I'm not fit to do this job. I could let you down again and—'

'Oh shut up,' Hillary said. 'You did fine, and I'd go out in the field with you again any day of the week.'

'Me too,' Claire chipped in.

'Now, give me a full report. Where was I? Oh yes, DI Farrell?'

Gareth looking both touched and relieved, visibly pulled back on his poker face, and stiffened a little.

'Yes, ma'am,' he barked. 'DI Farrell must have heard your shouted warning about the suspect having a weapon, because less than a minute later he broke the door down. By then I had Philpott on the ground and disabled, and the DI cuffed him and took him away.'

'Damn,' Hillary said. That meant that even now Farrell was probably making the formal arrest and charging him. And would no doubt bag the right to do the first interview. Even if she got there as fast as Claire could drive them, she doubted that her superintendent would agree to her muscling in on the interview anyway. He'd say she was in no fit state.

And he was right, damn it. She felt very much as if all she wanted to do was go home to the *Mollern* and take a nice long nap. Under a warm soft duvet.

She sighed. 'OK. Back to HQ.' She got her feet under her and stood up, experimentally. Her legs felt about as substantial as her arms, but at least they held her weight. Claire, without a word, came to one side of her and waited to see if she needed someone to lean on.

Gareth Proctor followed on behind as the two women walked slowly out of the house. In the hallway he found a set of keys resting in a bowl on a small console table and locked up carefully behind him. He was sure that a team must be on the way to process the house and the last thing they needed was to find burglars had been in and had a feeding frenzy.

* * *

Back at HQ they all trooped straight to Rollo's office. There, the superintendent told them that Robin Farrell was indeed interviewing their witness. Since Kevin Philpott had been stupid enough to attack them, he had been charged with assault, which meant they could take their time dealing with him and gathering the evidence for further, more serious charges.

'Well, that's something, I suppose,' Hillary grumbled. 'DI Farrell is only going to be interested in what Philpott has to say about his dealings with Spence. Once he's got that out of him, it'll be our turn.'

'You mean *my* turn,' Rollo Sale said flatly. 'You're going to go home and rest.'

Hillary nodded, but didn't actually say out loud that she agreed to go.

Claire shuffled in her seat. 'Are we saying, then, that Kevin Philpott killed Michael Beck?' she asked tentatively.

Rollo, realizing only then that the two younger members of the team hadn't been filled in, glanced significantly at Hillary, who sighed wearily.

'Yes, that's our belief,' she said. 'I think it probably went down something like this. We know from his own mouth that Michael Beck and Kevin were best mates, and that even after Michael left to go to university, they'd still meet up whenever he came home for the holidays. And that they'd hang around together, indulging Michael's hobbies, whatever the latest hobby was, and generally hang out. We also know from the Becks and his own father that Kevin was a bit of a dreamer and a moocher who probably wasn't ever going to amount to much.'

She sighed again and leaned back in her chair. 'So, on the day Michael left his home for the last time, he was on his bike, without his metal detector, which led his parents to think that he was probably heading into Oxford. But I don't think he was. I think Kevin (who had an old work van that he used for his various business ventures) had agreed to meet up with Michael that day for a spot of treasure-hunting, probably at a site not far from Woodeaton. It would make sense for Kevin to have charge of the equipment, since Michael only had his bike. Also, I suspect Kevin probably "borrowed" the metal detector on a regular basis in the hopes that he might strike it lucky while Michael wasn't using it.'

Rollo nodded. 'I have a friend with one of those things. He says that using it can get to be very addictive — a bit like gambling. Especially if you make one or two finds. It doesn't take much, he says. Finding someone's lost wedding ring, maybe, or a broken gold chain. It's that thing of making money without having to work for it.'

Hillary thought that he was probably right. 'Anyway, that day, I think he and Michael met up and finally found that significant find that Michael had always been looking for. Just how big or significant it was, we can't say unless or until we find out where Kevin's hidden it. But I think we can be fairly certain that it was something well worth finding. Now, from what we've learned about Michael so far, what do you think his reaction would be?'

'Jubilation,' Claire said at once. 'His research was vindicated, and he'd just given himself a real leg-up on the academic ladder if he wanted to teach either history or go into archaeology in any big way. Being the one to make a big discovery was almost a guarantee that he'd be able to forge himself a successful career. Not to mention the kudos of having the collection named after him or whatever.'

'Right,' Hillary agreed. 'But as a young man who'd grown up in a well-to-do family and had always known that he'd never have to worry about money, the fact that he'd hit gold, literally, probably wouldn't have mattered to him so much, from a purely monetary point of view.'

'Oh, he would have been happy about that as well, though, surely?' Claire objected. 'Who doesn't dream of coming into your own money when you're in your twenties? Or at any age, come to that!'

'Of course, I'm not saying it didn't matter to him *at all*. Just that it wouldn't have been his *primary* consideration. As you pointed out, a great deal of his jubilation would have come from his research being vindicated and the prestige that came with it. However, shift that focus to Kevin Philpott. Kevin came from a working-class background and had no financial security net underneath *him*. He didn't have Michael's brains either. We know from what the Becks said that his own father didn't rate him very highly and never thought he'd do well for himself. That sort of thing has to hurt, and must have affected him psychologically, no matter how much he probably laughed it off. Nobody's ego can take that sort of constant knocking without it getting to you. Now, on top of that, say that at this point in his life, he'd been trying and failing to earn enough from self-employment. Which meant he was going to have to admit he was no entrepreneur and get a "proper" job. Which for someone with no particular skills or qualifications probably meant going from one sort of dull, boring job to another. Thus fulfilling his father's contention that he was a good-for-nothing. But here he suddenly was, in a field, with a fortune literally at his feet. How does *he* feel?'

'It's the best day of his life, ma'am,' Gareth said quietly. 'He would be picturing his father having to eat crow, and could see his whole life changing from there on in.'

'Exactly. He wouldn't have to work for a living at all! The good life beckoned. Holidays abroad. A fancy car. Pretty girls, the whole lottery-winner fantasy. No more business venture failures for him. Nobody laughing at him when his get-rich-quick dreams bit the dust.' Hillary sighed again. 'No more being the loser, the fat, lazy, useless kid. He'd be *someone*.'

She paused, and thought about his modest home in Headington. 'Even if the stash didn't turn out to be worth actual millions, maybe, say only a quarter of a million, it still meant a life of relative ease and comfort for a working-class lad. And then Michael starts talking about calling in the coroner's office. Letting the landowner know, so that he or she could get their share. Calling the academics, who'd maybe make a case that it should be donated to a museum. Who knew what might happen then?'

'He wouldn't like it,' Rollo said, in massive understatement. 'He'd go from the high of thinking he was set for life, to the gut-wrenching fear that he might get nothing at all.'

'Bad psychology,' Gareth muttered.

'Yes. So he loses his head. We know he's prone to do that,' Hillary said ruefully, still feeling the soreness in her chest from the taser. 'His first instinct would be to try and talk Michael round, and persuade him to keep the gold for themselves. Sell it on the black market maybe.'

'But Michael wouldn't wear it,' Claire said, as caught up in imagining the scenario as everyone else.

'They argue, and the argument gets more vociferous,' Hillary nodded. 'Until, eventually, in sheer frustration, he lashes out.'

'With what?' Claire asked. 'The forensic pathologist could never find a murder weapon that quite matched his head wound.'

'I think he hit Michael with a spud planter,' Hillary said.

'Huh?' Claire blinked. 'What the hell's one of those?'

Hillary grinned. 'What it sounds like. It's a device for digging a divot out of the ground into which you can plant a spud. Or, in Michael and Kevin's case, a device for digging out potential finds. It's smaller and less cumbersome than a spade, requires less hard work because you wouldn't have to dig out a big area. And because it's basically a big tube at one end, it would leave an unusual-shaped wound.'

She explained what she'd found out on the internet about its use by nighthawks.

'So Kevin loses his rag, bangs his best friend over the head in a fit of frustration and then, what? Dumps his body in the river?' Claire asked.

'Why not? He knows the area around Woodeaton and Islip. He knows the river is there and available, and that the fields are often lonely and little used, and mostly out of sight of the road. He had the van. He could easily use it to cart Michael's body to the dump site. All he'd have to do is use the detector to make sure he got every last artefact, then load the loot, Michael's body, the equipment and Michael's bicycle in the back and who would be any the wiser?'

For a moment, all of them considered this in silence.

'He then dumps his friend in the river, goes into Oxford and leaves his bike somewhere unlocked where it's almost guaranteed to be stolen, and there he is. Free and clear with a fortune in ancient gold artefacts,' Hillary concluded.

'It was only once we knew that Michael's latest hobby had been treasure-hunting that it gave us the actual motive at last. And once I'd considered the possibility that he'd actually found a genuine hoard of treasure, it wasn't hard to see who was the most likely candidate to be his killer. Who hung out with him and might have been on hand when he found something? Not Mia — they'd split up. Not his tutor, who would have been as fascinated by the find as Michael, but who was, by then, in disgrace and the last person he would have confided in.'

Rollo nodded. 'It all hangs together all right, and I'm not saying you're wrong, but this is all sheer speculation.'

'Yes, sir,' Hillary agreed readily enough. 'But let's go on anyway. We have Kevin now in possession of a small fortune. He has enough intelligence to wait until it's clear that the investigation into his friend's death is going nowhere, and that he's safe and unsuspected. He now needs to sell some of the items if he's going to start living the good life. He might have been smart enough to realize that he couldn't just sell a whole lot of stuff at once and buy himself a house without attracting unwanted attention. So he decided to sell a bit now and then — just enough for him to indulge himself and rent a decent place without being too ostentatious about it. What does he do?'

'He needs a fence, guv,' Claire said promptly.

'Enter Simon Newley,' Gareth put in.

'Right. He asks around, someone points him to Newley being his man, contact is made, and the deal is done. And for nearly ten years, all goes well,' Hillary said. 'Every now and then, Kevin took him an item to sell on, and Kevin lived on easy street. His needs were relatively few, and I think he lacked the imagination needed to really fly high. I can see him just loafing around, making it clear to his family that he was "doing all right for himself" and that his imaginary business ventures were providing him with a nice little income, thank you. That alone must have been very satisfying for him. Seeing his relatives slogging away at regular jobs while he never had to.'

'So what went wrong?' Gareth asked. 'Why did he kill Newley? Because you think he did, don't you?'

Hillary nodded. 'Yes. I think we'll find that the head wound for both Newley and Kirklees will be a close match to that of Michael Beck.'

'But he won't have kept the murder weapon all these years, guv!' Claire immediately objected. 'He'd have ditched that the first chance he got!'

'Yes, I'm sure he did,' Hillary agreed amiably. 'But don't forget, Kevin isn't a professional crook,' she pointed out. 'As a killer, he's nothing but a rank amateur. So when he needed to kill Newley and Kirklees, he'd want to go with something that he knew worked — something that he was familiar with. And he knew for a fact that a sturdy spud planter would get the job done. It was both innocuous and easy to handle. Also, he wouldn't know where to buy a gun, and using a knife isn't everyone's cup of tea. Too much blood, and too big a chance that your victim might get the better of you, and turn the tables with it! Besides, getting caught carrying a blade wouldn't be very clever. But he could buy a spud planter at any garden centre, and if it was ever found on him, so what?'

She paused, imagining Kevin thinking things through. 'But the last time he'd killed had been a totally unpremeditated affair, a spur-of-the-moment thing, done in a white-hot rage or a moment of burning frustration. Michael was hit almost on top of his head, so he was probably kneeling down at the time, presumably examining the ground. In any case, he wouldn't be expecting to be attacked. But killing someone else in cold blood — especially a hardened crook like Kirklees — well, Kevin would have quickly realized that he'd need something else other than the spud planter. After all, Kevin was overweight, unfit, and hardly used to physical fighting. He'd need to come up with something significant to help tilt the odds firmly in his favour.'

'The taser,' Gareth said grimly. He still hadn't got the image out of his head of Hillary Greene stepping in front of that thing to take the hit.

'Yes. Like I said, he wouldn't know where to buy a gun — and probably wouldn't have had the guts to use it, if he had — but tasers are far easier to get your hands on,' Hillary was saying. 'Plus, it had the added advantage of not being as noisy as a gun either. And once again, if he was ever caught with it on him, although still an offence, he almost certainly wouldn't be looking at doing jail time over it. He would just claim that he felt safer having it for personal protection.'

She paused, rubbed a finger thoughtfully across her chin, and sighed. 'So, his MO was simple. Take them by surprise at a carefully chosen spot that he'd decided on beforehand, fire the taser before they knew what was happening, then bang them over the head when they were down. Then instantly run away. Leaving behind no murder weapon, no witnesses, and very little — if any — forensics. So long as he chose his time and place well — and he did, you have to give him that — it was as neat, if unconventional, as you could ask for.'

'But why? What went so wrong that he had to kill his fence? And where does that vicious slug, Kirklees, come into the picture?' Claire demanded.

Hillary sighed. 'Sorry, Claire, but at the moment, we've no idea. We're going to need to go through Simon Newley's racket with a fine-tooth comb and see if we can come up with anything. Unless we can persuade Kevin to tell us, that is,' she added.

For a moment there was another silence as everyone debated the likelihood of that happening. Right now, DI Robin Farrell was grilling Kevin about the events of the past few hours, but none of them knew, as yet, how it was going.

It made Hillary want to spit. Being shunted aside when it came to closing her own case was galling, to say the least.

It was at that moment that there came a knock on the door. Rollo Sale called out for whoever it was to come in, and a constable stuck his head around the door.

'Sir! A Dr de Salle has come in, demanding to speak to DI . . . er . . . Mrs Greene,' he said smartly.

'Has she now,' Rollo said dryly. 'In that case, you'd better have her shown to an interview room then.'

'Yes, sir.'

Hillary felt her heart sink a little. Any chance that she might have of going back to her boat and having a nap was now no more than a pipe dream. On the other hand, it beat sitting around here waiting for Robin Farrell to do her job for her.

'I can talk to her on my own, Hillary, if you're not feeling up to it,' Rollo offered, but Hillary was already shaking her head.

'Believe me, sir, you don't want to do that. She's an odd one.'

'You can say that again,' Claire said with a grimace, and put a finger to her temple and made a twirling motion. It was very politically incorrect, but everybody knew what she meant.

'All right. But I need to sit in on the interview at least,' Rollo pointed out. He was, after all, the only one present with any official standing.

* * *

Mia de Salle looked up fiercely as Hillary walked into the room and she started to open her mouth. Then her gaze flickered towards Rollo as he appeared behind her, and her shoulders slumped a little.

'Who's he?' she demanded at once.

She had her long dark hair swept up in a complicated chignon and was wearing well-tailored black trousers and a crisp white blouse. As before, she wore no make-up or jewellery. She'd never looked more severe, or more oddly attractive. Her eyes, though, looked manic, almost ablaze, and Hillary didn't like the look of them one little bit. She was also all but fizzing with some kind of suppressed emotion that didn't bode well for a well-conducted, text-book interview.

Hillary unhurriedly took a seat, set the tape rolling, and introduced herself, Mia, and the superintendent for the benefit of the tape, hoping that her slow, deliberate actions would calm her witness down a little.

Mia looked at the tape deck, frowned, then gave a slight shrug.

'Dr de Salle,' Hillary began pleasantly. 'You wanted to see me?'

'Yes. I know who killed Michael, and I want to tell you.'

Hillary saw and felt Rollo jerk a little in his chair. She was feeling a mite surprised by the boldness of the statement herself.

'I see,' she said cautiously. 'And how do you know this, Dr de Salle?'

'Because I saw it happen. Well, not literally with my own eyes, but I know it must have happened, because later I heard that Michael was dead.'

Hillary bit back a groan. If this was an example of what was in store, then this was going to take some time. Before, this woman had been almost monosyllabic. Now she was clearly going to be all over the place.

'Perhaps we should start at the beginning,' she tried gently. 'Let's go to the day that Michael died. Where were you?'

'Watching him, of course,' Mia said. 'Where else would I be?'

Hillary smiled. Having had some experience of this witness before, she was not quite so surprised by this admission. But she suspected that her superintendent's mind was probably boggling right now.

'You were — what — parked in your car a little way from Michael's home?' Hillary asked.

223

'Yes. I saw him leave on his bicycle and waited a bit and then followed him, as usual. He drove to this field the other side of Islip.'

Michael had been killed close to home after all, Hillary thought, momentarily distracted.

'That's where he met up with *him*,' Mia informed them dramatically, sharply focussing Hillary's mind once more.

'And who was that exactly?' Hillary asked, making sure she sounded unimpressed. She needed to keep this woman's feet on the ground, not indulge her self-aggrandisement.

'My soulmate, of course,' Mia said impatiently. Then cocked her fine head to one side, and made an obvious mental adjustment. 'Although I didn't know that at the time, naturally,' she felt compelled to point out. 'I thought, at that point, that it was still Michael.'

'I see,' Hillary said, although she didn't — not yet. 'So you saw Michael meet up with your soulmate. We'll need his name for the tape, Dr de Salle,' she said prosaically.

'Kevin Philpott.'

Hillary sensed Rollo perk up at that.

'He'd arrived in his van?' Hillary asked, very conscious of the tape recorder, and her need to try and keep this interview on as even a keel as possible. If this interview was going to be used as evidence, all sorts of legal experts were going to study it. And the more calm and rational she could keep her witness, the better.

But she had a sinking feeling that she was on a hiding to nothing as far as that was concerned.

'Yes, yes,' Mia said impatiently. 'He'd parked it on the grass verge. I watched through my binoculars as Michael got that silly metal detector thing off him, and they set off over the fields towards the river.'

Hillary nodded. She was used to watching Michael through binoculars and following him without drawing attention to herself. No doubt about it, she'd definitely been stalking him.

'I see. And then what happened?' Hillary asked calmly.

'Well they were in the field for hours. I could see them, crossing and re-crossing, quartering the ground with the detector. It's what they always did when they met up in the countryside somewhere. And then they went behind some trees and I couldn't see them anymore. They were there for so long that I eventually had to move the car to a different spot in order to try and get a different view of them. But I just couldn't find them again, and then I saw Kevin's van driving away down the road about a quarter of a mile in front of me.'

'How long were they out of your sight do you think?' Hillary asked, hoping none of her tension showed in her voice.

'Oh, it had to be nearly an hour, all told.'

Hillary made some swift calculations. That was enough time for them to get a big hit on the detector. And if the treasure had been confined to one spot — say in a now rotted-away wooden casket or a leather bag of some kind — and hadn't been buried too deep, just how long would it have taken them to unearth it? Another ten minutes? Twenty at the most? Then say five to ten minutes for Kevin to passionately argue that they keep the find for themselves, and lose that argument.

Hitting someone over the head in sheer frustration would take mere seconds. Then what — a few more minutes of dithering as Kevin realized his best friend was no longer breathing? A few minutes to panic. Then he'd have to gather the gold in whatever receptacle they used for keeping their finds in.

Then he'd have the task of getting the body into the water. And how long *that* took would depend on how near they'd been to the river when Michael was killed.

But Kevin was a hefty lad, and desperate to get away. He'd have been motivated to dump his friend's body and scram with all possible speed.

Yes. It was enough time.

'What did you do when you saw Kevin's van?' Hillary asked next.

'I waited for Michael to come along, of course. But Michael didn't appear. I thought he must have gone on somewhere else, or perhaps got in the van with Kevin, so I went back to work. It was only later, when I heard Michael was dead, and where he'd been found, that I realized what must have happened.'

'That Kevin had killed him and put him in the river, you mean?' Hillary asked curiously. And when Mia nodded emphatically, said carefully, 'But that's a bit of a leap, isn't it, Dr de Salle? How do you know that Michael didn't go on somewhere else and was killed later?'

'Because I figured it out.'

Hillary went very still. 'Figured out what, Dr de Salle?'

'That Kevin had killed him for me.'

Hillary took a long, slow breath. 'Killed him for you?' she repeated carefully.

'Yes! Don't you see? Kevin knew Michael had treated me shabbily, so he killed him for me. Michael had wronged him anyway, by coming between us in the first place. Kevin knew that it should always have been him and me, though *I* hadn't realized it before then. I felt so ashamed, and still do, that I made such a mistake!'

At this point, Hillary reached for a piece of paper and wrote the name of the psychiatric doctor the police used whenever they needed someone to assess a suspect or a witness's state of mind. She pushed it towards Rollo, who read it, and nodded in agreement. He got up, walked to the door, and left.

Hillary stated that fact for the tape.

He came back less than a minute later and resumed his seat, and again Hillary stated that out loud. Mia de Salle had remained silent throughout this, apparently without any curiosity about it, but she was shifting on her seat and impatient to continue.

'So you believe Kevin Philpott killed Michael Beck because . . .' Hillary paused, knowing that she would have to jump in.

'Because he was my soulmate,' Mia said angrily. 'Please, try not to be so unintelligent.'

'My apologies, Dr de Salle,' Hillary said. 'Let's move on. Did you tell Mr Philpott that you, er, saw him meet with Michael that day? The day Michael was killed?'

'Of course not!' Mia sighed impatiently. 'Really, you are being so dense!'

'Why not?' Hillary asked, ignoring the insult.

'There was no need! He knew. He must have known. He always knows when I'm close.'

Hillary nodded, but in truth, she was beginning to feel as if she was in danger of going down the rabbit hole along with Mia de Salle. Trying to sort out fact from fiction was fast becoming impossible.

Then she remembered Kevin saying how he'd often seen Mia around town. Hillary thought she knew the real reason behind that now.

But did *he*?

To hear Mia talking now, you'd assume that she and Kevin had become an item soon after Michael's death. But *had* they, Hillary wondered? Or was it all just in Mia's head? She knew that lots of stalkers believed they had a relationship with the object of their affections when, in reality, none existed. This was especially true when it came to film stars or other famous personalities. Some fan would become obsessed and begin stalking them, always trying to catch sight of them, and would eventually believe that they were a couple. Of course, they self-rationalized away any inconsistencies. Their relationship had to be kept secret, so the press didn't find out, for instance. But in their own mind, the object of their affection would call them up and talk to them, or send them Valentine's cards, take them out for secret romantic dinners or what have you. The celebrity being stalked didn't know they even existed.

'Dr de Salle, after Michael's death, you say you realized that Mr Kevin Philpott was really your soulmate?' Hillary began carefully.

'Yes. He killed Michael for me. He avenged my honour. He was my Heathcliff after all! I know he isn't classically handsome, but what does that matter?'

Hillary swallowed and hoped that the doctor would arrive soon. She was getting well and truly out of her depth here!

'Yes I see. And so you . . . er . . . began following Mr Philpott then?'

'Yes! I just had to see him, you see. Oh, I knew we couldn't acknowledge our love, not in the open. He was still in danger.'

'Of being charged with Michael's murder?' Hillary hazarded.

'Yes! They'd have thrown him in prison! We couldn't have that. We had to be patient. I knew that. But it's been so long,' Mia wailed. 'And now he's abandoned me, just as Michael did. I'm here to betray him,' she said. 'It's the only thing I can do.'

Hillary blinked. 'Er, yes, of course. Dr de Salle, did you ever *tell* Mr Philpott of your devotion?'

'I parked near his home and watched him walk by.'

'Yes, but did you ever *talk* to him? Declare your love? Your devotion?'

'No, I told you. We couldn't be seen together. But he knew. Whenever our eyes would meet in the crowded street, we both knew.'

Well, Hillary mused, since Mia was in such a talkative mood, she might as well see if there was anything that was actually helpful that she could tell them. 'Dr de Salle, when you followed Kevin, did you see him meet up with a man called Simon Newley, or go into his antiques shop?'

'That horrible man in that dreadful shop? Yes, he would go and visit him about four or five times a year. I don't know why though. He never bought anything in there. But it was an appalling place, full of old tat, so I'm not surprised.'

Hillary nodded. And although she knew her testimony would probably never be used in a court of law, at least it was helping to confirm her theories.

'I don't suppose you were watching him one night when he stopped at a house in north Oxford?' She cited Lionel Kirklees' address and the date of the night he'd been killed, but her luck didn't stretch that far.

Regretfully, Mia de Salle told them that she didn't 'meet' with Kevin in the hours of darkness. 'I can't see his face, you see,' she explained simply.

'I see,' Hillary said blankly. Then gave herself a mental shake. Talking to this woman for any length of time could seriously play havoc with one's mental wellbeing. 'Well, thank you, Dr de Salle,' Hillary said gently. Then looked across at Rollo. 'I'm going to have your statement typed up. If you wouldn't mind waiting, we'll need you to sign it for us.'

'Of course,' she said calmly. 'I understand.'

Hillary signed them off on the tape and they left in utter silence. Only once they were outside did Rollo allow himself to show any emotion.

'Damn it, her testimony is going to be useless,' he said bitterly. 'A defence lawyer would rip her to pieces, even if we could get her signed off as competent to give evidence, which we won't! In my opinion, I think that woman is going to be sectioned, and is probably due a long spell in an institution.'

Hillary regretfully agreed with this assessment.

'It's galling to actually have a witness at last, and not be able to use her!' Rollo sighed. 'If she was mentally stable, her eyewitness testimony putting Philpott at the scene of the crime, at the right time, would nail him good and proper. As it is . . . it's useless!'

Hillary, feeling all in, leaned against the wall and then slowly began to smile. 'Ah, but Kevin Philpott doesn't know that, sir, does he?'

CHAPTER SEVENTEEN

Rollo, who had been pacing agitatedly up and down, immediately stopped and looked at her. He noted her smile and his eyes narrowed. 'What are you thinking, Hillary?'

Hillary took a deep, weary breath. 'I think that Kevin Philpott lacks a backbone, sir. I think that DI Farrell is softening him up for you nicely right now, asking him all about his dealings with Larry Spence. Trying to dodge and dance around that is going to wear him out for a start. Then I think it's only a matter of time before we find that safety deposit box or other hiding place that he must have somewhere or other, and when we find it, we're going to find his precious Saxon gold. And when he learns that his nest egg is gone, he'll be feeling *really* sorry for himself. And if we can prove that he bought a spud planter not long before the two recent murders, even better. And on top of all that, if you then let him know that we now have an eyewitness that puts him and Michael together at the time of Michael's death, near the river where his body was later recovered, I reckon he's going to crack.'

The superintendent began to look a little less angry, but not totally convinced.

'Don't forget, sir, he's had ten years of thinking that he'd got away with it. That nobody even knew for certain the exact spot where Michael was killed. If you give him all the details Mia just gave us, he'll know better, and I think it'll be too much for him.'

Rollo leaned against the wall beside her, thinking it over, and then sighed. 'I hope you're right,' he said at last.

Hillary laughed wearily. 'So do I, sir.'

'We still don't know why he killed Newley and Kirklees though,' he pointed out.

Hillary sighed. 'Well, you can't always have everything, sir,' she said philosophically. 'And, technically, that's DI Farrell's problem, not ours.'

* * *

But in the next few days, the joint CRT case and Robin Farrell's double-murder case quickly resolved itself, with most of Hillary's predictions coming true. They found Michael Beck's hoard of Saxon gold when a careful search of Kevin Philpott's house turned up documentation for a safety deposit box in a bank in Witney.

A clerk at a garden centre near Burford came forward after they ran a request on the local news channel, along with a photograph of Kevin Philpott, asking for anyone who'd sold him a spud planter to come forward.

Mia de Salle had signed her statement but was currently being treated at a mental facility. Luckily for her, she had a rich aunt who had died eight years ago and left Mia her entire fortune, so she could afford the best of care.

And Kevin Philpott, unable to withstand the stream of evidence being gathered against him, finally admitted his guilt.

He even told DI Farrell just why he'd been forced to kill Simon Newley and Lionel Kirklees.

Although Hillary hadn't been able to sit in on that particular interview, Rollo had, and had been more than happy to fill her in on all the details later.

Apparently, Simon Newley had hit a bad patch financially, and was being squeezed by Kirklees for repayment of a loan that Newley had unwisely negotiated with him. Finding himself unable to pay it off, the fence had instead tossed the client he referred to in his books as 'Teddy Bear' under the bus, by selling him out to Kirklees in lieu of paying the loan. Newley could prove that Teddy Bear (who'd probably earned the nickname due to his cuddly figure and deep-set dark eyes) was a regular client who always had very valuable items for sale.

Naturally, Lionel Kirklees had then put the frighteners on Teddy Bear, having him beaten up and telling him to hand over the gold, or end up floating face down in the Cherwell. Thus leaving Kevin Philpott facing the very unpalatable fact that his easy lifestyle was now over.

Unless he could get rid of Kirklees.

It was a bold move, for there probably wasn't a crook in Oxford — save perhaps Larry Spence — who'd have dared to have a go at tackling a thug like Kirklees. But here, ironically enough, it was Kevin's very innocence and lack of understanding at just how dangerous Kirklees was that allowed *him* to do something so dangerous.

Of course, before he could kill Kirklees, Kevin reasoned that he needed to get rid of Simon Newley first, since he felt sure that Newley would guess who was responsible when Kirklees turned up dead. He wouldn't hesitate to give an anonymous tip to the police and drop Kevin in it, if it meant keeping himself safe from a murderer out for revenge.

So Kevin had bought the taser and spud planter, made a note of the men's various habits, and then laid his plans. He killed Simon Newley the moment he opened his back door, and then killed Kirklees under cover of darkness in his front garden that same night.

As Kevin had told a gobsmacked DI Robin Farrell, he needed to kill Lionel before he got to hear about Newley's killing. He didn't want Kirklees being forewarned.

Rollo Sale had had to laugh out loud when he described Robin Farrell's chagrin and disgust when he finally had to admit that Larry Spence had had nothing to do with their deaths after all.

* * *

It was getting on for eight o'clock in the evening, and Hillary Greene was sitting in a deckchair on the tiny deck at the rear of her narrowboat. It had been a warm day, and the evening was turning out to be pleasantly warm too. Soon the sun would set, and the bats would come out, and she would go inside and settle down with a good book.

She was drinking a small glass of wine. She no longer felt sore from the taser, and she was well and truly back in Rollo Sale's good books, with the CRT sharing the glory with Robin Farrell's team for the closure of three murder cases. Four, if you included the killing in Reading.

She had assigned Gareth the job of going over to Woodeaton to tell Michael's parents the news that their son's killer had been caught and would be brought to justice. She thought, after all he'd been through, the former soldier needed reminding that he could still be of so much use in the world. That there were still people — good people — who were relying on them all to do their jobs properly.

Hillary found herself in a philosophical mood, however. Had she done the right thing in saving Gareth from committing professional suicide, after his friend had committed the real thing? She wasn't altogether sure. She knew that some people would argue — quite rightly — that she had stepped over the line there.

But would it have been better for her to have followed the letter of the law and see a good man ruined? A man who had fought for his country, and been injured in the process? A man who had only been trying to do right by his dead friend?

She didn't think so.

But she didn't really know for sure. How could she? How could anyone really be their own judge and jury?

She sipped her wine and sighed. Her job had never been easy, and it could certainly take its toll at times, but she couldn't see herself doing anything else.

And if she made mistakes along the way . . . well, in the end, she knew that she was as imperfect as any other member of the human race, and as long as she could look herself in the mirror every day she shouldn't really complain.

When it came right down to it, she supposed, feeling just a touch melancholy, she could only do her best, and hope for the best.

She took another sip of wine.

And if there was a better way of going about life than that, then she didn't know what the hell it was.

THE END

ALSO BY FAITH MARTIN

DI HILLARY GREENE SERIES

MONICA NOBLE MYSTERIES

JENNY STARLING MYSTERIES

Thank you for reading this book.

If you enjoyed it, please leave feedback on Amazon or Goodreads, and if there is anything we missed or you have a question about, then please get in touch. We appreciate you choosing our book.

Founded in 2014 in Shoreditch, London, we at Joffe Books pride ourselves on our history of innovative publishing. We were thrilled to be shortlisted for Independent Publisher of the Year at the British Book Awards.

www.joffebooks.com

We're very grateful to eagle-eyed readers who take the time to contact us. Please send any errors you find to corrections@joffebooks.com. We'll get them fixed ASAP.